Sangrita

Jessica Watts Southwest Suspense Series

Kathryn Dodson

Renegade Reads

Contents

Chapter 1

Jessica let the mental exhaustion take hold for a minute, then shook it off. Eighteen months to go. If she survived that, she'd be a lawyer with real cases instead of a paralegal who people constantly hit up to solve weird and dangerous mysteries.

She settled into her chair. "I'm back," she called to her boss. Linda owned the one-person firm housed in a quaint old home turned law office in downtown El Paso. Jessica ran her fingers across the antique, inlaid cherry desk. She'd started here less than a year ago, but she already loved this place.

"Hey, how was the test?" Linda strode into the room and plopped down in front of her. A perfect-fitting Armani suit and a blond blowout softened the toughness shining through Linda's blue eyes. The creases in her face told the world she'd faced a few battles.

"Tough, but I'm pretty sure I passed," Jessica said.

Linda smiled, then cocked her head, a question appearing in her eyes. "I bet your father would be proud."

Jessica bristled, a dull ache returning to her shoulders and prickles of tension running across her skin. Linda hadn't brought up Jessica's dad since the first time they met.

Jessica hated how her father's conviction for destroying evidence in a drug case shaded her pending law career. He'd been El Paso's district attorney at the time. That embarrassment had held Jessica back for too many years. She'd gotten past it, mostly, especially since her father's passing.

She shrugged her shoulders in response, then willfully changed the subject. "Has it been quiet here?"

"Surprisingly so. But who knows what will walk in the door next?" Linda glanced out the large window as if she expected to see someone trotting up the steps. She turned back to Jessica. "Do you have any new projects on the horizon?"

Jessica's reputation for finding things, missing people, murderers, had ratcheted up since she started working with Linda. She shook her head. "No more wild cases for me. I need to keep my head down and finish school. I keep getting waylaid by these other projects. It's too hard to focus on law school and my work here when I'm off solving someone else's mystery."

Linda studied Jessica. "Maybe, but I think you like striking out on your own, solving someone's problem, and coming back a hero. I just hate how much danger you come across. Practicing law is so different than that. It's tedious and requires an extraordinary amount of patience while the wheels of justice turn."

Did Linda doubt her aspirations? Not every law case would be exciting, but lately, she could use a little less excitement in her life. Fortunately, she'd escaped every tight spot without a problem.

"Perhaps," Jessica said. "But you're a lot less likely to be confronted by people pointing guns at you or burning down the house you're trapped in."

"True. At least most of the time."

Jessica wondered about her answer. "Is that why you left the police force and became an attorney?" She had heard about Linda's first career from Jaime Castro, a sergeant on the El Paso police force and one of her oldest friends. Based on the admiration in his voice, Linda had excelled as a police officer.

"Not really." Linda's gaze softened, as if remembering something from long ago. "The problem with police work is that you don't get to choose your cases. When they don't seem fair, it becomes hard to put your heart into the job."

Jessica waited for an explanation. What kind of case would make someone as tough as Linda walk away? For a minute, Jessica thought she would say more. But instead, her boss changed the subject. "Why don't we go over the upcoming cases?"

When they finished, Linda headed back to her office. Jessica had just turned to her computer when she spied someone coming toward the door. Someone she did not want to see.

Tomás Garcia loped up the steps and opened the door before Jessica could escape. If only her test had taken longer.

"Hi, Jessica. It's good to see you." He sat in the chair Linda had just vacated as if he owned the place.

He didn't. And when he'd tracked her down at a party a few weeks ago, she'd told him she didn't want to see him again. Yet here he sat. The audacity of rich men never failed to surprise her.

"Why are you here?" She threw all the surliness she could muster into her voice.

"Is that any way to treat a potential client?"

"Tomás, I made it clear that I would never work with you again. You do remember you tried to kill me the last time." And the time before that, she'd almost died at the hands of someone he'd forgotten to tell her dealt drugs.

"I wouldn't have killed you. I am not a murderer. I was just angry. I thought you had taken something I considered mine."

"That something was a human being, and she didn't want to be with you. You've lost your chance with me."

He steepled his fingers and stared across the desk. "We have a long history, and we've worked well together in the past." Arrogance wafted off him like a bad smell.

Jessica scanned her desk for something to throw at him or stab him with. Life was way too short to tolerate assholes like this.

He held his hands up in surrender, as if he could read her mind. "You're right. That last time was horrible. I shouldn't have done so many of the things I did then. I'm sorry. I promise I'm a different man now. And I need your help."

Fire lit in her veins. She had already taken too many chances with Tomás. Jessica took a deep breath and tried to keep from spitting at him. "You need to leave. There is no way in hell you've changed enough in the last few years for me to consider working for you." She wouldn't physically attack him, but she tried her best to stare daggers into his soul.

"Please. Let me explain. I'm married to a wonderful woman now. We have a son, and he's the most important thing in my life. Becoming a father changes a person. I'm a much better man today. Also, I lost my mother a year ago, and I'm worried about losing my father. That's what I need to talk to you about."

Of course, curiosity gnawed at her, but it wasn't enough. She loathed this man.

"You do realize that waltzing in here expecting me to listen to you after I've already told you no means you're still the entitled jerk you've always been."

"I'm not. I swear. Please, just hear me out. I think someone is trying to kill my father."

"So. Go to the police."

"I have, but I can't get anywhere with them. My dad remarried just a few months after my mom died. His new wife has completely denied me access to him."

"Didn't you hate your dad? How many times have you told me you wanted to build an empire even bigger than his? Maybe he just doesn't want to see you."

"Things are different now. After . . . after what happened with Doraliz, I had to change. I wasn't a man I could be proud of, and I certainly wasn't a son my mother could respect. But she didn't give up on me. Instead, she helped me see what a terrible person I'd become and gave me a way to recover."

"Whatever. I don't care, and I want you to leave." Jessica refused to buy his rich boy sob story. He should have ended up in jail.

He leaned forward, hands on his knees, blue eyes staring her down, probably his attempt at acting earnest. "I know how selfish and hurtful and conceited I was. I know, and I hate that version of myself. I understand why you don't want to work with me, but my father's life is on the line. You have a knack for solving mysteries. I've seen you do it. I need your help to save my father."

"It's not going to happen. And if you don't leave, I'll call the cops." Jessica picked up her phone and hit the timer, then turned it to face him. "You've got sixty seconds to get out of this office."

Exasperation crossed Tomás's features. He sighed and started to say something. Then he shut his mouth, rose, and walked out the door. She hoped she'd never see him again.

Linda emerged the minute he left. From the look on her face, she'd heard the conversation.

"I didn't know you had such a long involved relationship with Mr. Garcia." Linda sat in the probably still warm chair.

"Yeah. Unfortunately." Jessica said nothing more, hoping Linda would drop it. She preferred to avoid the whole sordid tale.

Linda watched Jessica for a long moment but didn't press her for more information. "You do know that you're always welcome to work on outside cases. Soon enough you'll have your own legal cases."

"I look forward to that, but not with him."

"Fine. You should head home early tonight. Go celebrate finishing midterms with that handsome husband of yours."

"Thanks." She did want to celebrate, although she'd stayed up so late cramming, she'd require a second wind to do anything other than crawl into bed. Or maybe a shot or two of tequila to help her forget torts. And Tomás's visit.

Chapter 2

J essica and Angus sat at an outdoor patio just starting to fill with people. They had first come to Aceitunas with fake IDs in high school and then more legitimately in college. As she looked around at the under-twenty-five crowd, thirty suddenly felt old. But they had a trough full of ice filled with the coldest beer in town, paper containers overflowing with nachos, and some of the best music in far west Texas. Plus, she got to hang out with the best person she knew.

"When does Robbie go on?" she asked. Their high school friend still had a band that made the local rounds. In high school and college, Angus had been the guitarist and singer of the popular local rock band, but all the original lineup except Robbie had given up shows for stable jobs.

"Not for another hour." Angus took a bite of a hot dog smothered in white cheddar and green chile. Jessica considered stealing it from him.

Instead, she piled a tortilla chip with the perfect amount of beef picadillo and a fresh jalapeño slice, then shoved the nacho in her mouth. Chewing bought her time while she figured out whether to tell Angus about Tomás or her plans for tomorrow first. He wouldn't be happy with either story.

She washed down the nacho with a swig of beer. "Linda let me knock off work early, and I spent the afternoon scouring Google Maps for ponds and water basins out in the desert. Quite a few areas fit the description Mari and Angela gave us about where their families were murdered." Since she'd saved the cousins in the desert, she'd spent months trying to piece together their story. They'd been kidnapped shortly after crossing the Mexican border. Their captors massacred the rest of their family in the desert night. Angela told Jessica it had happened near some kind of pond. Jessica had sworn to get justice for the cousins.

Angus kept his eyes on her as he slowly set down his hot dog. "And?"

"I thought I'd go check out one of the locations tomorrow," she said. Angus's face showed exactly the cold reception she'd expected. His pride for her rescuing the girls vied with his concerns about her safety. But some things were worth the risk.

"You want to drive into the desert, alone, and try to find a murder scene? That sounds safe," he deadpanned.

"Well, I figure the bad guys won't be around during daylight hours."

Angus rolled his eyes at her. "Jaime said he'd keep looking into it. Have a little patience."

Jessica had called Jaime Castro, as soon as she'd had phone reception the night she found the Guatemalan girls in the desert. Their gruesome story and narrow escape from a psychopath had tied Jessica to them, and she'd promised herself she'd stop the men who'd hurt them. Angus certainly knew she wouldn't stop looking for answers. So did Jaime. "There's only so much he can do. The El Paso Police Department has no jurisdiction out there."

"Can't you take some time off during the week? That way I could at least go with you."

"I already take so much time off for school that it's not fair to Linda. I promise, it will be safe." She couldn't help it that their jobs had almost zero overlap. He taught kids rock and roll when they weren't in school, which meant evenings and weekends—her time off work.

"You can't promise that. You have no idea what's out there. If you're determined to go tomorrow, then promise me something realistic, like you'll take someone with you."

Jessica whirred through her list of friends but couldn't think of anyone who'd want to spend Saturday morning driving over an hour east into the nothingness of the Chihuahua Desert. She'd figure it out. "I'll find someone. I promise."

He nodded, although she doubted he totally believed her. She hardly believed herself. The yearning to make some progress on the case pulled at her. Time to move on to other sore topics. "There's one more thing. Tomás Garcia came to the office today."

"Well, it wouldn't surprise me if that guy needed legal help," Angus said. "What did he want?"

"He wanted me to do a job for him. Something about his father."

"Fuck." Angus shook his head, then suddenly stood up. "I need another beer for this conversation. Want one?"

"I told him no." Jessica said the words to Angus's retreating back.

Angus had hated Tomás since she first worked with him in college, when he owned a string of nightclubs in Juarez. She approached him about showcasing Angus's band. Somehow, that led to her being chased through the streets of Juarez by an American trying to break into the local drug scene. The second time they worked together, he'd set her up to find the missing daughter of a Mexican business mogul. That time, she'd almost died. Angus had reason to be upset. But she had survived, and as long as she stayed away from Tomás, she'd be fine.

She leaned back in her seat and looked around the bar while she waited for him to return. The patio's high walls protected patrons from the evening sun, not to mention the busy road lined with strip shopping centers. The bar had survived in the same location forever. Her mom had mentioned that she and her dad had more than one date here. Jessica had always imagined her parents meeting in classier locations, but evidently, even back then, it had drawn young clientele from across town. When Jessica told her they'd updated the bar with a beer garden and koi pond, she didn't think her mom would ever quit laughing.

Angus strolled back, an icy beer in each hand. He handed one to Jessica and sat.

"I told him no," she said before he could get settled. "I never want to work for that guy again."

"I'm really glad. Tomás is an ass."

Angus lifted his beer and Jessica clinked hers to his. "Agreed," she said. Now if she could only figure out who could accompany her tomorrow.

Chapter 3

After Angus left for work the next morning, Jessica sat on the couch, drinking coffee and double-checking Google Maps to plot her route to the reservoir. Tela, her Catahoula Leopard Hound, curled next to her, occasionally sighing and resting her head on the laptop keyboard. Jessica complied with her request for ear scratches while trying to keep the device stable.

She had no idea who to call for such a strange errand. She'd learned that small, dry reservoirs dotted the far west Texas desert. Formed to stop soil erosion, some obscure state department managed them. Several lay between the US/Mexico border and where she'd found Mari and Angela.

According to the story they told the authorities, the cousins had crossed the border with their families in the middle of the night. The Texas border stretched over twelve hundred miles, and the infamous border wall that allegedly stopped pedestrians blocked less than a third of that length. The wall, an ugly metal barricade, split El Paso and Juarez but petered out not far to the southeast. Just east of El Paso, the town of Fabens faced the Valle de Juarez, one of the most dangerous areas in Mexico, with no wall between them.

The cousins and their families could have crossed anywhere. Jessica's finger traced a straight line from the ranch where they'd been held to the border with the Valle de Juarez. She found two reservoirs on the path, one less than five miles from Interstate 10. She could be there in an hour, check it out, and be home before noon.

She'd promised Angus to take someone. The dog licked her hand, asking for attention. *Of course.* Tela had a huge bark and would probably bite anyone who tried to attack Jessica.

"Let's go for a ride." She used her excited dog voice as she slammed the laptop shut. Tela leapt from the couch and ran to the front door. She definitely wouldn't get this kind of enthusiasm from anyone else she knew.

***

Jessica pulled off the freeway at Exit 68. This part of Texas lay sixty-eight miles from the New Mexico state line, and maybe two miles from the Mexican border. Tela perked up as the truck slowed. She looked out the window, probably hoping for a destination.

Red and white barricades and a "road closed" sign kept anyone from turning south toward the border. Jessica headed north and crossed the freeway. Low desert hills stretched for miles. The world's best steakhouse hid somewhere out here. She'd visited Cattleman's a few times. People revered the German cattle farm turned fabulous restaurant.

Tela would have loved a steak. Instead, they drove into a no-man's-land where the road turned to dirt at the bottom of the overpass. Jessica crossed a cattle grate. The official sounding name of the reservoir along with its management by the State of Texas had led her to believe the government owned the land. Instead, she found herself on private property.

She debated turning around, but she'd already invested more than an hour on this search. Sometimes asking for forgiveness beat wasting a bunch of time looking for an owner who probably didn't care anyway. Or just might care too much.

She hit a fork in the road, and GPS told her to veer right. The site's proximity to the interstate and fifty-mile sightlines meant decent cell phone reception, even out in the boonies. Another right turn, and she saw the reservoir's dam ahead. Calling it a dam seemed a stretch. Really, it was a long pile of gray rocks that blocked a completely dry wash. The dam's color clashed with the buff-colored sand surrounding it. The gravel road continued up the barrier, and Jessica pulled the truck up it and stopped at the highest point.

The reservoir didn't hold a drop of water. A few plants grew in the seams of the cracked, dry dirt. El Paso's high desert climate received fewer than eight inches of rain a year, and the vast majority of those came during the monsoons of July and August. Mari and Angela had crossed the border in November. Now spring, months had passed since the last downpour.

Jessica scanned the area. Craggy red hills jutted just a few miles to the north. The water from those hills would pass through here on its way to the Rio Grande. At least it would have before the stone dam. The reservoir looked to be only an acre or two in size. Tire tracks crisscrossed the dry bottom, sometimes forming circles as if kids had done donuts in the dirt.

In the harsh morning sun, she couldn't imagine eight grisly murders taking place below. No crime scene tape or chalk outlines of bodies marked the cracked dirt. No pools of dried blood stained the ground. But if the crime had occurred here, surely, she could find some evidence.

The narrow road atop the dam had steep gravel slopes on either side, making it too dangerous to turn the truck around. Instead, she backed down slowly. Just a few yards past the bottom, tire tracks veered off to the left. Jessica followed them, and the truck climbed a shallow rise, then dropped to the reservoir. She parked by a scrubby bush, then opened the door and stepped down into the sand.

Tela bounded out of the truck and ran to do her business, then trotted toward the center of the dry reservoir. Jessica followed. The dog darted from place to place, her nose to the ground. Jessica took a quick three-sixty-degree video of the spot, then started looking for evidence. Creosote, sage, and other desert brush surrounded the reservoir, except for the side walled by the dam.

She figured she'd walk the perimeter of the space, but first she followed Tela out to the middle. The caked dirt beneath her feet varied from the surrounding sand, probably because of silt brought down from the hills.

Tela ran to a point opposite the dam and started barking. Had she found something? The dog had a nose for trouble. Not long ago, she'd found a buried skeleton in a pecan grove that had turned into Jessica's most recent case.

Instead of stopping and digging, like when she'd found the skeleton, the dog ran around the dirt churned up by vehicle tires, occasionally stopping to bark. Jessica couldn't see anything unusual, but Tela's nose had found something.

Just then, the sound of tires crunching on gravel reached her. Shit. She and the dog were completely exposed. Jessica watched an SUV climb the gravel wall. She hoped the vehicle didn't contain a pissed-off property owner with a gun, or worse, the murderers who haunted her dreams.

"Fuck me," she said to the dog and the universe as the vehicle turned enough to expose the black and white paint and bold lettering on its side. This wouldn't be her first run in with the county sheriff. While whoever drove the vehicle probably wouldn't kill her in cold blood, there was a good chance she'd be taken to jail for trespassing. That had happened before out in this desert, and it had cost her her job and the trust of the man she loved. Damn it. And of course this happened when she'd brought Tela as her wingman.

The window of the SUV rolled down, and Jessica caught the glint of a pair of binoculars. She couldn't see inside the cab. No telling whether she'd run across the deputy before, or if she'd have a chance at talking her way out of the situation.

The driver's window rolled back up, and the vehicle continued across the dam and down the other side, quickly rolling out of sight. That seemed more ominous than the driver getting out and yelling at her.

Tela, who'd raised her head when the vehicle stopped, went back to exploring. Jessica was about to do the same when she heard the crunch of gravel again. She watched the vehicle ascend, then slowly cross the dam. She felt like the only duck left standing in a carnival shooting game. Nowhere to run. Nowhere to hide.

She might as well keep searching while she had the chance. Perhaps she'd find something to convince the deputy she had a reason to be here. Tela darted back and forth, then started barking at a small mound of dirt.

Jessica walked over and examined it. No bones. Nothing but dried mud. She kicked at it. It didn't look any different than the rest of the churned-up soil. Meanwhile, Tela had grown bored and trotted off in a different direction.

Jessica glanced back to where she'd parked her truck, and sure enough, the SUV pulled in beside it. She called Tela to her and put her hands on her hips, waiting for whatever would come next.

Deputy Guerra stepped out of the vehicle, shocking Jessica. He'd arrested her. Months later, they'd had a confrontation in front of the county courthouse where she'd accused him ignoring the fate of the Guatemalan girls and their family. Now he was here. Perhaps at the site where it had happened. A prickle of fear started at the base of her spine, then rose to tense her back and shoulders.

They stared at each other across forty yards of dirt. Tela growled deep in her throat.

"Good girl." Jessica kept her voice soft enough that it didn't reach the deputy. Guerra walked toward her, his linebacker frame as much of a threat as his gun and handcuffs.

"Are you coming to arrest me again?" Her loud voice carried the twenty yards remaining between them.

"No," he answered, as if that were the most ridiculous thing he'd ever heard. "Why are you out here?"

"Are you stalking me?" she asked.

"Why would I do that?"

"I can't believe it's a coincidence that we're both here at the same time." She crossed her arms as he stopped five feet away.

"I think the better question is why you are here. I'm on patrol. This is my jurisdiction." He let the words hang in the air.

Jessica had no idea whether to let him in on her theory. He must be familiar with Mari and Angela's testimony. Perhaps he'd followed the clues the way she had. Although he certainly hadn't seemed to care back then.

But he could have followed her. For all she knew, the sheriffs had put a tracker on her car. Tomás had tracked her to Central America once through an app on her phone. Jessica had never trusted people much, but after that, everyone was suspect.

Tela chose this moment to betray Jessica and approach Guerra with a wagging tail.

"Hey pup," he said, squatting down to pet her.

Jessica fumed. She'd have to talk with that dog after this. Guerra might look like a pro football player, but he seemed more like a happy kid as he petted the dog. Maybe he wasn't so bad after all, although she'd be less quick to judge than her dog.

"I think I know why you're here," he said as he stood back up. "One of the Ortega girls remembered being near a pond when the outlaws gunned down her family. There's only so many places to find water in the desert, and this one is near a notorious illegal border crossing."

He didn't look angry. Or threatening. Although just his presence was a menace. He'd probably make her leave, hopefully in her truck not his SUV.

"Okay," she said. "We can both use Google. So what?"

"Well, if you were a real detective, you'd understand the need to gather evidence."

What a jackass. "Why do you think I'm out here?"

"You mean why do I think you're trespassing on private property again?" He cocked an eyebrow at her. Was he making fun of her? Someone was about to learn that was a big mistake.

"Well, someone needs to do something," Jessica said. "If I'd left it to the sheriff's department, who knows what would have happened to those girls."

He deflated as if all the fight had left him. "What you did out there that night. The way you saved them. That took guts. Thank you."

Was that admiration in his eyes? Jessica shook her head, knocking the idea away. First he arrested her, then he argued with her—this must be an act. "Why are you looking for evidence out here? You sure didn't want to help before."

He stiffened, a muscle moving along his square jaw. Black eyes bored into her, but she stared back defiantly. "I was wrong before. If crimes were committed, I need to investigate. But that doesn't mean you should be out here as a private citizen."

"I'm already here. I can help."

He looked around as if the sage or sand would tell him what to do. "Well, I don't really have time to arrest you. Especially since the owners haven't made a complaint." A corner of his lips hooked up in a smile, probably remembering when he'd arrested her after a ranch owner had complained about her, twice.

He was teasing her. Why? She came close to calling him a dickhead, but Angus's pleading with her to have more patience saved the day. She changed tack instead. "Who owns this place anyway?"

"An entity called West Texas Trust. They're based in Lubbock."

She hadn't heard of them before. "And they gave you permission to be out here?"

"I left a message for them. Should we each walk half the perimeter?"

While she preferred to work alone, the search would go faster with two people. "Sure. I'll start over there. Also, my dog barked at that dirt in the middle like she'd found something. I checked it out but didn't see anything." Jessica pointed to the dirt pile she'd kicked.

"Could be remnants of a deer carcass or some other animal. Might be nothing at all. What's her name?" He nodded toward Tela.

"Tela. What's yours? Your badge just says Guerra."

"You can call me TK. Or Keith." He turned and walked toward the rim of the basin.

Jessica did the same in the opposite direction. When she reached the rim, she wandered among the brush, hoping to avoid snakes, tarantulas, and other natives. Tela stayed in the reservoir, following trails of odor as she trotted determinedly from spot to spot.

Jessica found trash: beer bottles, Coke cans, a diaper. How was it that diapers always ended up in such strange places? It probably took them a century to degrade in the dry desert air.

"I think I found something," Keith said. At his voice, Tela jogged toward him. Jessica followed.

A pile of red plastic cylinders with brass tips lay on the ground. Dirt partially covered them, more like they'd been out here for while in the wind than someone had tried to bury them.

"Gun casings?" Jessica asked.

"Yeah. Twelve gauge. That's a lot of them." He pulled a latex glove from his back pocket, pulled it on, and picked up one of the casings, turning it over in his hand. "There's no way to tell when this was used. Not years ago, but not yesterday either."

"What do they shoot with that type of ammunition?" Jessica asked. Tela sniffed the pile.

He stood up and handed her the casing. "Everything. Quail. Gophers. Deer." His body blocked the sun.

Jessica studied the plastic sheath, one end shredded, the other hot metal. "People?"

"It's the most popular shotgun for home defense."

"How does this work?" She pointed at the casing. Jessica had promised herself to take a gun safety class—just as soon as midterms ended. Which was yesterday.

"The casing is full of buckshot. Round lead balls. Each time you pull the trigger, you send a casing's worth of balls into your target, if you're any good. Sometimes people use them because they're much more likely to hit and kill your target with a shotgun than a revolver or a rifle which shoots just one bullet."

Jessica closed her eyes and recalled the girls' story. They'd crossed the border and walked for hours. They made it to the pickup point where the trucks waited for them in the black of night.

Her eyes flew open. "This would be a great weapon for night hunting."

"We don't know what these shells were used for. They're popular with deer hunters." Concern crossed Keith's face. "But yeah, they'd be useful at night."

"Deer?" Jessica asked. "There are probably more pronghorn antelopes out here than deer." This wasn't a desert rich in large prey. "So, what now?"

"We keep searching."

Jessica no longer wanted to be out here. Shell casings weren't proof, but thoughts of bullets ripping through flesh disturbed her. She wished she could ask Tela if she smelled blood on the ground.

She glimpsed something yellow under a sage. "More casings," she hollered.

Keith headed her direction. "Twenty gauge. That's interesting."

"Why?" she asked. "And how can you tell?"

"Twenty-gauge shells are always yellow. You can't put these in a twelve-gauge gun. They'll fit, but they won't shoot. They'll explode instead.

They searched the area for another hour but found nothing else. Even Tela, not one to give up easily, left the search for the shade of Jessica's pickup. When Jessica had completely combed through her half of the reservoir, she returned to the truck. She swigged down part of a too-warm bottle of water, then poured the remainder bit by bit into her palm for Tela.

Keith approached, swiping a hand across his sweaty brow. "That might have been a bust since all we found were the shotgun casings."

"There are probably a half dozen more reservoirs around here. Should we search them too?" Jessica needed to act, to make something happen on this case. In the past, she'd attacked her cases with a single-mindedness that gave her quick results. This one had dragged on for months.

"Not today. Maybe not ever."

"What? You're going to give up after just one day?" Heat-fueled fury flashed through Jessica that had nothing to do with the midday sun. "Fucking sheriffs."

"I'm standing right here. And of course I'm not going to give up after one day. But I think we need to be more strategic about this. Or I do, anyway. This reservoir seemed like the best chance. There's one more that could be a possibility, but it may be too late to find something relevant at the scene. The desert wind destroys evidence."

Yeah, especially if you wait six months to look into a crime. If he'd intended to soothe her with his comment, the opposite happened. "You should have been out here the day after I found the girls. Eight bodies don't just disappear. Someone is responsible for this, but you guys aren't serious about finding them."

The jab must have hit home, because Keith's eyes narrowed. "I am proud to be a sheriff. My father and uncle were sheriffs, and I'm honored to follow in their footsteps. And by the way, we care about every case, and we have lots of them. I don't get to pick and choose the cases I think are important and ignore the others."

"It seems like eight murders should take precedence over a lot of other cases. There's like what, thirty or forty murders a year in El Paso—a city with almost 700,000 people? We've got one of the lowest murder rates in the world. Eight is a lot."

Keith shook his head. "Let the professionals handle this."

Jessica's frustration crawled across her skin. Something terrible had happened in this desert that left two girls orphaned in a Pecos, Texas detention center. They needed answers. Not that answers would bring back their families.

"Whatever." Jessica patted the seat of the truck so Tela would jump in. She shouldn't rely on sheriff's department employees to solve this case. In fact, some of them might be the bad guys, or might protect them.

"You should leave this to law enforcement," Keith said.

"I'd like to see a resolution in my lifetime."

"Are you always such a bitch?"

She'd gotten under his skin. Good. "Pretty much," she said, then pulled herself into the truck and slammed the door shut.

If it took being a bitch, being a little short on patience, to get some movement on a case, Jessica was the girl for the job.

Chapter 4

As soon as she arrived at the office on Monday morning, Jessica tried calling the land trust that owned the reservoir. She'd verified Keith's information. The trust owned forty thousand acres of land including two reservoirs, the one they'd explored and a smaller one farther from the border.

Neither person nor machine picked up at the land trust, so Jessica jotted the number on a sticky note to try again later. She wanted to visit the second reservoir. For that, she'd prefer to have permission to access the property. She also really needed to find someone to go with.

She'd told Angus the truth about using the dog as her companion on her first trip. He'd rolled his eyes instead of getting angry. She appreciated that he trusted her to make her own decisions. But he had brought up a few good points. The dangers in the desert extended far beyond men with guns to things like rattlesnakes and heat exhaustion. A dog couldn't dial a phone or drive a truck. If only.

She turned back to her work, focusing on what paid the bills. As she did, she noticed a woman pushing a baby stroller down the street. It surprised Jessica when the woman stopped and opened the front gate to the office.

Linda took plenty of women clients, in fact, she specialized in helping them. Usually, the women they worked with didn't have the glossy hair, perfect makeup, or a Gucci handbag like the woman rolling the pram toward the building.

Jessica opened the front door, wondering how the woman would get the buggy up the two front steps. She didn't even try. Instead, she reached into it, undid a few hooks, and lifted a baby to her hip. Great. Jessica hadn't planned on dealing with a baby this morning.

"Hi," Jessica said. "This is the Linda Reed Law Firm." Surely the woman had come to the wrong address.

"Then I'm at the right place." She breezed past Jessica and into the building.

"Linda's not here right now."

"I'm not here to see her. I'm here to see you."

"Do I know you?" Jessica asked. But she did know her from somewhere. She racked her memories for where she'd seen the woman.

"I don't think so. Is there somewhere we can talk?"

"This is my desk. You're welcome to have a seat." Jessica gestured toward the lone chair in front of her desk as she slipped behind it and sat.

"I'm Claudia. Claudia Garcia."

Recognition slammed into Jessica as the woman said her name. "I do know you. I talked to you at a party a couple of years ago at Federico Rubio's house in Juarez. You were upset when they ran out of peach seltzers." Far from sober, Claudia had tried to help Jessica find information about the missing heiress Jessica had a contract to locate.

Shortly after Claudia had asked some of her friends about the missing woman, the woman's ex-boyfriend had led Claudia away. Jessica lost sight of her, and soon after, someone, probably Federico, spiked Jessica's drink, killing her memories of the rest of the night.

Claudia sighed heavily and looked at the baby in her arms before addressing Jessica. "I hope he never hears those stories about his mother. I used to drink far too much and tried way too hard to fit in."

"You and me both. At least the drinking too much." Jessica had never cared about fitting in, at least not after her father's conviction. Best not to care about things you couldn't change.

Claudia examined Jessica. "I don't remember you, but I used to hate those parties full of beautiful women I could never compete with. You look like you'd fit in perfectly. Well, with the right makeup and hair."

Her honesty shocked Jessica. Back then, Claudia had come across as pudgy and not nearly as put together as the other young, wealthy women from the city across the border. Things had changed. While not svelte, she looked beautiful and content, like some kind of fertility goddess with a baby leaning across her shoulder happily sucking its thumb.

"You look better than those women," Jessica said. Not usually one for uncalled for kind words, something about Claudia made Jessica want to connect.

Claudia's smile lit her entire face. "Now, I am exactly where I want to be, living the life I'd always dreamed of. I wanted to be a wife and a mother. This is Cinco." She leaned the baby toward Jessica.

Was she supposed to shake its hand? She sure as hell wasn't going to hold him. Thank god for wide desks. She opted for a small wave. "Hi, Cinco. Nice to meet you."

The baby reached a hand toward her. Jessica had no idea how old he was. One? Two? He didn't look like he could walk yet, but she wasn't sure. He did have big blue eyes and blond hair, and looked nothing like his raven-haired mother. Also, why was he named for the number five?

"How can I help you?" Jessica asked.

"I am concerned about the health of my father-in-law and would like to hire you to check up on him."

This sounded too familiar. "What did you say your name was again?"

"Claudia Garcia. Tomás is my husband."

"Oh, no. I've already told him no on this." She couldn't believe Tomás had sent his wife in to do his dirty business. Actually, she could. The guy was an ass and hated to be told no.

"Please," Claudia said. "Can I at least tell you what happened?"

The baby pulled his thumb from his mouth and slammed into his mother's chest. It looked painful. Jessica sank back into her chair and crossed her arms, willing but wary.

"I am afraid of my new mother-in-law. I think she killed Tomás's mother and now she might be killing his father."

"That's a little different than the story Tomás told me."

"Tomás doesn't think Letty is capable of something like that. She partially raised him. I think he thought of her as a part-time nanny, at least until she married his father." Claudia paused and looked down at her son. He had stilled again and rested his head on her. His eyes started to close. She kissed his forehead, and the eyes snapped open once before completely shutting.

Jessica would not let the sweet, almost saccharine scene get to her. Tomás had likely set this whole thing up, hoping she'd cave to his wife. It wasn't going to happen. "Since Tomás hates his dad and sees this woman as a nanny, then I suppose he wants me involved because he's worried about his inheritance now that Daddy has a new wife?"

"No. It's not that. I swear." Claudia looked earnest, but Jessica had a hard time buying it. "I'm worried about Letty. She's some kind of nurse or pharmacist. They brought her into the house when Sofia, Tomás's mother, got sick. Sofia became sicker and sicker after Letty started taking care of her. After she died, his father became very depressed. But he wasn't sick. Then he and Letty married just three months later, and we've hardly seen him since. Now, she says he's so sick that she refuses to let us see him." Her voice wavered and grew louder with her pleading. The baby didn't stir.

"I thought Tomás said his father didn't want to see him anymore. If that's true, how do you know he's sick?" Something in the story didn't add up. Not that Jessica cared. She would not get involved.

Claudia sighed, her frustration blowing through the room. "Tomás received a letter from his father saying he didn't want to see him. Let me show you." She leaned forward and swiped her Gucci bag from the floor.

It amazed Jessica how the baby stuck to her chest, never stirring through all the commotion. If only she could get through a night like that, dead to the world instead of constantly worrying about books, school, and missing people.

Claudia pulled a rumpled envelope from the bag and put it on Jessica's desk. "This is the letter."

Jessica picked it up, thinking she should tell Claudia none of this would work. Nothing would make her take this case. She unfolded the single sheet of white paper.

Tomás,

Now that your mother is gone, we no longer have to live the farce of our strained relationship. I am happy with Letty and do not wish to see you again.

Tomás Garcia Obregon

The typed letter bore an ink signature. Jessica almost smiled. Looks like the poor little rich boy finally got his due. "That sounds about right. I think Tomás's father feels the same way about him as I do," Jessica said.

Claudia's eyes popped open. "You should not be mean. Besides, I thought you were good at your job. Why would his father have typed this out? It's just two short sentences. Why wouldn't he have called, texted, or handwritten him a note. Also, why did he sign his full name instead of writing "Papá" like a normal person?"

The valid questions didn't make Jessica curious. Not much anyway, although it was odd that he'd used his complete name with his son. He must really hate him. Jessica had to get this woman out of her office before she let the case intrigue her.

"Look, I appreciate that the feud between Tomás and his father has put you in an awkward position, but there's nothing you can say or do that would make me work with him again. Honestly, I can't imagine why you even married him. You seem really nice, and he's not a good person."

Jessica expected the woman to either start crying or jump out of her chair and flee. She didn't enjoy showing her meaner side, but it often resulted in action. Instead, Claudia's nostrils flared slightly, and a fire lit in her eyes.

"You do not know Tomás. He has changed. I grew up around the arrogant man you speak of, but I have hardly seen a trace of him in years. What happened with Doraliz shattered him, not because he loved her, but because of who he'd become. He proved that the worst things people said about him were true, that he cared about success above everything else. He spent a lot of time with his mother after that, trying to figure his life out. With her help, he got therapy and began atoning for all he'd done wrong."

Jessica gazed at the woman in shock. People from the upper echelon of Juarez society didn't talk about psychotherapy, especially the men. She couldn't imagine Tomás approving of his wife's indiscretion.

"When we began dating, I promise you, his ambition changed. Now, he cares about his family above all else. Including his father. They repaired their relationship before his mother's death. I'm sure Tomás's father didn't write this letter."

"But that is his signature?" Jessica asked.

"Yes, but it is not how he would have signed a letter to his son."

Jessica shook her head, then folded the letter and returned it to the envelope. She looked Claudia in the eye as she slid the paper toward her. "You can believe Tomás has changed. But I still won't work with him. Besides, I find it extremely convenient that he's concerned about his father when his inheritance is on the line."

Claudia tried again, staring at Jessica as if she were a lifeline. "Tomás doesn't care about his dad's money, he's made plenty of his own. My family has money also. Besides, we live modestly here in El Paso. You don't seem to understand that a man is in danger."

"There are probably a thousand people you could hire to check on Sr. Garcia. Call one of them. Tell your husband I won't work for him."

"Tomás doesn't even know I'm here. He had to travel to Mexico City this morning. Surely, you can work with me." The woman's voice had gone quiet, as if in a last, desperate plea.

"That's not how this works. My answer is no." Her refusal to help might seem unkind, but if Jessica shared what she really knew about Tomás, it would likely devastate Claudia.

The harsh words finally seemed to get through to her. Claudia picked up the envelope and dropped it into her bag. She took Jessica's business card from the holder on her desk and dropped it in also. Finally, she stood. "There is a crime happening, and you don't even care."

That cut. She'd accused Keith of the same thing. "I do care. But I have my boundaries, and working with Tomás Garcia is one of them. I do wish you luck."

Claudia turned to leave, the child still attached to her, dead asleep. A tear spilled down her cheek, but she left without another word.

Chapter 5

Jessica stared at her computer screen, eyes going bleary. She still had two legal cases to get through for homework, but not tonight. Beside her on the couch, Tela snored quietly. Angus strummed an acoustic guitar in a nearby chair. His head gently bounced with the rhythm, and the way his fingers caressed the strings set her heart, and other parts of her body, racing. She really did have everything. Except enough time for sleep.

"Hey, everyone. Eleven o'clock. Time for bed," Jessica said.

Tela yawned and stretched, then hopped off the couch. Jessica shut the cover of her laptop and set it on the coffee table. She rose, then sauntered over to Angus and rested a hand on the guitar's neck. He lifted it to her, and she placed it on the stand before dropping into his lap.

"You ready for bed?" she asked, planting a soft kiss on his lips.

He slipped his hands under her T-shirt and stroked the bare skin of her back. His guitar-playing hands felt like suede on silk, and she felt her body come alive. "Come on, cowboy. Let's go have some fun."

Jessica pulled him toward the kitchen, where Tela waited beside an empty water bowl. She reached for the bowl and slipped her phone from her pocket, asking Angus to plug it in. As she set the bowl down, Tela licked her cheek in a doggie kiss.

Jessica pulled her shirt off as she entered the bedroom and used it to wipe her cheek. Angus stood at the nightstand, her phone still in his hand when it rang.

"Unknown number, but El Paso," he said.

"Answer it. Put it on speaker." Jessica unhooked her bra and let it slide down her arms. She loved how Angus's eyes grew big when he looked up from her phone. Neither of them spoke.

"Hello. Hello. Is Jessica there?" A wail accompanied the voice emanating from the phone.

"This is Jessica? Who's this?" She covered her breasts with her arms. She'd expected a sales call she could quickly ignore.

"It's Claudia. She's here. I saw her face in the window. Letty is here, and I'm so afraid."

"For god's sake, call the police." The panic in Claudia's voice infected Jessica. Although at the same time, she couldn't imagine why Claudia had called her.

"What if she gets in the house?" The baby, Jessica assumed, screamed again, and Claudia shushed him and then began sobbing. "I'm so afraid. Tomás is still in Mexico City, and I can't get Cinco to be quiet. What if she breaks in?"

"It's going to be okay. I need you to calm down and call the police." Jessica pulled the dog slobber T-shirt back on. "Where are you? Are you someplace safe?"

"I'm hiding in the kitchen. I don't think she can see me here. Please come help." More sobs and wailing.

"We have to get the police there. What's your address?" She motioned to Angus to pull out his phone.

The woman began shushing in regular beats. Whether she tried to calm herself or the baby, Jessica couldn't tell, but the noise seemed to work on both of them. After a few seconds, Claudia's breathing slowed. "We live at 2828 Broadmoor, near the country club."

"Okay. We're calling the police. They'll be there soon." Jessica nodded at Angus to make the call.

Angus slipped his phone out of his pocket, eyes wide. He shrugged at Jessica, then bent his head to dial. The sounds from Jessica's phone quieted, then she heard thumping.

"Someone's knocking at the door." Claudia's voice returned to panic mode. "You have to come save us."

"Do not open the door. Stay where you are." Jessica practically shouted the words, praying Claudia would listen. "Don't open the door until the police arrive."

She heard Angus connect to 911. He nodded toward the door, and they scrambled through the house and into Jessica's truck.

"Stay on the line with me," Jessica said, setting the phone beside her. "The police are on their way, and we'll be there soon."

"Thank you," Claudia whispered through the phone. The baby was eerily quiet.

"Is Cinco, okay?" Jessica asked. She glanced at Angus, who had just wrapped up his call with the police.

"Yes. I'm letting him eat. It comforts him."

Didn't need that detail Jessica thought. She pointed the truck up El Paso's mountain, driving faster than the speed limit allowed. "Angus, put the address into your GPS."

Jessica heard the sirens when they were less than a mile from the house. Broadmoor wound between different sides of the country club's golf course, snaking its way further and further up the mountain.

They only passed one car coming down the street, a nondescript silver sedan. It looked like it had Chihuahua plates, the Mexican state just across the border. That, of course, meant nothing. It was almost as common to see Chihuahua plates in El Paso as it was to see Texas plates on the streets of Juarez. For millennia, people had crossed this border, and it remained porous. Employees crossed in each direction every morning, Mexicans drove to El Paso to shop, eat, and party, and El Pasoans did the same heading south. Still, it was almost midnight. Jessica wished she'd gotten a better look at the plates.

A police car had parked in front of an enormous modern home just two houses down from the country club. Jessica saw an officer at the door speaking with Claudia who clung to the baby the same way she had at the law office.

Jessica strode toward the front door, still wondering how Claudia had convinced her to come. She didn't want to step into this world. She'd grown up from the girl who'd once believed Tomás's lies. She'd put herself in so much danger then.

And now this woman, his wife, feared for her life. Each footfall toward this house took her the wrong direction. But she had to make sure the woman and her baby were all right. She glimpsed Angus beside her, at least as determined as she to set things straight.

"There she is. Jessica will help me." Claudia pointed at her and the police officer turned.

After introductions, the police officer offered to walk the grounds and check inside to make sure no one had entered the house.

"Please. I saw her standing right there." Claudia pointed toward a large picture window. The home looked new, all flat concrete and metal beams. Jessica had seen more and more of these modern homes replacing the stucco and red tile roofs of an earlier era.

"Please come in," Claudia said.

She led them through a soaring two-story entryway featuring a brightly lit chandelier twisted like a double helix. A long living room with two separate seating areas stretched into darkness, except for the pulse of the police vehicle lights. The picture window gave a perfect view onto the lawn and street. It must have terrified Claudia to see someone peering in through that window in the dark of night.

Rooms opened onto one another as the party made their way toward a light at the back of the house. Jessica followed Claudia into a great room that must have spanned the width of the home. A wall of windows placed at right angles to each other formed jagged scenes along both sides. To the left hulked the black mass of the Franklin Mountains topped by a midnight sky. The opposite side opened to an infinity pool hovering above the golf course which stretched gently toward the valley below. Claudia opened a door leading to the pool. The officer went outside, and Angus followed him.

In an alcove at the back of the massive room, a black marble island long enough to hold six chairs on one side divided the room from the kitchen. Claudia walked behind the island.

"This is where I hid," she said, staring at Jessica.

Jessica met her behind the island and turned around. She could still see out the windows on both sides of the room. Odd place to hide. She turned to Claudia, about to ask the question, when the woman dropped to her knees.

"Down here," Claudia said. Gripping the baby now asleep in her arms.

Five feet of cold white marble lay between the island and the biggest range Jessica had ever seen. No one outside could have seen her hidden there.

"Good thinking," Jessica said as Claudia rose. "You're sure you saw your mother-in-law?"

"Letty. Sofia was my mother-in-law. I'm positive it was her. That bruja."

"I'm sure calling her a witch endears you to her." Jessica's curiosity drew her into the intrigue of the relationship.

"She is a bruja. She was trained in nursing and used to work at a school in Chihuahua but was fired after a girl died. I heard stories about her in Juarez. Lots of the women there know her."

"Did the girl die because of Letty?"

"Nothing was ever proven. I think Tomás's family paid for the story to go away."

"Why?"

"Because Sofia and Letty grew up together. Tomás's grandfather, Sofia's dad, started a pharmaceutical company in Chihuahua. His younger brother, Letty's father, was the black sheep in the family. He was given a position at the company but was caught stealing drugs and reselling them. He was fired, and Letty came to live with Sofia. She worked at the company for years, then got her nursing degree."

Something didn't make sense. "How unusual that they let her work in the company. Did Sofia work there also?"

Claudia softly laughed. "No. I'm sure my mother-in-law never worked. Her role was to represent the family in society and then to build her own family. I looked up to her long before I was interested in Tomás. I strived to be like her."

Angus and the police officer reentered the house. "There's no one in the back yard. In fact, I really haven't found anything pointing to a person trying to break in. Do you want to file a report?"

At the sound of the male voice, the baby woke and started crying. Claudia bounced and shushed him, but it only seemed to ratchet up the cries. Claudia looked at the baby and then back toward the officer. "No. I guess there's not really anything to report. But thank you for coming."

"Anytime. Please call us again if there's any trouble. I'll show myself out."

As the officer left, Angus headed straight toward Claudia. "Hey, little man," he said in a soft voice.

The baby looked at him with big eyes and ceased crying. Angus smiled and waved, then made a funny face. The baby laughed.

"I think he likes you," Claudia said. "Would you like to hold him?"

"Absolutely," Angus replied with far more cheer than necessary. He swooped the baby up and held him above his head. "What are you doing up there?"

The baby laughed. Jessica couldn't believe it. She'd married a baby whisperer. Now he'd probably want one himself. This whole night was a bad idea. She needed to quickly extricate them from this situation.

"Is Tomás gone a lot?" Jessica asked.

"Not that much," Claudia said, her eyes never leaving Angus and Cinco. Angus swung the baby up and down and the child laughed incessantly.

"Perhaps you can hire security. If you're really afraid of this woman, you shouldn't stay here alone." It seemed an easy solution and personal security guards weren't uncommon along the border.

Claudia sighed heavily and turned to Jessica. "We moved to El Paso to get away from all that. I didn't want Cinco growing up the way I did with drivers and security guards never leaving our sides. I wanted him to have a normal childhood."

Jessica glanced around the enormous room with its spectacular views and stunning artwork. Sure. This kid would grow up normal. Not to mention, his dad was an asshole.

But she understood Claudia's concern. Juarez had become a hotbed of drug war violence in the mid 2000s. For many years it wore the title of most dangerous city in the world. Things had calmed down in recent years, but most wouldn't consider it a safe city.

The violence in Mexico, rarely seeped over the border. Speculation held that the drug kingpins didn't want the US government shining a light southward, so they kept crime out of the city. Also, many wealthy people moved from Juarez to El Paso to avoid the violence. Jessica believed they shielded the city from the worst of the drug war to protect their own families.

"I'm going to go talk to Letty," Claudia said as if she'd just made the decision.

"Why? Ten minutes ago, you were terrified of her." Jessica stared at the woman in disbelief.

"She can't come here and threaten my family. I am going to stand up to this."

Jessica looked at the tiny woman who maybe reached five-foot-four in heels. Defiance lit her eyes. At the moment, she looked like she could take on the world.

"I'm not sure that's a great idea," said Angus, now rocking the baby in his arms. Cinco had his thumb in his mouth and stared at Angus like he was a superhero.

Jessica was in trouble. Who were these people? Claudia had gone from passive mom to warrior, and Angus had transformed into a . . . She would not think about this right now. Sure, Angus taught children music for a living, but she didn't know this alarming version of him.

Children terrified her. She'd spent half her life hating her parents after they abandoned her following her father's conviction. She didn't come from stock that should be put in charge of small humans.

Jessica turned back to Claudia. "If you can find someone to take care of Cinco tomorrow, I'll go with you to see Letty. She lives in El Paso, right?"

An enormous smile crossed Claudia's face. "Thank you, Jessica. Yes. She lives on the Eastside. Maybe we'll even get to see Tomás's father. I'm really worried about him."

"You still need to hire a security detail, at least for when Tomás is gone."

"I'll call my father tomorrow. Believe me, he knows people."

Jessica wondered at that comment. She didn't know much about Claudia, but clearly her family moved in the upper echelon of the Juarez elite. She could learn more tomorrow.

"I'm helping you out, but I'm still not working for your husband." Jessica needed to clarify the situation, to Claudia, to Angus, and to herself.

"I will pay you to help me. This has nothing to do with Tomás."

"You don't need to pay me. Hire a security detail, then we'll go see Letty tomorrow. That's all I'm in for."

"Thank you. I really appreciate it. What time works for you?"

"Noon. Let's go during my lunch break. Angus and I should get going since we have work tomorrow."

"I'll pick you up at your office." Claudia's bright smile made Jessica worry she'd walked into something from which it would be difficult to extricate herself.

The two women turned to Angus, who was singing softly to the baby now asleep in his arms. *Damn it*. Angus would be a great dad.

Chapter 6

Claudia pulled up in front of the office in an indigo Porsche SUV right at noon. She wore bright red lipstick and hid behind giant bedazzled sunglasses looking every bit a wealthy young woman.

Jessica pulled herself into the car. It smelled like expensive leather.

"Good to see you," Claudia said. "Thank you for helping last night. And today. Please tell your husband thank you also. He's really great with kids. Are you planning any?"

Great. Way to jump right into it. "We haven't been married that long."

"Tomás and I married eighteen months ago and wanted to have kids right away."

"Isn't he like fifteen years older than you?" When Jessica saw Claudia at the party, she'd have pegged her at eighteen.

"Thirteen. I'm lucky. Most guys my age don't want to settle down. Tomás was ready. Plus, our families have known each other forever. We were a natural couple."

Except that her husband used to be obsessed with a different woman. One who graduated from Harvard and then disappeared from the bonds of the Juarez aristocracy. But Jessica had no reason to mention that.

"I know about Doraliz," Claudia said, as if reading her mind. "I also grew up with her. Certain families in Juarez are very close knit."

But did she actually know everything about Doraliz and Tomás? It wouldn't help to tell her. Claudia had made her decision and cemented it with a child.

"You must have started dating Tomás right after all that happened." Right when Jessica had gotten her shit together and married Angus.

"Our mothers set us up. I don't know that Tomás saw it as a love match at first. I think he needed to atone for the man he'd become. At least that's what he told me. But we are in love now, and he is a fantastic father."

Jessica had no response. Maybe Claudia spoke the truth. Maybe Tomás remained evil. Jessica didn't care. She'd help Claudia out today, then she'd back away from this and hopefully never see Tomás again.

They drove down the busy freeway past the exit to Juarez, the crowded malls, and all the other crap visible from the freeway. Everyone Jessica had ever met who'd driven through El Paso and never made it off Interstate 10, or maybe just stopped for gas and a hotel, had hated the city. Visitors saw the worst of it from the freeway. Dusty, dirty, run down. It wasn't until one left the thorough-fare and turned up into the desert canyons, or drove into the green valleys, or visited the vibrant downtown, that the city came to life.

They turned onto Lee Treviño Avenue, a street that once marked the outskirts of the desert metropolis. But like most Texas cities, it outgrew this boundary and now stretched east toward San Antonio, just five hundred and twenty miles away.

"What is your family's business in Juarez?" Jessica asked, steering the conversation onto safer ground than babies and husbands.

"Waste removal. And real estate. Two of my brothers consider themselves property developers, but my dad and oldest brother think they're just wasting family money."

"And you had no desire to go into the family business?"

"No. Zero. I wanted a family. But watching my brothers helped me understand the relationship between Tomás and his father."

Jessica looked out the window, convincing herself she didn't care about the relationships between Claudia's brothers, much less that between Tomás and his father. The strip malls and gas stations lining the road gave way to homes as they moved farther from the freeway. Eventually, they passed one of the city's golf courses, the grass mostly straw yellow as winter turned to spring, but green shoots had started to peek through the thatch. Jessica had run out of things to talk about and hoped they'd reach their destination soon.

"Tomás and his father are too much alike." Claudia continued her analysis as if she needed to fill the dead air. "They both want to be the jefe, the boss, not because they are controlling, but they constantly need to prove themselves to each other. It causes misunderstandings. The son wants to build his own business to prove himself to the father, while the father thinks the son doesn't respect what he's built because his son won't become part of his business. It's like walking on the treadmill at the gym, it just goes round and round forever."

"Just push the off button." Jessica said with a tone as dry as the yellow grass. Rich people problems.

"Families don't have an off button," Claudia sounded sad, and patronizing, like Jessica didn't understand families.

"Sure they do. Mine left when I was sixteen." Jessica threw the personal grenade into the vehicle mostly in hopes it would get Claudia to shut up. She immediately regretted the comment and wished she were back at her desk working on other cases.

Claudia braked hard and turned to Jessica. Someone behind them honked. "What do you mean? That's terrible," she said.

"Keep moving. You're going to get us killed." Geez. Claudia had to be the only person in a fifty-mile radius who didn't know Jessica's story. The SUV rolled forward.

"What happened?"

"It was a long time ago. My dad was the DA, and he was convicted of a crime. He and my mom moved to Fort Davis after that." There. A simple explanation.

"And you didn't go with them?" Claudia sounded astonished, but to Jessica, it had all happened so long ago. She'd gotten over it. Eventually.

"I was sixteen. At sixteen, El Paso already seemed like the middle of nowhere. And Fort Davis was 250 miles closer to hell."

"But who took care of you? Were you all alone?"

Jessica shook her head and rolled her eyes. She should never have started this conversation. "My lawyer lived with me. I was fine. Are we almost there?"

As if listening, the car's navigation system told them to turn right at the next light. Surely, that meant the trip would soon end and Jessica could escape this conversation and Tomás's grip, which seemed to tighten around her as they drove.

"Jessica. We have to talk about this. Your past is important. I study families because I want to break these traumas that occur generation to generation." Claudia's eyes stayed on the road as she turned the vehicle, yet Jessica felt them peering into her nonetheless.

"I'm good. Let's check on your father-in-law and give you a chance to lay into Letty about scaring you last night. Then we're done."

Claudia stopped talking, and Jessica stared glumly out the window. She'd once come to east El Paso often, when she had an industrial real estate career and constantly shuttled between the airport and industrial parks on both sides of the border. Often, she had a Midwest factory owner in tow who'd just landed in El Paso for the first time. The mountains, long sight lines, and sheer size of the sky with few trees to hem it in always seemed to impress them. But those same features made the office buildings and apartment complexes they drove by now seem dinky in comparison. Away from the intersection, houses began again, but modest ones, built in the sixties and seventies. The low-slung brick ranch houses differed greatly from Claudia's mansion on the mountain's west side and from the grand estates of the Juarez elite.

"I'm surprised your father-in-law lives in El Paso." Even more so that he lived in this particular neighborhood.

"We were surprised also. The family home in Juarez is quite luxurious. We only discovered they'd moved when we went to visit them in Juarez—to stage an intervention. But when we arrived, the staff told us Letty had decided to move to El Paso, and they hadn't seen Tres in weeks. Tomás was very angry. I'm just worried."

"Tres is Tomás's father's name?" Jessica asked.

"No. All the male children are named Tomás. Tres is the third Tomás. Cinco is the fifth."

That explained it. She wondered if anyone ever called the Tomás she knew Cuatro.

The vehicle told them to turn again, and they eased up a large hill that must have backed up to the golf course. The Porsche seemed out of place on a street filled with mid-class sedans and nondescript minivans.

"Tomás tried calling his father's cell phone that day, Claudia said. "Tres didn't pick up. Letty did. She told him his dad didn't want to talk to him again. Ever." She sighed with such sadness, Jessica worried she'd begin to cry. "Just like in his letter."

Claudia followed the GPS directions and pulled in front of a squat brick house barely visible behind a red brick wall topped with spiked wrought iron bars. Raw concrete took the place of grass in the yard. It looked like a mini fortress. Or a jail.

"Oh, no," Claudia said. "This isn't very nice. I can't imagine Sr. Garcia living here. He is a very elegant man with," she paused . . . "refined tastes."

"What does that mean?" Jessica asked, although the unwelcoming building pretty much answered the question.

"It means he only wants the best of the best for his family. Beautiful things and beautiful people." A trace of anger laced Claudia's words. "But he is family, and we are here to help him."

Claudia's hands gripped the steering wheel as if it tethered her to the present, and she pressed her cherry red lips into a firm line. Until this moment, she'd seemed like the type of woman who appreciated her circumstances without overthinking her status. There was a lot more going on under the surface than Jessica realized. It took her back to the party where Claudia had seemed drunk, loud, and out of place among the aristocracy she very much belonged to. Jessica had been drawn to her, just a regular kid at a party, looking for another drink.

"Do you still like peach seltzer?" Jessica asked.

Claudia turned to her, and Jessica could see the line of eyebrows rise above dark glasses. One side of her mouth hooked up in a wry smile. "I did, once. I drink wine now. Good wine. It's classier, more refined."

Claudia's desire to fit in, then and now, pulled at Jessica, who'd long preferred pushing people away to impressing them. But that could be a lonely existence. Claudia seemed the opposite, bending more so she could build a family she loved.

"How old are you?" Jessica asked.

"Twenty-two."

She'd accomplished a lot in the few years since Jessica had seen her last. They both appeared far more comfortable in their lives, less desperate. Jessica had outgrown her worst habits, and perhaps Claudia had done the same. A new kind of kinship drew Jessica to this woman.

"I think you and I are completely opposite yet totally the same."

"What do you mean?" Claudia asked.

"I think we want completely different things in life. You want motherhood and family. I want to work and make a difference in the world. But I've got a feeling we both go after what we want, take risks."

Claudia lowered her sunglasses, and her eyes sparkled beneath them. "Hell, yes. Now let's go pry my father-in-law out of the claws of this bruja."

Jessica slipped from the car and a gust of wind slammed the door closed. Uh oh. El Paso's bad weather wasn't thunderstorms, hurricanes, or tornadoes like most of Texas. It suffered from two things: summer heat and spring winds that blew thousand-foot-tall walls of sand across the city. Afternoons tended to be the worst, although in recent years some of the dust storms lasted for days.

Jessica and Claudia stopped at the chest-high metal gate—apparently the only entrance to the property. It had neither latches nor levers, just a lock that required a key. Attached to the gatepost, a metal contraption with a camera watched them.

Jessica had encountered these in industrial buildings. She pushed the lone button and heard the intercom connect.

"Hi, this is Jessica Watts. May I speak with Sr. Garcia?"

Silence.

Claudia pushed her aside. "Letty. It's me, Claudia. I need to talk to you. Let us in."

Still nothing. Jessica waved at the camera. "Are you sure this is the right house?"

"Yes. The staff in Juarez gave us the address. They had to bring things over here." She pushed the button again, repeating Letty's name.

Jessica strode to the house next door, which had a yard filled with colored gravel instead of grass, an El Paso specialty. She grabbed three pebbles. When she returned to the gate, she heaved the first stone at the door. It hit with a thud. She chucked the second at the door as well.

"What are you doing?" Claudia asked.

"Knocking."

Jessica threw the final rock, this time hitting the door handle with a ping. She returned to the video intercom. "We've knocked politely. Please open the door."

"Jessica! They're going to call the police on us."

"That's a great idea," Jessica said. "If you're absolutely positive that your father-in-law is here, and he's sick, you should call and get a wellness check." It would beat the hell out of standing here in the wind with no one responding.

"Do I call 911?"

"No. It's not an emergency. I have a friend on the police force. I bet he can help."

Far more than a friend, Sergeant Castro had lived next door to Jessica after her parents left. Over the years he'd given her advice, chased boyfriends away, and had always been there when she needed help and didn't have parents to turn to. Years later, she learned her parents had set him up there to watch over her because they feared the drug cartel might retaliate against the family.

She found his number and dialed. Fortunately, he picked up on the first ring. She explained the situation then handed the phone to Claudia for the details.

While Claudia gave details to the officer, Jessica peered at the house. The windows along the front had louvered blinds closed tight against the outside world, making it impossible to tell if anyone was home. The lowered garage door had its own metal gate. Other than having the key or scaling the wall and wrought iron, getting in looked impossible.

"He wants to talk to you," Claudia said, holding the phone toward her.

"Hey," she said, putting her phone to her ear.

"You really think there's an issue with the father-in-law?" he asked.

If she'd had to rely on Tomás, she'd have said no. But Claudia clearly had no idea what had happened to the man. "I think they are worried about how sick he may be. Frankly, I think they'd love to know he's still alive. Something's off here."

"Okay. I'll coordinate a wellness visit and be back in touch. Send me Claudia's contact information when you get a chance."

"Sounds good." Jessica ended the call.

As soon as she slipped the phone into her pocket, Claudia stepped up to the intercom. "Letty, this is Claudia. I saw you at my house last night. Do not ever threaten me or my child like that again. I've already contacted the police."

Jessica moved beside her and hit the button again. "By the way, she's got security now. The shoot first, ask questions later kind. Welcome to Texas."

Claudia thanked Jessica the entire ride back, even though Jessica kept telling her to wait for results. When she finally pulled up in front of Jessica's office, Claudia grabbed her by the wrist. "I mean it. Thank you. I'll call you as soon as I hear from Sergeant Castro."

When Jessica thought about Tomás, she wanted to turn away and forget the entire adventure. But Claudia had drawn her into the case with subtle skill and a big heart. Hopefully, whatever Jaime found would be enough for Jessica to get away.

Chapter 7

Happy to have the office to herself when she returned, Jessica dove into work. She didn't want to think about this case that had lured her in despite her best interests. She'd always found it easy to walk away before.

She'd walked away from far too many one-night stands. She'd severed her relationship with her parents at sixteen and didn't speak to them for twelve years. But she knew their location and could have reached out to them. She'd constantly received letters from her mom, even though she threw them away unopened. But she'd always had the power to reconnect. Claudia didn't have the choice with Tres.

Jessica still bore many scars from that time, almost all of them self-inflicted. She didn't trust, reached for anger and venom before understanding and kind words. Self-medicated with booze. But she'd made progress since she'd repaired the relationship with her parents.

Time had waited for her psyche to grow up, and she'd established a new bond with her father before he passed. It took longer to forgive her mother because she had to learn to forgive her earlier vengeful self first.

She hoped that hard-earned lesson would dull her sharp edges, maybe give her a leg up on that patience Angus longed for. If her parents had truly disappeared, or died before she caught up to them, her life would have remained a hollow, desolate place.

That's what Claudia, and yes, Tomás faced. Tomás deserved it. He earned whatever bad came his way. But Claudia seemed to truly care about her father-in-law. And Jessica wanted to help.

***

Jaime texted just after five o'clock and asked her to meet him at Claudia's in an hour to discuss the wellness check. Claudia wanted Jessica there. She, in turn, invited Angus, a buffer to help keep her at arm's length.

A part of her longed to immerse herself in the mystery of what had happened to Tres Garcia. It would take her away from boring textbooks and a paralegal/receptionist/jack-of-all-trades job that didn't exactly fill her days with excitement, even if she enjoyed the work, and especially working with Linda.

Angus worked evenings but quickly found someone to cover for him. She stopped by the rock and roll music school he owned to pick him up. He came out to the parking lot, high-fiving kids showing up with electric guitars. His face lit up with each interaction, and the kids clearly adored him. They probably thought of him as their own personal rock star.

It almost made her sad, watching him with the children. She had good memories from before her parents left, but so much of her youth she'd spent howling at an unfair world. She didn't want to pass that trauma on to another generation.

Angus opened the door and sank into the passenger seat. His welcome smile banished all negative thoughts.

They drove up the mountain, sharing the mundane details of each other's days. She didn't mention how this case pulled at her, and how much she hoped Jaime and the wellness visit had resolved any issues. Or how that sliver of her earlier self that desired dark places to explore and a mystery to solve had lodged itself in her spine.

Jaime's cruiser sat at the curb in front of Claudia's house. He and another officer hopped out as soon as she and Angus did.

"My partner and I did the call ourselves," Jaime said as they approached. "Clint, this is Jessica Watts and Angus Delgado."

"Nice to meet you." Clint reached out to shake Jessica's hand.

She'd met Jaime's earlier partners and had recently heard about Clint when the mayor and city council honored them for solving a cold case.

He matched Angus's height at about six feet and sported a slightly trimmer version of Jaime's gym-honed body.

They approached the front door, and Jessica stepped back to let Jaime knock. The second the door opened, she regretted coming. Tomás.

"Fuck," she whispered. She thought she'd been almost silent, but Clint turned to look at her.

"Thank you for coming," Tomás said, all magnanimous charm. "Please come in."

Jessica glanced back at Angus. He wore a tight mask of barely hidden anger. They'd almost been friends once, back when Angus played in Tomás's clubs. But Tomás had repeatedly shown a willingness to put Jessica's life in danger.

As they walked through the doorway, they might as well have entered the viper's den. The house had a completely different vibe in the evening light. Where last night had been shadows and ghost-like fears, today the space seemed properly grand with soaring ceilings, a herring-bone wood floor that appeared hand-hewn, and copious amounts of leather, iron, and glass adorning each room.

When they reached the great room, the space opened to a spectacu-lar view. The floors perfectly matched the desert exterior, leading to the mountains beyond as if the glass wall didn't exist. Jessica swept her eyes to the right where a navy-blue pool perched above the lush greens of the golf course. Not a whiff of the terror from the night before remained.

The stark comparison between this mansion and the homely brick house and beige golf course they'd seen that morning made Jessica worry even more about Tres. Surely, his wealth bought him this kind of luxury, in fact, it might have even bought this house.

The squeal of an infant turned Jessica toward the kitchen. The blond baby bounced on his mother's hip but reached toward Angus. Jessica couldn't hide her smile at Tomás's stormy look as Angus swept the child into his arms.

"We visited your father-in-law's home today." Jaime addressed Clau-dia.

Jessica appreciated that he'd taken this personally. Plus, Jaime knew of Jessica's long past with Tomás.

"Thank you for going to see him so quickly. Please sit down." Claudia gestured to a sitting area on the pool side of the room.

They all found seats. Jessica perched on a cognac leather couch beside Angus, who still held the baby. Tomás sat on the arm of Claudia's chair. Despite the size of the room, tension hovered around them.

"We visited the home at approximately three thirty today," Jaime started. "Letty Garcia met us at the door and let us in. She seemed wary, but many people seem wary when the police show up."

"I'll bet." Tomás said.

His anger seemed to simmer beneath his features. Claudia put a hand on his knee, and Tomás looked at her, then took a breath. Jessica watched his features dissolve into calm, and he squeezed Claudia's hand. It shocked Jessica. For as long as she'd known Tomás, she'd never seen him look tenderly at anyone. People had been tools to him, a means to an end.

"When we asked to see Mr. Garcia, she asked us if we had a warrant," Jaime continued. "We explained that this was a wellness check called in by his family, and she relented and took us to his room."

Here, Jaime paused, as if trying to find the right words to continue. "Mr. Garcia appears to be a very sick man. He was in a hospital bed and was sleeping when we arrived. Mrs. Garcia woke him and explained that we were there. He looked at us and mumbled something, but he didn't seem lucid."

Tomás stood, his manner again stressed. "That can't be. Just months ago, he was fine. Sad about my mother's death, but healthy."

"He didn't look healthy today," Clint said. "He looked like a very sick man. But he did seem cared for. He was clean and Mrs. Garcia explained the medications he was on."

"Stop calling her that." Tomás almost shouted the words.

The baby started crying, and Claudia popped out of her seat to get him. He quieted immediately, and she returned to her place near Tomás.

"Isn't she married to your father?" Clint asked.

"Yes, but she manipulated him into marrying her. I'm sure of it."

"As his wife, the State of Texas considers her his legal guardian unless there are other arrangements in place," Clint said. When Tomás didn't mention anything, he continued. "In fact, she asked us about placing a restraining order on you and your family."

"That's ridiculous. We have got to get him out of her clutches." Tomás turned his back to them and stared at the glass wall. Jessica saw him rest his shaking hands on his hips as if he verged on losing control.

"That isn't something we can help you with. Perhaps you can contact an attorney," Jaime said. "And there's one other thing. While we were there, a man came by. He let himself into the house and became furious at our presence."

Tomás turned back to them, his face showing his eagerness for this information. "Who was it?"

"He said his name was Don Octavio Perales. Is he related to you in any way?"

"No, but I know him. He lives in the Valle de Juarez and has a bad reputation for procuring the illegal and immoral. There's no way my father would have anything to do with him." Disdain radiated from Tomás.

The policemen perked up. "What kinds of illegal items?" Clint asked.

"Women. Guns. Drugs," Tomás answered.

"Is he part of the cartel?" Jessica asked, a special sore place in her heart ached. Her father's downfall came at the hands of the cartel.

"No. He's a bit player, someone they hire last minute when things don't work out. He is useful to them, but not integral to anyone's operations."

"Like a convenience store for the crooks." Jessica shook her head.

Tomás looked at her, his eyes evaluating her comment. "Pretty much."

"We're familiar with the name," Jaime said. "And we left soon after his arrival. Letty hid behind him the moment he arrived. Your father didn't interact with him and didn't seem to recognize him. I'm not sure he was capable of that."

"You make it sounds like Tres could die at any moment." Claudia's voice filled the room with sadness. "Shouldn't he be in a hospital?"

"We're not medical professionals," Clint said. "He was alive and being taken care of, which is all a medical check is meant to uncover. Perhaps he prefers home care."

"That's not possible," Tomás said, turning back to the group.

"Our report is that he is alive and receiving care. Beyond that, it sounds like a family dispute." Jaime stood, quickly followed by Jessica.

Claudia rose as well. "Thank you so much for visiting him. We appreciate knowing that he is there. I'll show you out."

They turned to leave, and Jessica stood, grabbing Angus's hand and pulling him from the couch as well. They'd escaped without incident, and it looked like the end of this case.

"Jessica," Tomás said. "Can you stay?"

She stared into his eyes, seeing nothing but treachery. "No. I need to leave."

At the door, Claudia grabbed Jessica by the wrist, stopping her. The officers continued to their cruiser. A tear coursed down Claudia's face.

"I'm so worried about him," Claudia said. "You know that's not where he belongs."

I don't know that, Jessica wanted to say. But deep in her bones, she did. It didn't fit that a man used to wealth and luxury would want to die in that house, in a city that wasn't his.

"I'm sorry," Jessica said. And she was, but not sorry enough to work with Tomás. She needed to change the subject from what she wouldn't do, how she wouldn't help this woman she'd come to like. "Have you hired security? I don't see them."

"They'll arrive soon and stay all night. With Tomás home, we didn't think we needed them during the day." She paused and looked at the baby. "What are we going to do?"

Jessica wasn't sure which of them she addressed. "I don't know."

"How could he have become so sick so quickly? Tomás's mom passed away from cancer, but his father was completely healthy."

"It's true." Tomás spoke from behind her, and Jessica felt a sliver of the old trepidation run up her spine. Somehow, Angus noticed and rested his warm hand on her back. Jessica turned, needing to keep Tomás in her sights.

"He was not only healthy but continued to run his company after my mother died. For some reason, after her death, Letty stayed in my parents' house. They were married not long after, only no one was invited to the wedding, if there was one. But there is a legal document, signed by both of them." He sighed then, as if the weight of death and bad decisions held him down.

"Maybe he wanted someone to take care of him," Jessica said. Marriages had been made of less.

"Last week I was told he'd retired from his company and named Letty Chairman of the Board. There's no way that would have happened. She has no experience running corporations. That company was everything to my father."

Suspicion passed through her like smoke. That kind of decision was unheard of, but also, Tomás had never shown an interest in his father's company. Now he did. "Are you involved in the company?" she asked.

"No. Another board member let me know. That's why I went to Mexico City, to meet with our attorneys. Evidently, my father gave himself sole responsibility to appoint the board chairman position, and they had a signed letter from him doing so."

"Sergeant Castro said he wasn't lucid. Perhaps he wasn't capable of making that decision." After two years of law school, Jessica couldn't keep her brain from reaching for solutions.

"You're right," Tomás said, suddenly excited. He looked at his wife. "I may need to return to Mexico City."

"I thought you didn't care about your father's company." Jessica expected to see his conceit rise at her words, instead, she saw something else. Maybe honesty.

"I don't. You know I never have. But I do care about my father and his legacy. And I care about the future of this one." He stroked Cinco's cheek.

"If your father is as sick as they say, you'll probably want to check on the kid's inheritance as well." The comment came from Angus, but it sobered them all.

A dying man. A fortune. Whether Tomás's father had returned to the sticky relationship with his son earlier or whether the new wife manipulated him, a countdown clock began ticking, and it drew Jessica in with every second hand movement.

Chapter 8

Back home, too keyed up to sleep, Jessica cracked open two beers and let Tela into the backyard. She slumped into a patio chair, a recent gift from Angus's parents. Tela had jumped off the couch and bounced with energy when they returned, and the long, narrow yard provided the perfect place for the active dog to run. Normally, she and the border collie next door would race the fence until they collapsed in exhaustion, but he was likely inside and asleep.

The backyard and a cold beer usually meant instant relaxation, but Jessica's mind worked in overdrive trying to figure out the Garcia case. It chilled her to think of the old man spending his days debilitated in that house. And that Don Octavio guy. Was he the wife's lover? He sounded like bad news. Did he supply drugs to Letty that she used to disable her husband? Jessica's mind spun scenario after scenario.

Tomás's father was seriously wealthy. He'd owned the original bottling company in Juarez and parlayed that monopoly into real estate deals, car dealerships, and hotels. A small-time criminal like this Don Octavio guy would probably do anything to get his grubby hands on a fortune like that.

Letty also intrigued Jessica. She'd grown up adjacent to Tomás's mother, but it sounded like she'd never quite fit in. Still, she'd surely known Tres since his wedding. Were they involved in a long-term, salacious affair, or was something even more nefarious afoot? Could she have taken advantage of the man at a low point, the loss of his wife? Did she love him or his money?

"I can see your brain working," Angus said. He took a swig of beer.

Tela, lit by the back porch light, had sniffed almost the entire yard by now. She looked up when she heard Angus's voice. Her tail wagged exactly twice, then she trotted over to a yellow tennis ball, grabbed it, and loped toward him.

"Here we go again," he said as the dog laid the ball at his feet. He picked it up and threw it far into the yard. Tela bounded after it.

"You know, she'll do that all night." Jessica squinted up at him, enjoying the starlight on his features.

"Just like you'll puzzle over the Garcia case all night." He threw the ball again.

"It is interesting," she said. "A rich old man suddenly on his deathbed. A brand-new wife. A small-time criminal. I think I've seen the movie."

"You left out the asshole son," Angus said.

"That dude seemed really angry."

"I'd be upset if I couldn't see my dad."

"Yeah, but your dad is awesome. You two have always had a special relationship. And unlike the men in the Garcia family, he named you after his favorite guitarist, not himself. That says a lot."

It really did. Angus had the perfect family. Laid-back dad, occasionally overbearing but always loving mom. Close knit siblings.

Tomás's family had money, but they also passed down the family name like an obligation. For all of his earlier loathing of his father, Tomás had named his baby the same, continuing a long line of tradition. Or narcissism.

Angus continued to throw, and Tela chased each new ball as if it were a brand-new game. The night-time chill of the desert sank into Jessica's bones. She faced the western mesa, a sizeable blackness cutting through the dark sky. The tabletop of sand lay just a single mile and an entire state away in New Mexico. El Paso was made of borders. The one between Texas and New Mexico, another split by a river between the United States and Mexico. The city's mountains dividing the east from the west. Families split between love and greed.

Once torn apart, family relationships mended slowly. Jessica had learned this with her parents. But desperation sped the healing. Jessica had quickly repaired her relationship with her father, whose stroke-destroyed body threatened to take him away at any time. It did, but they'd had the time they needed to forgive and move forward.

Had Tomás's rift with his father healed due to his mother's illness and passing? Or had it festered, at least from the father's side, leading him to turn away from his son the moment the person holding them together passed? An elusive answer, given his father's condition.

"I feel for Claudia. She seems really nice." Angus's voice interrupted her thoughts.

"Yeah. Me too. I can't believe she's with Tomás. She says she knows about him, but she can't."

"I'm sure she sees a different side of him than we do." Angus sat next to her, letting the ball roll across the deck the next time Tela dropped it. "I'm glad you get to sit this one out." He reached out and stroked her arm.

"Good thing you chose the clean hand for that." She said looking at where his hand lay atop her skin. "That ball is disgusting."

She didn't respond to his comment about the case. She didn't have a role, yet it still knocked around in her brain, looking for a solution. It should be easy to solve. No one had disappeared. But if she divided the problem into bad guys and good guys, she had no idea who fell on which side. The answers had to be right there.

***

The next day, the wind howled through the city. Air currents gathered sand in New Mexico, Arizona, and possibly California, then shoved it into this corner of Texas. It hung in the air giving everything an orange hue, blasting the shine off cars, and sneaking in through cracks in windows and doors. The sun and mountains disappeared, and planes couldn't land at the airport.

Like siroccos in the Mediterranean or Santa Anas in California, the winds affected psychological as well as physical space. Some people hunkered down trying to outlast the storm, others used it as an excuse to go on tangents that would have been taboo on calmer days. The winds made Jessica want to leave her office and explore dirtier things. The movement of the air caused her to crave momentum as well. She took off early for lunch, got in the truck, and drove.

On the freeway, flying grains of sand tried to abrade the white from her truck. Wind attempted to muscle the vehicle into adjacent traffic. The blotted-out sun formed a hellscape in orange twilight. It exhilarated her to drive through such drastic conditions. It felt like humanity on hiatus.

She told herself she didn't know where she planned to go, but of course she ended up at the brick house on the golf course on the east side of town. She parked across the street, one house down, and stared at it through the dirt-filled air. Dust devils formed in the walled off, concrete yard and spun piles of orange sand into every corner.

A set of trash cans partially hid the truck from the house yet gave Jessica a clear view of the gate and windows. Blinds closed, doors and gate shut, the house closed in on itself like a turtle tucked deep within its shell. Yet a sick man in a hospital bed and his new wife/nurse-maid inhabited the home. Perhaps a criminal with an undetermined relationship to the occupants visited also. Or he might live there. She wanted to know, wanted the x-ray vision children believed in to illuminate their activities and bare their thoughts and feelings.

Was she drawn to them because she'd recently dealt with her own dying father? Was it her certainty that Claudia had made a bad decision? Was it boredom or her famous lack of patience? She wanted to start a fire to force them outside, then convince them to give her answers.

An extra strong gust of wind shook her truck and knocked over one of the trash cans. The gray bin spewed its contents across the street. Jessica saw a roll of gauze unfurl onto the pavement, then the wind picked it up and blew it away.

Thick plastic bags, like the ones that held fluids in a hospital, splayed near the can, one red, one clear. That was it. Hadn't Claudia mentioned the new wife worked as a school nurse? She grew up in the family's pharmaceutical business. A suddenly sick man. IV bags. There had to be a link between these bags and Tres's abrupt incapacitation.

Jessica opened the truck's door, and the wind wrenched it from her grasp and almost pulled it from the frame. It took her body weight to slam it closed. More gauze, white pads, and the bags scooted down the street as if on a mission to save someone—or to kill them.

Jessica knelt beside the trash can and peered inside. The evidence needed to either help or hinder a very sick man filled the can. She spied a plastic baggie full of used needles. Bloody pads. Empty plastic bottles of alcohol, which should have gone in the recycling bin, hid behind bandages. And small glass vials of medicine formed a trail into a plastic trash bag that had burst open.

She wanted to gather it all, present it to Jaime and close the case. She also refused to touch the biohazard zone with her own fingers. It was disgusting and even she knew of the procedures in place to deal with waste like this. Plus, the police would need a clear chain of evidence, something her gathering the materials would ruin. But if she left them here, they might blow away. Or be picked up by a trash truck, never to be seen again.

She debated too long, squatting beside the debris while wind-flung dirt threaded into her hair and burrowed into her skin. Finally, she decided to go back to her car and get her phone. She could take photos as evidence and call Jaime. If the trash truck came, she'd pull in front of it so they wouldn't take the bin away. Maybe she'd close the lid and push the container upright, although another gust could always come along and force even more evidence into the street to be vanished by the wind.

The vials and bloody pads certainly looked like a crime scene. She'd do everything she could to ensure the evidence lasted until Jaime had the chance to see it.

She rose, careful not to touch anything. Movement spun at the corner of her eye. She turned toward the house just in time to see the flat blade of a shovel swinging toward her.

Chapter 9

Pain pounded through Jessica, a slow never-ending drumbeat. A death serenade.

Slowly, she became aware of her body, mostly her throbbing head. But it beat in time to her heart, and once she knew she had a heart, she explored her gut, her legs, her fingers. She took a breath, and the pain almost ripped it from her. But the pain also told her she lived.

Almost pure silence surrounded her, just the ringing in her ears and a faint beeping from far away. She smelled nothing but dust and the iron scent of blood. Her hands and body rested on something soft, if uncomfortable. A bed, but not her own.

She tried to open her eyes, but the tiniest shaft of light hit her brain like a fireball, almost causing her to wretch. Jessica squeezed her eyes shut and tried to retreat from the burn.

In the next moment, or perhaps hours later, she swam back to consciousness. Her head still throbbed, pulsing like something alive but separate from her body. Afraid to open her eyes, she used her fingers to explore. She touched cloth, perhaps a sheet atop a narrow bed. Not home. Her mind searched for memories of home, of who and where she was, but her brain blocked every foray with a fresh stab of agony.

She stopped thinking, just tried to exist as a body on a bed. Thirst came, and she licked dry lips. Nausea followed, and she remained completely still until it passed. Ragged breathing reached her ears, her own, that and the faint beeping, like in a hospital. She pulled in each breath as if summitting a mountain, then forced it out again, following the pain back downhill.

She heard a creak, then footsteps. A prick. Then silence returned.

***

Jessica clawed her way back to consciousness, a symphony of pain ringing through her. The sharp jabs in her head, neck, and shoulders made her want to scream. But she knew who she was. She pried her eyes open expecting to see hospital white. Instead, a single light bulb glared at her from above.

She tried to turn her head to survey her surroundings, but pain shot through her skull, taking her breath away. Instead, she used her eyes alone. A bare ceiling but for the single bulb. Cinder block walls. No sounds except her own inhalations. The smell of dust and still air.

She had to sit up, to reclaim the use of her body. Each movement threatened to rip her apart, but she lifted herself onto her elbows. A surge of vomit gripped her, and she swung her upper body to the side to throw up. Her body heaved, targeting a bucket that someone had placed beside the bed, but nothing came out.

Halfway up already, she swung her legs over the side of the bed and slumped against the wall next to it. The surroundings, completely unfamiliar, looked more like a jail cell than a hospital or home. Cinderblock walls on all four sides, concrete floor, a metal door. Where the hell was she?

She closed her eyes to force the memories to come. Time passed, and when she opened them, a woman stood before her.

"Who are you?" Jessica asked, not sure her voice made it through her parched throat and chapped lips.

The woman's black eyes, framed by a heavy, black brow darted to her own. Deep lines creased her face, and two thin braids of gray hair dropped to her shoulders. She looked like a witch.

The woman handed Jessica a bottle of water. The weight of it slammed Jessica's hand to the bed. She stared at her arm, forced it to lift the small plastic bottle. Her strength had disappeared.

"Duerme," the woman said. Sleep.

Jessica lifted her eyes to see the woman walking toward the door.

"Wait. Espera," Jessica screamed, the words coming out harsh and raspy. The woman didn't slow, and Jessica watched her small, black-clad frame disappear behind the metal door. She heard the click of a lock.

It took many long minutes of frustration for Jessica to unscrew the bottle cap. She needed to get her strength back and process this situation. She took a sip of water, worked to hold it down.

I am Jessica Watts. Angus's face floated through her memories, and her heart jerked. Where was he? The memories came tumbling back. Angus, her dog, then Claudia and the baby. Sitting in Claudia's house surrounded by Angus, the police, Tomás. Something had happened there.

She closed her eyes against the bare walls, searching for a clue. The windstorm. It flooded back suddenly. She'd gone to the fallen trash can, found the bandages and vials, needed her camera, saw the object flying toward her. The blade of a shovel hitting her in the head. Her final memory.

She must be in the house in east El Paso. Whoever hit her must have dragged her inside. Was it the woman who'd brought her the water? Jessica had a hard time believing that. The woman seemed so small and thin. Could she have hit her hard enough to knock her out and drag her body inside? Probably not.

But surely that was Letty. Jessica's thoughts fogged. She couldn't pull apart why they'd bring her into the house or what they hoped to accomplish. If only she weren't so tired. The fog settled like a blanket, making her question unclear and answers impossible. She let her eyes close.

***

The next time Jessic woke, the world seemed sharper. Pain still jabbed at her as she opened her eyes, but she fought past it. She sat up in the bed, growing dizzy for a moment but better able to control her limbs.

She found the water bottle and took a long, slow sip. The water cascaded through her body, bringing the relief of rain in the desert. She finished half of it, each sip bringing her back to herself.

The questions came quickly. How long had she been here? Was she being held hostage? Why? It seemed like a stupid maneuver. The police had been to the house before. Jaime would come for her, probably soon. He'd experienced her curiosity, and her acting out on it, for many years. Why would Letty or Don Octavio want to be charged with kidnapping? Had something happened to Sr. Garcia? Had that made them desperate?

"Hey," Jessica yelled, the noise spearing her brain. No response. The thick walls did an amazingly good job of insulating the room. She couldn't hear a thing. Except that constant, slow beeping.

Jessica grabbed hold of the metal bed frame and heaved herself up. The pounding in her head almost slammed her back down, but she fought it. She crossed the small room step by sluggish step.

When she reached the metal door, she rested her forehead against its cool surface. She wanted to return to the bed and sleep until the stabbing pain in her head disappeared. But she had to get out of here.

She pounded on the door. "Hey," she called, then pounded again. Nothing.

Eventually she stopped. Each knock on the door skewered a burning poker into her brain. She put her back to the wall and slid down, unwilling to walk all the way to the bed.

As she sat beside the door, she heard voices. The gap at the bottom of the door let in sound. She leaned over and set an ear against it.

"You have to get rid of her," a man said in Spanish, making Jessica grateful for her grasp of the language. "It is too dangerous."

Murmuring from a woman reached her ears, but she couldn't make out the words. It matched the voice of the woman who'd brought her the water.

Jessica wanted to call out, to alert them to her. She could tell them the police were on their way, that they'd never get away with whatever scheme they'd planned. Jessica wished she had told someone about her visit to the house. But she hadn't planned it. Antsy in the howling day, she'd driven without purpose. Just like usual. This was why Angus always told her to be patient. She always just took off, to Central America to find a missing woman, into the desert at night searching for a missing girl. She forced things to happen instead of waiting for them to unfold. And now something had definitely happened. Next time, she'd be more careful.

"Just kill her!" the male voice roared.

"Not yet," the woman said. She didn't yell, but her steely voice didn't allow for argument. "I must secure what is mine first."

"He'll never agree," the man said.

"Trust me," the woman said. "In all these years, have I ever let you down?"

"You have two days to get them out of here. That is when the next transfer happens."

The woman didn't respond. Instead, Jessica heard noises like pots and pans in a kitchen. A door slammed, then footsteps approached.

Jessica scooted away from the door. Were they coming to kill her? Her mind whirred as she scanned the bare room. The space, maybe twenty by twenty feet, had no place to hide. The room held only the bed, the pail beside it, and a crucifix attached to the wall. And Jessica.

The footsteps stopped outside the door. Jessica held her breath, expecting another shovel hit, a gun, or worse. Keys jingled, then the lock turned.

The woman started when she saw Jessica crouched near the door. She recovered quickly, her eyes going from shock to steely hate in a millisecond. She had a tray in her hands and set it on the floor just inside the room. Then she slammed the door shut and locked it.

Jessica hadn't seen much behind the woman. This room seemed to open onto a hallway near a sparse kitchen area. Jessica couldn't imagine the floor plan of the house.

She examined the tray. It held a paper plate with rice and black beans and another bottle of water. No utensils. Her stomach growled and she couldn't remember the last time she'd eaten. And she wouldn't eat now.

The woman had probably laced her food with some kind of drug. Jessica remembered the pinprick from one of the times she'd woken. She looked at her arm and saw a faint bruise above a buried vein.

She had to think, to figure out how to get out of here, but her mind wouldn't work. Exhaustion overtook her, and the savage pounding in her head returned. The bed seemed so far away. Jessica crawled across the floor and pulled herself onto the narrow mattress. She had to escape, would figure it out before that man returned and tried to kill her. But now she needed sleep and to pretend she could snuggle into the love and safety of Angus. He must be wrecked with worry.

Perhaps he would arrive like a white knight and save her. Or maybe Jaime would come before she woke and rescue her. Those sweet dreams brought comfort instead of the loneliness of having to save herself. She let her eyes close and drifted off to faint beeping.

Chapter 10

Jessica hadn't opened her eyes yet, but the thin foam mattress and distant beeping gave away her exact location. It was time to get the hell out of this place.

She swung her legs off the bed and stood. Her skull hurt like it was stuck in a vise. She brought her fingers to her temple. Sore and swollen. And she probably had an enormous bruise. But she had far greater things to worry about. The untouched food and water still sat on the tray.

She lurched over to it, her limbs clumsy with disuse. She wouldn't eat the food but needed the water. Surely, help would arrive soon. If not, she needed an escape plan.

She uncapped the bottle and chugged the entire thing. Just like the first bottle this one had a Mexican label. Immediately, she needed to pee. She pounded on the door. "Hey, I need to use the restroom."

No one responded. She glanced around the room. She'd have to use the bucket. Disgusting. But better than peeing in her pants. She'd leave the bucket for someone else to deal with—maybe then they'd let her use a restroom.

With her needs taken care of, she returned to the door. She stooped down to the crack and listened. Silence. As if no one was home. She jiggled the door handle. Locked tight. Maybe she could find something to jimmy it, like a wire from the bedframe.

She noticed the cross again when she looked at the bed. A potential weapon. Jessica could reach it by standing on the bed, but it seemed to be glued to the wall and barely moved when she yanked on it.

She slammed her palm against it until it hurt too much to go on. The perpendicular pieces of wood barely budged.

She needed a different tool. She crawled under the bed. Springs and wire held it together, but the taut springs and thick wire wouldn't budge under her fingertips.

Frustration overwhelmed her. Her drive for action accelerated, yet she could find nothing productive to do. She had to fucking get out of here. Desperation mixed with the constant pounding in her head, creating a cocktail that threatened to tip her over the edge. She wanted to tear the room apart, but there was nothing to tear. Wanted to pound her body against the impenetrable cinderblocks. Wanted to slam herself into the metal door until either it broke or she did. Her entire body trembled with the need to get out of this damn room. Jessica wiped a tear from her cheek. Maybe she could escape by dissolving into a puddle of tears and evaporating into the dry desert air.

A growing dread hollowed her out, but she refused to sink into nothingness. Instead, she crawled back to the door and listened.

***

She waited minutes or hours, although it felt like days before she heard someone. Her ears strained at the faint sounds—a door opening, footsteps, voices. She'd hoped so desperately for the police to arrive that she'd surely pulled them here with her mind. But no, only the familiar voices she'd heard before, presumably Letty and Don Octavio.

Why hadn't the police come? Something was wrong. Days, or at least twenty-four hours must have passed since they'd kidnapped her. She had no way to tell. Less than a day had passed between the visit with Claudia and Tomás before Jessica had barreled back to Letty and Tres's house. Surely, everyone would guess she'd gone there. It fit her M.O.

The bulb in the ceiling never turned off, and the room had no windows. She'd never felt claustrophobia before, but the walls pushed at her now, beckoning her to a new level of fear. She had to get out.

Linda would have noticed if she hadn't returned to work. And Angus. She tried to avoid thinking about how terrified he'd be. He'd become her best friend in kindergarten. Had remained her strongest support in the years after her family had left. In the past, her bad habits had almost broken their friendship. But then she'd gotten her act together, promised to always love him, married him. She hadn't strayed then and never would. He'd always feared something would happen to her, worried that she wasn't careful. Guilt mixed with hope.

Surely, Angus would have alerted Jaime by now. Given her past behavior, Jaime would know she'd returned to Letty's house. She could never leave things alone and always went off on her own trying to solve cases. Jaime had complained about it. Angus too. If she ever got out of here, she'd never go off half-cocked again.

Pots and pans banged in the kitchen. Jessica focused on the conversation now close enough to hear.

"Why do you feed her?" the person Jessica assumed was Don Octavio asked.

"She is part of my plan. I can use her to lure Claudia and the baby." Letty said.

"Eres tonta. There's no way you'll succeed. Tomás is too smart for your games."

It stunned Jessica that he called Letty a fool. Tomás must be right; Don Octavio must be the brains behind the operation. Claudia had feared Letty, but she didn't seem to have much power in this relationship.

"You are wrong. I raised Tomás. Even though he never respected me, I know him. I understand how to get things from him. He won't risk losing his wife, and she's not smart. It will be easy to manipulate her. Claudia is the one you should be calling tonta."

The puzzle pieces came together in Jessica's head. Letty was right. Despite her marrying Tomás's father and him making her the head of the company, Tomás would fight to protect his inheritance unless he had a good reason not to. If Jessica had to bet, she'd guess Letty had Tres's will changed as well. She'd need leverage with Tomás, and Claudia might unwittingly provide that.

"The son is not a man if he won't fight for his legacy. Your plan won't work." Don Octavio's voice boomed.

"He is a changed man," Letty said. "He used to be hard, like his father. But my cousin made him soft. When he came back home, she treated him like a child. She hated that he went against his father, had his own ambitions. When she had the chance to ensnare him, she demanded he forgive his father and marry that ridiculous girl who just wants to play housewife, just like Sofia did."

A plate clattered to a counter or table. "Bring me the salsa," Don Octavio said.

Jessica smelled the food Letty cooked, and her stomach growled so loudly she feared they'd hear it through the door. Her body needed food, craved it as if she hadn't eaten in a week. Perhaps she hadn't. No, it couldn't be that long. She shook her head to clear the fog, but the movement sent knife blades through the backs of her eyes.

The voices quieted. Jessica heard the clatter of silverware. Occasionally, Don Octavio asked for something: more tortillas, water. Letty seemed to do his bidding. Jessica lay on the cement floor, letting the cold creep into her system.

"How much longer does the old man have?" Don Octavio asked.

"Not too long," Letty answered. "Days, not weeks."

"Aye, mujer. You only have until Friday. Speed it up."

The words arrived with an onslaught of questions. What would happen on Friday? Did Letty really think Tres was so sick he'd only survive a few days? And why did he call her *mujer*, a term usually reserved for one's wife?

"I can't go faster. His death must look natural. I will stay here until he's gone."

"No!" A loud smack meant he must have slapped the table. Then, Don Octavio's anger-tinged voice echoed. "These people are too dangerous."

"We will make more money with my plan. People cross all the time. What's a few days? The coyotes can hold them in the desert until we're done. They can cross next week."

"I told you, I do not control this. These coyotes would just as soon see us dead as change their plans. They need this location and pay me well for it."

"Tell them they can use the land but not the house." Letty's voice held steel. She might take occasional digs from Don Octavio, but she could also hold her own.

"It's impossible. If you don't have them out of here by Friday night, I'll kill the girl and the old man myself."

Jessica's stomach roiled again, but not from hunger this time. She tried to make sense of the words and came up with the worst of answers. She wasn't at the house in El Paso. They'd brought her to Juarez, or somewhere else in Mexico.

The term coyotes sealed it. Immigrants hoping to cross into the United States to flee persecution, find work, or reunite with family, often paid coyotes—the men, not the animals—to help them safely across the border. Some coyotes did their jobs. Others took the money and left their victims to die in the desert. Or killed them.

This place must be a waystation on the trip to the United States. It made sense. Jessica had wondered why anyone would have built a room with raw cinderblock walls inside a regular house. They hadn't. And she could be anywhere. Her hope faded.

The US/Mexico border stretched almost two thousand miles. Given Letty's interest in Tomás and Claudia, Jessica would bet they were within a hundred miles of Juarez. This also explained why the police hadn't found her. No one knew where she was. Her heart ached for Angus and her mother. They loved her. If she survived this, she'd prove her love to them.

What the hell had she done? No one had asked her to go back to that house, to search for evidence. She was always acting first and thinking later, and now that might get her killed. Fuck. She'd claim the mantle of tonta for herself.

"Fine," Letty said. "I'll get Claudia. Tomás won't be able to resist saving the mother of his child." Footsteps, then clattering.

"I told you, they have security now. I've seen them. You can't get to her. Your plan is falling apart. Kill the woman and the old man and take your chances with Tomás."

"Claudia will come to me. She may not trust me, but she needs me."

The footsteps neared, and Jessica heard the swishing of fabric then the metallic clink of keys. Shit. She scooted along the wall and away from the door. It opened partially, then swung further toward her. The woman bent, and a tray clattered to the ground.

Jessica wished she'd stood instead of staying crouched against the wall. She could probably take Letty in a fight. Although Don Octavio sat steps away, and he had already threatened to shoot her.

Letty pushed the door open until it thudded against the wall. Her black eyes found Jessica, but Jessica could barely see her as she'd slitted her own eyes closed and slumped against the wall. She kept herself as still as an opossum. With no plan and nothing to defend herself with, she hoped pretending to be unconscious would buy her more time.

Jessica felt Letty's gaze on her for long seconds. It prickled the hair on her arms, but she didn't move. She forced herself to breathe regularly, if more slowly than the situation warranted. Eventually, Letty grabbed the old tray and pulled the door shut.

Relief washed through Jessica as the tumblers in the locks rotated into place. She wanted to escape from this room as much as she'd ever wanted anything. But she needed to plan how to escape and live, not just go barreling from a current danger into a greater one.

Letty had left another tray of food, and the aroma pulled Jessica toward it. First, she opened the water bottle and took two deep sips. The water heightened her senses, and she could almost taste the rice and beans. She bent over the tray. Inhaled.

Her lips hovered above the beans. She wanted to gulp the food down like a dog. She shoved herself backward. Letty had drugged her before. Jessica would never forget that pinprick. And Letty had no reason not to drug her again. It would probably be the easiest way to kill her.

Of course, if she went too long without eating, she'd die anyway or not have the strength to save herself. She sat against the wall and rested her head in much the same position she'd taken when Letty had entered the room. Only this time, she felt the exhaustion she'd pretended earlier. She wanted to give in to the hopeless situation. Give up. Only that wouldn't accomplish anything. She had to keep her wits about her, and they were fraying fast.

Patience. What was the smart, patient thing to do? Maybe she could eat some of the food to fuel her body. Jessica would discover if Letty had laced it with drugs, but hopefully not ingest a fatal amount.

Her singular focus on food annoyed her, but it had taken over her thoughts. She approached the tray again. She'd eat one quarter of the food. As she examined it, she noticed a tortilla under the rice and bean mix. That should be fine. Letty hadn't been in the kitchen long enough to make tortillas, which meant she'd probably stopped by a tortillería.

Jessica pulled the warm corn disk out from under the food and wrapped it around one fourth of the mixture. Her hand shook as she brought it to her mouth, hopefully due to anticipation, not weakness. She sank her teeth into the soft taco and almost moaned in pleasure. Too soon, it was gone.

She grabbed the water bottle and retreated to the bed. The urge to finish the food and lick the plate clean overwhelmed her, but she couldn't let it happen. Not until she'd completed her experiment.

The situation reminded her of stories about tasters back in the days of medieval kings. Constantly afraid of someone poisoning them, they assigned people to test their food before they ate it. If no one barfed or dropped dead, then they dined. Jessica had to be her own taster. But at least she was being careful. Unlike so many times before.

She lay down and rested her head on the pillow. The faint beeping continued to make its way through the cinder walls. It sounded so much like the machines in a hospital room. Tres probably sprawled in his hospital bed one room over. If the noise was his bed, then they'd brought him to Juarez as well. Perhaps the visit from the police had scared Letty and Don Octavio back across the border. If so, did Jessica have an obligation to save him as well as herself?

No. Already old and sick, he'd slow her down too much. What was she supposed to do, push his hospital bed through the streets of Juarez? They'd both be better off if she escaped and went for help.

What about Claudia and Cinco? Jessica's thoughts muddled. They were safe at home. She didn't need to rescue them. But her brain wouldn't leave the thought alone. Something Letty had said made Jessica worry they wouldn't be spared. Her thoughts couldn't follow a straight line from those remarks to potential outcomes. Drowsiness swooped in and claimed her before she figured it out.

Chapter 11

Letty had drugged the food. Waking up felt like swimming through Jell-O. It took effort to make Jessica's sluggish thoughts coalesce into ideas that made sense. She forced herself to relax, told herself she had nowhere to be. The beeping reached her consciousness. That had to be Tres. Another instrument wouldn't carry on so seamlessly night after night. Or sleep after sleep. Time was an illusion. Only fear and death were real.

As her brain sharpened, she realized its dull edges had tried to fool her. Patience only mattered when time existed, and she'd run out. Her body wouldn't last, but it might outlast her mind.

She needed sharp thoughts and a honed weapon. But she'd have to use the tray. That would mean overpowering Letty. Or befriending her and then overpowering her. Or maybe she could convince Letty to let her go. But Letty had barely spoken to her. And Don Octavio wanted to kill her. She'd have to find a time when he was out. Which seemed like never.

She sat up and took a sip of water. The room whirled around her, whether from weakness or the drugs, she didn't know. She couldn't afford to wait any longer. She slowly rose from the bed, struggling as if all her muscles had decayed. She dragged herself across the room, moved the bucket, and slid down the wall next to the door. She'd be right there the next time Letty opened it, and in the meantime, she'd listen in on their conversations.

Jessica waited for what seemed like forever. Each minute, her emotions swung between fear, rage, determination, and defeat. What she wouldn't give for her watch or her phone. Her phone. Was it still in her car, parked in front of the El Paso house? If so, it would at least point to Letty and Don Octavio. Maybe that's why they'd come here. Her truck in the street compromised the El Paso location, forcing them into hiding.

Jessica dozed some, leaning against the wall. She'd never slept so much in her life, not that she had anything else to do. So many movies showed imprisoned people exercising to gain strength so they could beat the enemy. Maybe the drugs or the shovel to the skull made her lazy, but she had no desire to move. Or sweat. Especially when she only had access to the occasional bottle of water. She'd have to rely on her brains more than her brawn to get out of here.

Heavy footfalls neared. A key slid into the lock with the accompanying jingle. Jessica held her breath as the door slid open. She had to look up, way up, to see his face. And she wished she hadn't.

A bald man stared down at her. He had a pockmarked face and a full, grizzled beard, neatly trimmed. His gun seemed tiny in his giant hand. He didn't point it directly at her. His thumb rested in his waistband, while his fingers wrapped around the metal. The black button down and dark blue pants he wore had a slight sheen to them, as if he'd gone clubbing or had just left a mafia meeting.

Fuck. He did not look like a guy who wanted to be crossed. And he'd already talked about killing her. He seemed surprised to see her by the door. Not that she could escape through his bulk. Plus, the gun.

Jessica went on the offensive. "Don Octavio?"

He jutted his chin out in an approximation of a head nod but didn't say anything. They stared at each other.

Jessica's only relief came from the unaimed gun muzzle. She'd be incredibly easy to kill. Becoming Scheherazade might be her only chance to survive until morning. She definitely wouldn't survive one thousand and one nights.

"What's it going to take for me to get out of here alive?" she asked.

He chuckled and raised an eyebrow. "I don't think that's an option."

"The people you're working with don't like trouble. Especially the kind of trouble that results in international attention. Murdered white women tend to do that."

"No one has to find the body." He said it with such nonchalance, like he talked about such things daily. Jessica shivered.

"But you already know the police are looking for me. They visited Sr. Garcia. The officers told me about it, and they knew I'd gone back to the house to look for clues." If only she had warned someone. Next time. She would find a way to survive this. Leaving Angus with no explanation wasn't an option. Her longing for him hurt. She winced as if a stiletto had actually pierced her heart.

"Not feeling well?" he asked. "Perhaps I won't have to kill you. Maybe you'll just die on your own. That's Letty's specialty."

"It's not really dying on your own if someone poisons you."

"We're the only ones who have to know that." He chuckled again and reached for the door.

"Wait." She didn't want him to leave without giving her any helpful information. "Are those beeps from Sr. Garcia's machines?"

He bent down, sticking his big ugly face in hers. "I don't know what you're talking about." His breath stank of fish.

She wanted to turn her head and hurl her empty guts at the odor. She looked at him with all the fierceness she could muster, instead. "Who's coming on Friday?"

He straightened, laughing loudly this time. "You won't have to worry about that. You'll be long gone."

The door slammed shut with a whoosh of air. Despite his laughter, she'd seen a brief glint of fear in his eyes. The people coming scared even this tough guy. Jessica sighed. She'd learned long ago about bigger fish with sharper teeth. She really needed to get out of here.

***

The next time the door opened, Jessica had returned to the bed. The unforgiving concrete had numbed her ass while sending spikes of pain up her spine. She sat there, legs crossed, wondering if she'd get another tray of inedible food or a guy with a gun. If only there were a door number three.

This time, both Letty and Don Octavio entered the room. They carried a passed-out Claudia between them.

Jessica jumped off the bed and skittered into a corner. They dumped Claudia onto the mattress.

"Where's the baby?" Jessica asked out of sheer panic. Letty shook her head, and they left the room. Shit. Did that mean they'd killed Cinco?

Jessica approached Claudia, laid a hand on her. Her chest rose and fell with her breath. One small positive in an increasingly desperate situation.

Jessica tried to make her as comfortable as possible, rearranging her limbs and smoothing her hair off her face. Unlike Jessica, she didn't seem to have any wounds. Maybe her injuries were internal. Maybe Letty had just drugged her. Jessica might not know for hours.

Surveying the room with renewed energy, Jessica searched for a weapon that didn't exist. She'd find one, find some way of getting them out of here.

She scrambled over to the door. The one thing she needed more than a weapon was information. Sliding down she held her ear to the open space, waiting for any slips of conversation.

"You've made things worse." Don Octavio quickly rewarded her with his outburst. "Now we have three people to get rid of."

"It's the only way. I deserve my inheritance, and now I can force Tomás to give it to me." Letty sounded proud of her accomplishment. How could anyone be proud of destroying this family?

"You stupid bitch," Don Octavio roared. "No one owes you a legacy. No one owes you a dime."

"My grandfather started that company, and my father helped it grow. He was entitled to a life of luxury, and yet they let him die in the street like a dog. Then, she stole the man who should have been *my* husband." Passion and pent-up anger flew through the air.

"Your father was a drug addict who stole from his family. And that man dying over there, he never loved you, even when you threw yourself at him. Remember, I was there. You've fabricated a past out of your dreams."

A long pause ensued. Jessica pressed herself into the cool concrete hoping for more. "Maybe they are dreams." Letty spoke so slowly that

Jessica might have imagined the words. "But after all this time, it is my turn to live my dreams. They took everything from me. My past and my future. It is fitting that I take what I deserve."

Another pause. "Fine. Take whatever you want and pay me my share. Just make sure you're out of here by Friday." Don Octavio's footsteps faded away.

Jessica heard a moan from the bed. Claudia shifted her head back and forth. Jessica went and sat beside her.

"Claudia, it's Jessica. Can you hear me?" Jessica clasped the other woman's hands. They were icy.

She didn't wake, and Jessica eventually scooted her over to make room for them both to lie on the single bed. She could have slept on the floor, but Jessica needed to do everything she could to protect her strength for the coming battle.

She woke to the key in the lock and sat up. Letty entered with a single tray in her hands, quickly placing it on the floor and lifting the old one. She stared at the women. Jessica stared back.

"You need to let us go," Jessica said. "You can have whatever you want, just get us back to our families." She wondered what key would unlock this woman's heart.

Letty had dyed her hair. Instead of mostly gray, it now shone onyx. Instead of tied into braids, locks fell about her shoulders as if fresh from a blowout. She might have tried to turn the clock back, but the lines on her face didn't lie.

Letty shook her head, then set the tray down. Fury overcame Jessica. "Did you kill that baby? Or do you plan on leaving him motherless? What the hell is wrong with you?"

Letty froze, but said nothing. Her black eyes sparkled, and Jessica remembered her passion from when she'd talked to Don Octavio.

"I heard you," Jessica said. "I heard how they stole everything from you. I understand how family can hurt you and how that anger can fester for years." She did, but she would have said it anyway.

Letty didn't speak, but she didn't move either. Jessica tried again. "My father made mistakes, mistakes he had to pay for. I grew up alone because of that, and it made me so bitter." She shook her head at the memory, the years of misspent youth as she fought her way through the world with only booze and men to mend her broken heart.

"It took a long time, but things got better for me. Let me help you."

Jessica watched the woman's face change from open and listening to haughty and completely closed off. It was as if two different women lived inside Letty, and the mean one had just taken over. Jessica's gut pinched. She'd said the wrong thing.

"You are nothing," she said. "I am Leticia Garcia, heir to the Garcia fortune. I do not need your help." She turned and shut the door, locking them inside.

"She's gone mad," Claudia whispered.

Jessica turned to her. Claudia's eyes remained shut, but she'd spoken. Relief sank through Jessica, but dread quickly pierced it. The child. "Are you okay? What happened?" she whispered.

"Ay Dios," Claudia said, rubbing her eyes. "I'm so tired."

"It will wear off. You're going to be okay." Maybe.

Claudia sighed. "I'm so sorry for dragging you into this. She told me if I came with her, she wouldn't kill you. I don't know why she had to drug me."

Jessica's head filled with questions. Claudia's words made no sense. But only one question mattered. "Claudia, where is your baby?"

"He's with my mom."

Jessica almost collapsed with relief. Anything else she could handle. Sure, her job had just become twice as hard. Now she had to figure out how to save Claudia as well as herself, and she probably needed to do that before Don Octavio decided to shoot them, or coyotes overran the place. But at least the baby was safe.

"You need to tell me exactly what happened," Jessica said, returning her focus to Claudia. "Somehow, we'll figure a way out of this mess."

But Claudia was sound asleep. The room seemed lonelier than ever as the burden of saving this woman as well as herself fell on Jessica's shoulders.

Chapter 12

Jessica had loosened the cross somewhat when she heard yelling from the other side of the door. She jumped down from the bed, not waking Claudia, who'd slept through her tugging on the pieces of wood attached to the wall. Letty had some good drugs. Jessica dropped to her knees and pressed an ear against the open space beneath the door.

"Why did you bring her here?" Don Octavio yelled. Now that she'd seen him, Jessica could picture his scowl.

"It had to be here. Everything is here. Now that I have Claudia, I will convince Tomás to leave us alone. He's got his own money. He doesn't need his father's wealth, but he does need his wife to raise his son."

Jessica wouldn't make that bet. She still didn't believe Tomás cared about anyone above himself. Well, maybe his son, but wives were easily replaced. Besides, he'd been forced into marrying Claudia after the Doraliz fiasco.

"Do it today. There is no more time." Don Octavio's tone dropped in volume but became far more menacing. It went perfectly with the ruthless face Jessica remembered.

He must have left, because Jessica heard a door slam and then kitchen sounds. Soon, Letty's footsteps approached. But they didn't stop to open the metal door. Instead, they continued, stopping further away, she heard a different door open, no lock, and the beeping noise became clear.

"Hola, mi amor," Letty said, and then the door shut.

She must be talking to Tres. The saccharine voice Letty had used with him surprised Jessica. The words spoke of love, the tone of manipulation. Jessica shuddered at a sudden chill. Three people to save.

The thought motivated her. Giving in to hopelessness was not an option. She'd come close when alone, but her desire for freedom had ratcheted up with others to save. If she had a chance at survival, it meant action. And the patience to wait for exactly the right moment to strike. A moment that would arrive shortly.

Energy to do something, anything, filled her. She glanced at Claudia, who gently snored on the bed. Best to let her sleep, she'd need her strength for the escape. Jessica finally understood the allure of working out while trapped. She had to funnel her stress somewhere while she waited for an opportunity.

Thinking of every prison movie she'd ever seen, Jessica tried a pushup. Fuck. Range of motion, three inches. She really needed to get in shape. Instead of pushups, she sank to the ground and rolled over, glad her now filthy jacket protected her against the cold floor. She made it through eight sit-ups, an exercise she probably hadn't done since middle school P.E.

She stood and did twenty squats before giving in to the burn in her thighs. At least she ended on a high point instead of the three-inch pushup. She normally bled off excess energy by taking Tela for a run. Sadness shot through her heart as she thought of her dog.

Thinking of Tela goosed her determination. She would fucking survive this. She had to. Besides, what she lacked in muscles she made up for in cunning and sheer determination. She'd met worse than Letty, worse than Don Octavio, and she'd survived. Barely, but no reason to dwell on that now.

Finally, Claudia stirred. Jessica offered her the last water bottle with only a couple of inches of liquid remaining. Claudia raised her head and drank, then pushed herself up.

"How are you feeling?" Jessica asked.

"Like someone ran over my head."

"Tell me what happened. Then, we've got to come up with an escape plan." Jessica hated the desperation in her voice, but she hoped it would motivate Claudia.

"Letty called me and told me she had you. She said she'd let you go if I met with her."

"Why would she call you? She didn't even let us in the yard when we visited." Jessica needed logic to grab onto, and this explanation didn't have it.

"When we met, she said she could secure her inheritance if Tomás thought she'd kidnapped me." Claudia seemed nonplussed, at least until her face suddenly crinkled and tears came to her eyes. "I wonder where Tres is and how he's doing?"

"He's next door." To Jessica, this seemed like the least important part of their dilemma.

"Oh! I have to go see him." She swung her legs over the side of the bed.

"Wait." Jessica couldn't understand Claudia's lack of concern for her own predicament. "We are in danger here. You don't seem to understand that."

Claudia sighed, her breath ruffling her bangs. She gave Jessica a sheepish look. "Letty won't hurt me."

"What the hell are you talking about? A few nights ago, you were terrified when she showed up at your house." Was everything she'd been told a lie? "Was everything that happened in El Paso some kind of game?"

"No. Not at all. I was scared of her that night. After she married Tres and pulled him away from us, I thought she had changed. But when we met earlier, I saw the old Letty."

"What do you mean the old Letty? How well do you know this woman?"

Claudia refused to meet Jessica's eyes, suddenly interested in her own palms instead. "I've known her for years, just like most of the women I know in Juarez." Claudia paused. "She supplies us with weight loss drugs."

"What the everlasting hell." Jessica's head hurt, and not from the shovel this time. Was this even about Tomás and his father? It had to be, yet Claudia had spun everything in a different direction. She forced herself to calm down and be firm. "Explain."

"I was a fat kid. My mom started me on Letty's compounds when I was eleven. Even so, I was always fatter than everyone else."

Jessica remembered her as the plump girl from the party a couple of years ago. While she hadn't been as svelte as the others in the room, she'd been cute and far friendlier than the waif-like beautiful women. Claudia hadn't preened or posed like the others, and she invited real conversation, or could have if she'd been more sober.

"What does any of this have to do with us being trapped in this room?" Jessica asked.

"Two years ago, Letty started giving me a new drug, a semaglutide. It worked really well. I was finally pretty. I'm sure it's the only reason Tomás noticed me. Or agreed to marry me."

The words disgusted Jessica. That sounded like Tomás. She shook her head. He'd tried so hard to convince her he'd fallen in love, that he'd changed.

Claudia must have caught her look. "It's not like that. Tomás loves me completely, now. You couldn't possibly understand how it is for women like me. Look at you. You're five foot ten, skinny, and have big blue eyes." She waved her hand down her own body. "I'm five four and have always struggled with my weight."

Jessica shook her head. People didn't decide to love others based on a scale.

But Claudia hadn't seen the motion. Instead, she stared at her belly, grasped it in both hands and squeezed a bulge of fat. "Look at this. I can't take the drugs right now because I'm breastfeeding. But the second I stop, I'm getting my good body back."

"Stop." Jessica couldn't take any more. "We have more important things to deal with right now. Also, I don't think love is based on weight."

"It's not." Anger laced Claudia's voice. "But you don't get a chance at love if you don't look good. Tomás fell in love with me as a person. But he wouldn't have gotten to know me if I'd been fat. His mother wouldn't have seen me. He wouldn't have seen me. You don't understand because you've never dealt with it."

Jessica wouldn't win this argument. And Claudia wasn't wrong. Jessica had spent a fair number of years picking up men in bars. Highlighting certain parts of her body made it extremely easy to get her reward—a few hours with a stranger that made the emptiness of her life recede for a while. Until not even that worked.

Not that her memories or this conversation got them any closer to freedom. Still, she could be a little gentler with Claudia. She squeezed the other woman's hand. "How did Letty convince you to meet her?"

"She called. I told her I was really upset that she scared me that night and that she wouldn't let us see Tres. She said that she was mad that we'd opposed her marriage to him. She also reminded me that she and I had a relationship before I became involved in the family. And she told me she knew I would need her services again. Both are true. But when she told me about you, I knew I had to meet her."

"Why didn't you call the police? And did you meet her in El Paso or Juarez?" Jessica needed more facts, and fast.

Claudia's desperation-filled eyes bore into Jessica. "She told me if I wanted to see you again, I needed to meet her at the Pronaf parking lot in Juarez. And she wanted me to bring Cinco. I lied and told her I would, but I dropped him off at my mom's place. Then, we met. I had to get you out of this since I brought you into it."

"You should never have agreed. Now she's got us both trapped." The pressure closed around Jessica like a vise.

"It will be fine, although I'm really upset that she drugged me. She didn't need to do that." Claudia must have sensed Jessica's concern, "But don't worry. She just wants money. Tomás will agree, and then she'll let us go. Kidnappings like this have happened in Mexico for years."

Jessica stared at the other woman, wild confusion running through her brain. People died in Mexican kidnappings, sometimes even after the payoff. Claudia couldn't be that naïve.

"I can tell you don't believe me," Claudia said. "I promise, Tomás will let her inherit Tres's money, and then we'll be free.

Perhaps Claudia was right, although Jessica doubted it. "We have another problem," Jessica said, remembering what Don Octavio had said about the coyotes. "What day is it?"

"It's Thursday. Now, I need to go to the bathroom." Claudia scooted off the bed and stood."

"There's a bucket."

Claudia looked at Jessica in horror. "I would never." She marched toward the door and knocked on it, calling Letty's name and letting her know she needed to go to the restroom. Soon, Letty opened the door and took Claudia out, locking the door behind them.

Shit. Was that all it took? Had Jessica peed in a bucket for nothing? But she had pounded on the door before. Something had shifted in the prisoner/guard relationship. Jessica began pacing, wondering if Claudia would return.

A few long minutes later, she did. As soon as Letty had locked them back in their cage, Jessica pounced. "What's it like out there?"

"It's just a tiny house," Claudia said. "Two bedrooms, one bathroom, and a kitchen/living area. I wanted to see Tres, but she said not until she'd talked to Tomás. Oh, and she's bringing us lunch soon."

"Don't eat it. She drugs the food."

Claudia turned toward the door and banged on it. "Letty, don't put drugs in the food or we won't eat it."

It stunned Jessica how Claudia treated their kidnapper like a servant. Was she not that smart, or were class roles just so ingrained in her she didn't see how she acted?

"When is she calling Tomás?" Jessica asked.

"Soon, I think. I don't want to be here very long."

"Listen to me." Jessica hoped the graveness of the situation echoed in her voice. "It needs to be very soon. I don't know exactly where we are, but earlier, Don Octavio told her we had to be out of here by Friday because some very bad coyotes were bringing immigrants through here. He said they'd kill us if we remained."

Fear passed over Claudia's features like a wave. "What? Please tell me we are not in the path of the cartels."

"I'm afraid we are."

Claudia spun back to the door and began pounding on it violently. "Letty!" she screamed. "Letty. I want to talk to Tomás."

Chapter 13

Letty did not come back for hours. At least it felt like hours. Jessica had resumed her position at the bottom of the door. Claudia sat on the bed, looking ill.

Finally, Jessica heard what she now thought of as the front door. Multiple sets of steps. She thought about letting Claudia know but wasn't sure pounding on the door would help.

"Tomás better decide quick," Don Octavio said as the voices neared. "It's almost time to move them. Or kill them."

"It won't be much longer. Have patience." Letty's remark cut Jessica. People always told her to have patience, and she certainly didn't want to share any traits with Don Octavio.

"You need to get it done. Now." His voice seethed with aggravation.

Jessica jumped up from the floor. They needed to be ready. She didn't want to attempt an escape with Don Octavio in the house, but they might not have a choice. "I think they're coming."

Claudia looked up, hope in her eyes. "Good. I need to see my baby."

Both stood in the middle of the room when the door opened. Letty stared at them while Don Octavio loomed above her.

"Come with me. We need to talk to your husband." Letty said.

Claudia left with Letty. Instead of going with them, Don Octavio entered the room and closed the door. He crossed his arms and leaned his long frame against the wall. His dark eyes raked down her body, then slowly moved back up. She might as well have been naked.

Jessica stood her ground. If she backed up, she'd near the bed, which would definitely send the wrong message. She also didn't want to approach him. Thinking about him touching her made her gut roil. She crossed her arms and glared at him, hoping it would keep him away.

"You're feisty," he said, raising his brows. "I like that."

"Stay away from me, you fucking asshole."

He laughed. "You don't make the rules here. I do."

She didn't move, wouldn't retreat or let fear take over. Instead, she glowered into his face and vowed to kick, bite, scream, and scratch if he laid a hand on her. She'd wound him, kill him if she could. She briefly wondered if she could grab his gun if he came for her. His snug-fitting jeans and T-shirt meant the only place a gun could hide would be his back waistband.

Their standoff lasted long seconds. He looked as if he couldn't decide what to do with her. She hoped she looked like she wasn't worth the trouble.

"Get on the bed," he finally said.

"Fuck no. If you touch me, I will kill you. I'll bite through your arteries, gouge my fingers into your eyes, and make sure that's the last time you ever try to use your dick."

He laughed again, but it took him a minute, and it looked like it cost him something this time. "I could shoot you right now."

She wouldn't dignify that with a response. He could shoot her, but for some reason he hadn't yet. Perhaps because of Letty. But if Letty had wanted Jessica so she could lure Claudia to whatever hellhole this was, then Jessica's usefulness had ended. Maybe he would shoot her. Just one more reason for her to figure a way out of this situation.

A flush of doubt crept over her skin. What if she'd finally found the situation she couldn't escape? In past scary circumstances, luck had always ridden beside her. That couldn't last forever. Here, she had no weapons, no element of surprise. Worse, they'd caged her. In the streets of the city or out in the desert badlands, she had a chance.

A froth of anger and fear surged through her veins. She wanted to charge him, attack and take her chances, try to do something, anything, besides wait. She forced her muscles to remain motionless. Her mind might find brief relief in playing offense, but she couldn't beat him in hand-to-hand combat, less so if he had a gun.

So she waited, half-crazed with the need for action. This must be the patience people had always talked to her about, and damn if it didn't hurt like a physical wound.

Perhaps she looked half-crazed as well, because he didn't make a move. She could tell he wanted to and wondered whether he feared her or Letty the most.

Finally, when Jessica's feet and back hurt so much from standing that she'd actually considered retreating to the bed, Claudia and Letty returned. Claudia entered first, tears streaking her cheeks. Letty jerked her head back when she saw Don Octavio as if surprised to find him there. She glanced back and forth between him and Jessica before pushing Claudia forward.

"Let's go," Letty said to the man. He obeyed, and she locked them back in their cinderblock prison.

"Oh, Jessica," Claudia said, then started sobbing.

Jessica wanted to hear what had happened to Claudia, but the conversation between Letty and Don Octavio might be more valuable. "Sit on the bed and be very quiet for a few minutes."

Jessica sprinted toward the door and dropped to her knees, ear to the open space. The next few minutes were crucial.

"But Jessica," Claudia wailed.

"Shh." Jessica's sharp tone and angry look did the trick. Claudia shuffled to the bed and sat with her head in her hands.

"He needs time," Letty said.

"Time for what? He doesn't need time. He just doesn't want to give up his inheritance. I told you this wouldn't work." Don Octavio's voice rumbled, and Jessica could picture him spitting the words at Letty.

"He wants his lawyer to draw up the agreement. I told him he had one hour. Everything will be fine."

"It won't be. You're cutting it too close. You need to get them out of here. Now." Don Octavio raised his voice.

"Stop telling me what to do. You told me I had until tomorrow," Letty yelled back.

"That was when I thought you could get the deal done. I never should have listened to you about this. You're not smart enough to pull off something this complicated."

"Shut up!" Letty snapped. "I've always been the smart one. You would have nothing if not for me. You've taken half of my income for fifty years, and all you ever do is complain. My concoctions have gotten you out of every problem you've ever encountered, from pregnant women to men you needed to kill before they killed you. You owe me."

Jessica heard a slam, like palms hitting a table. Or a body hitting furniture.

"I owe you nothing," Don Octavio said. A sharp scraping noise like a heavy chair on concrete reached her. "Tomás will never let you have that money. You're playing out of your league. I'm out of your league. You rely on me for contacts, for muscle, for physical intimidation. My fifty percent take isn't close to enough. The only reason you're here is because this payoff had potential. Fifty percent of Tres's estate is a lot of money."

"You won't get half of that. I'm his wife. That money is mine."

Don Octavio laughed. "His wife. I know better than that. All I have to do is tell the right people about you and you'll get nothing. Double-cross me and I'll kill you." The sneer in his voice sent a chill through Jessica.

"It's not a double cross. That money is not yours. You did nothing for it."

"You bitch."

A thud sounded, then Letty cried out in pain. "How dare you!" her voice contained surprise and rage, but no fear.

"It was easy," Don Octavio said.

A sharp boom echoed through the house. Jessica flattened herself against the floor, shimmying back from the door. "Get down!" she yelled, expecting another gunshot.

Claudia dropped from the bed to the floor and then crawled to Jessica. The women lay there, but for long moments, nothing but silence reached them.

Some kind of shuffling or dragging reached Jessica's strained ears. She and Claudia cowered against the wall several feet from the door. Silence returned for what seemed like forever. Eventually, she heard faint footsteps. A faraway door closed. Then the quiet returned.

"What happened?" Claudia asked after minutes more of quiet seeping from under the door.

"I don't know. I think someone got shot." But who? Don Octavio had a gun, but he probably would have torn through their door and tried to rape them both with Letty out of the way.

"I don't think anyone's home right now." Jessica stood then rolled her shoulders and neck, both sore from so much time crouched on the floor. She offered a hand to Claudia. They relocated to the bed, using it like a couch. Jessica's parched throat ached, but at least her weary muscles found some comfort on the aged mattress.

"Tell me what happened when you made your phone call to Tomás, and then we'll figure out what to do next." Jessica hoped her tone didn't convey the distress behind her rapidly beating heart.

Claudia sat up, wrapped her hands around her knees, then dipped her head to them. Her whole body trembled. "I'm so scared."

What could Jessica say? Lie and pretend everything would be okay? Tell her not to worry, she'd save her? Jessica wasn't sure she could save herself. She didn't have a single tool to help her escape, much less free someone else.

"Being scared sounds reasonable." It was all she could think of in the end. "Tell me what happened."

"Letty called Tomás from my cell phone. At first, he was so worried, asking if I was okay and wanting to know where I was. Then Letty started talking. He went from loving to furious in a second."

"She told him she'd gotten the letter from his lawyers contesting her control of the corporation and his father's new will. She said she'd kill me unless he gave her what she deserved."

Claudia shook her head and drew her legs closer into her body. "He was furious, said she'd never have a cent of his father's money. That his child deserved that money. It was like he didn't even care about me."

Jessica wished she could act surprised, but she'd learned the truth about Tomás long ago. "I'm sorry."

"It's okay. He remembered eventually. He said that if she touched a hair on my head, he'd hunt her down and kill her."

Claudia seemed to retreat into herself for a moment. She'd been through a lot, but Jessica needed to know how this story ended. Would Tomás save them?

"What happened next?" Jessica asked.

"Tomás wanted to know if I was okay and what the conditions were. I told him that Letty had you, and that's why I had to meet her. He wasn't happy about that. Just like you, he said I should have told someone."

"Yeah. I've made that mistake before. Too late to worry about it now. Is he going to give her what she wants? And if so, how do we get released?"

Claudia looked at her and bit her lower lip. It did not look like good news.

"He said he needed to think about it and discuss it with his lawyers," Claudia said in a small voice. "He said he just needed a couple of hours."

Now Jessica understood the tears. Claudia had just discovered Tomás's true nature. Jessica rested her head against the wall, eyes closed. *Think.* There had to be a way out of here.

"Who was shot out there?" Claudia asked, nodding at the door.

"I'm not sure. Don Octavio is the only one I've ever seen with a gun, but it didn't sound like his heavy footsteps leaving."

"Leaving? Are we here alone? Did they leave us to die?"

Good question. Jessica hadn't thought about that scenario. Although it didn't seem likely. Don Octavio didn't want them here at all, alive or dead. And Letty wouldn't kill Claudia, not if she hoped to reach a deal with Tomás.

"Someone will be back."

"I hope it's not that Don Octavio. He looks mean."

"That's putting it mildly. The guy's a real dick."

Jessica stood and walked into the center of the room. The door was the only way in or out. It had to be how they escaped. That needed to happen the very next time that door opened. Unless Letty reached a deal with Tomás that would deliver them to safety.

She wished her head didn't hurt and begged for her stomach to quit gnawing on itself from hunger. But the sooner she got out of here, the sooner she'd eat. And see Angus. And pet her dog.

"I need your help," Jessica said.

Claudia nodded with determination. It relieved Jessica that she didn't seem to let her broken heart get in the way of what needed to be done.

"We have a few scenarios. Maybe no one died, and they just quit fighting after the gunshot. We might also have to deal with either Letty or Don Octavio." Jessica didn't mention the final scenario, the one where the coyotes showed up. They'd stand no chance against professional criminals like that.

"If it's Letty, she'll probably take me to talk to Tomás again. Then maybe everything will get resolved." Claudia looked almost hopeful.

"It's a possibility, but not one we can count on. If anything at all goes wrong, we have to escape. I think I can overpower her, but I'll need you to lure her as far into the room as possible."

"Okay," Claudia said. "What do we do if it's Don Octavio?"

Great question, and she feared Claudia wouldn't like the answer. "He has a gun, and we have to assume it will be in his right hand. We also have to hope I can identify that it's him as he comes down the hallway. He has louder footfalls than Letty and a wider stride, so he takes fewer steps. You stay out of the way, and I'll try and disarm him." The ridiculous idea had almost zero chance of working, but she'd run out of options.

***

Time dragged slowly. Jessica held her post at the door, seemingly for hours. Claudia lay on the bed and napped some, or pretended to. Jessica occasionally saw tears leaking from her closed eyes.

Finally, the sound of an outer door opening reached her. Then footsteps, but this time the click of heels echoed on the floor instead of quieter footfalls.

"I'm not sure who it is," she said to Claudia. "It's definitely a woman."

Claudia stood and combed her hair back, then ran her hands down her pants to smooth them, as if anyone cared how they looked. Jessica rose, wondering if she should stand behind the door as it swung open. She could use it as a weapon by slamming it into whoever opened it, but if Letty, or whoever, didn't see her, they might become suspicious. She didn't want Claudia getting hurt, and she also feared someone locking them in permanently. Jessica could throw herself against the door for days and probably not dent it. Not to mention, they didn't have days.

By the time the door opened, Jessica stood in the middle of the room with Claudia. She gaped at the figure at the door. Letty had changed almost beyond recognition. To go with her recently colored and styled hair, she wore a navy pantsuit with images of large silver roses seemingly melted into the fabric, plus a matching silver blouse that looked like hammered silk. Her face appeared years younger, plump and smooth and now sculpted with makeup. Who was this woman?

"Letty?" Claudia asked, clearly as confused as Jessica.

"You seem surprised. You overlooked me just like everyone else."

"Who overlooked you?" Jessica asked, hoping to get the woman to talk while she formulated a plan.

Letty dismissed her with a glare, then held out a hand to Claudia. "It's time to see what Tomás has to say."

Jessica counted the seconds they were gone. She'd tried patience, not that she'd had much choice. Hour after hour, she'd sat in this room, waiting for an opportunity to escape. This had to be it. She hadn't heard Don Octavio since the gunshot, and whether he'd left or been shot, hopefully they could avoid him.

Letty might have a gun, but she seemed to prefer chemical weapons, drugs that would at best knock them out and at worst be fatal. Fortunately, she'd have to get close enough to them to administer the drugs. That's when Jessica would overpower her.

The interminable waiting would end soon. She just needed to hold on a little longer. Learn if Tomás had come through or not. But no matter what, she couldn't let Letty close her in the room one last time.

Hunger, thirst, and worry coursed through her. She'd had plenty of rest, but without food and dehydrated from too little water, her body would fail her if she didn't act now.

Each second dragged slower and slower, but finally she heard footsteps. And crying.

"He said he just needs another hour." Claudia's tear-stained voice echoed against the walls, painting them with fear and sorrow.

"He doesn't get another hour. He's not using that time to save you. The greedy bastard is using it to talk to his lawyers about how to cheat me out of what I deserve."

"But you told him you'd kill me. If I disappear, everyone will know that you did it."

Smart. Jessica approved of Claudia putting Letty on the defensive. Her plan to abscond with the Garcia fortune would unravel thread by thread.

Jessica prepared for battle. She wouldn't trust Letty or Tomás to resolve things in an hour. She pressed herself against the wall next to the door, willing Claudia to remember to lure Letty inside. The keys jangled, then slid into the lock. The tumblers clicked into place.

"You will have to stay here," Letty said. "Although I no longer have faith in your husband. It seems he'd prefer to let you rot or die instead of guaranteeing me what I'm owed. I practically raised him, but he is ungrateful just like his father and mother.

"No, they're not t . . ." Claudia started to argue.

The door began its swing, and Jessica grabbed it, heaved it open, then flung her body around the door's edge and into the two women. Claudia took the brunt of it, backing into Letty and tumbling her over.

Claudia screamed, and chaos erupted as Letty tried to shove the two women off of her. Jessica swung, her fist connecting with Letty's cheek in a burst of pain. Somehow Jessica scrambled over Claudia or Claudia scampered out from between them. Jessica dug a knee into Letty's gut and pressed her arms into the floor. She used her superior length and weight to hold the woman down.

"What are you doing?" Claudia screamed at Jessica.

"Getting us the fuck out of here." Pure adrenaline surged through her. "Help me. Come hold down one of her arms. Put your knee on it."

Letty surged and bucked under Jessica, far stronger than she appeared. Claudia stared at Jessica as if she hadn't understood the order.

"Claudia, snap out of it. Now!"

With a quick jerk of her head, Claudia acted, holding down one of Letty's arms while Jessica pressed her body into the woman.

"Kneel on her, with your knees," Jessica said.

"But I'll hurt her."

"And she will kill us if she gets away."

Finally, Claudia immobilized Letty's left arm. Jessica rolled off her, and Letty surged up, almost ramming her head into Claudia's chin. Jessica used the opportunity to grab the arm Claudia didn't hold down and wrench it behind her back.

With Claudia's help, they wrestled Letty's other arm back behind her and pulled her to her feet. Letty fought like a cat about to be dumped in water but couldn't regain control.

"Find the keys," Jessica commanded, before noticing that they still hung from the lock. She shoved Letty forward, into that horrible room etched forever in Jessica's mind, then closed and locked the door.

"Let me out!" Letty pounded the door and screamed. "You don't know what you're doing. The men out there will kill you."

"What men?" Claudia asked.

"She may be bluffing, but I think coyotes are bringing a load of immigrants to cross the border tonight." Maybe soon. Jessica had no idea what time it was.

Claudia didn't seem to register the response. Instead, she turned to the locked door and put her palm on it. "Why did you do this? Why did you steal me away from my family. They're your family too. They took you in when you were young and treated you like one of their own." She sounded heartbroken.

"Let me out and I'll tell you."

"I can't do that," Claudia said. "I no longer trust you."

"Please, Claudia. I've known you since you were a baby. You've known me all your life. I have helped you, and now I need your help." Letty's voice calmed, pleading replacing panic and rage. "I had to do it. It was the only way to secure my future. Tres loves me. He loved me before he even knew Sofia. We kept it a secret for many years."

"That's not true," Claudia said.

"It is mija. I promise." Letty said, using the term daughter. Jessica could feel the manipulation at play, but Letty no longer held the keys.

"Come on. Let's go." Jessica rested a hand on Claudia's back.

Claudia started to cry, pressing herself against the door as if she needed it to hold her up. "You shouldn't have done this."

"I'm on your side," Letty said. "The same way Tres and Sofia treated me, that is how Tomás treats you. He didn't want to save you. He didn't care that his son might grow up without a mother. Instead, he wanted time to find a way to cheat me out of my money. He only cares about himself. You and I need to work together to secure your son's future."

What a bunch of fucking bullshit. Jessica had never witnessed manipulation on this level. Unfortunately, it looked like it was working. Tears streamed down Claudia's face, and she slumped as if she'd lost all hope.

"Let's get you back to your baby," Jessica said.

That turned Claudia's head. "Yes. Let's do that." She sounded completely defeated.

This whole situation sucked, but at least Claudia now understood Tomás's priorities. Jessica pocketed the keys and turned toward the rest of the house.

She stepped from the hallway into a large room with a kitchen along one wall and a table in the center. A shotgun rested on the table, and a pool of blood with drying edges spread toward a door. Jessica saw a few trees and a silver sedan in the light thrown off by the window beside the door. Night had fallen.

Jessica forced her eyes back to the floor, where a wide trail of blood led from the table to a door on the opposite side of the room. Her stomach lurched, not that she had anything to throw up. She shut her eyes, but it didn't help, as the metallic tang of blood flooded her nostrils. Claudia's panting shallow breath reached her over Letty's pounding and screaming.

Jessica opened her eyes and spun back to the short hallway. Jessica headed past the prison door to the next one. She stepped inside and the thick cinderblock walls muffled Letty's outraged sounds.

Jessica hadn't realized the beeping had stopped. An old man lay in the bed, either sleeping or dead. The monitor beside him had gone dark. Jessica approached the man, reached a hand to his chest. He was warm, and faintly breathing, but he didn't wake at her touch.

"Sr. Garcia," she said, first softly, then louder. She moved her hand to his chest to gently shake him. "Wake up, Sr. Garcia."

Jessica heard someone enter the room and turned to glimpse Claudia. Her eyes had gone big in the dim light.

"Is he dead?" she asked.

"No. But's he's in a deep sleep, maybe even a coma. I can't tell."

"We have to get him out of here."

"Yes. Let's figure this out. You stay with him. I'm going to find Letty's car keys."

Back in the kitchen, a cell phone sat on the table, along with two boxes of shotgun shells. Red and yellow. The same colors as the ones in the desert. Coincidence, or were the coyotes the connection?

Jessica continued her search in the kitchen's cabinets and drawers, all while she avoided stepping in the blood. Nothing. She asked Claudia to help her, and they ransacked the house but didn't find the keys.

With no other options, Claudia approached Letty's door. "Where are your car keys?"

"In my pocket."

"What's wrong with Tres?" Claudia asked next.

"He's dying. In fact, if you don't let me out to give him his medication, he'll die today and his blood will be on your hands. Open the door and I'll give him the medicine, and then we can arrange for Tomás to see his father before he passes.

Claudia sobbed once and looked at Jessica. Jessica shook her head. This woman manipulated people with mastery. Jessica bet she'd practiced for years with her weight loss patients.

"We'll figure it out," Jessica said. She went to the cell phone on the table, tried to open it. "Hey, Letty. What's your phone's password?" she called out.

"If you let me out, I'll tell you."

Of course. This night just kept getting better. "We'll have to walk until we find someone to help us," Jessica said. "Come on, we better get going. It's already night."

The women headed toward the front door, Suddenly, headlights illuminated the front window. "Stay there," Jessica whispered, then ran to peek out. A line of headlights, at least four cars, headed down the driveway, right toward the house.

Chapter 14

Jessica grabbed Claudia by the arm and wrenched her away from the window. She spun, searching the room for options, then followed the trail of blood that led out the back door.

"What about Tres?" Claudia asked.

"We've got to save ourselves. Then we can come back for him."

Jessica didn't look at Claudia, didn't want to see whatever pain or betrayal hid in her eyes. Fortunately, Claudia didn't balk. She followed Jessica like a shadow.

They slipped out of the house and into a junk-filled yard that threw shadows chaotically across the dirt. Jessica waited a moment to let her eyes adjust to the dim light. An old car rusted beside them. In front, some sort of solid-walled corral formed a circle. A few trees grew on the sides of the property, then the land faded into desert.

"Let's get behind the corral," Jessica said. "It will hide us if they drive around back."

"Are those the coyotes?" Claudia asked.

"We have to assume so." Jessica trotted toward the structure, her eyes scanning the ground for things that might trip her.

The corral gate lay ajar, beckoning them inside, but Jessica turned to the left, skirting the exterior. She never wanted to be trapped inside anything again.

Engines roared and then stopped. Car doors slammed. Voices spoke in Spanish. They'd enter the house first and find Letty and Sr. Garcia. Jessica bet Letty would talk them into searching the grounds. They had to move, and fast.

"Claudia. Let's go. Now. I don't want to think about will happen if they catch us."

Claudia's eyes glowed with terror in the dark night, but she nodded. Jessica took off, trotting across the yard and praying the corral would block anyone's view. At least for a while. Of course, nothing would cover the footsteps they left in the dirt.

"Do you have any idea where we are?" Jessica asked.

"No." Claudia huffed behind her.

The lot seemed to go on forever, but as her eyes fully adjusted to the night, the starlight and a slim moon paved a silver path before her. Each step away from the hulking fear of the house and toward the scent of salt cedar unlatched the dread of the past hours and days.

Salt cedar. The scrubby trees grew at the river, lining the channeled banks. It smelled like desert parties and long walks along the levee. Could they be near the Rio Grande?

Without slowing, Jessica scanned the horizon for mountains. At night, they became shadows slightly darker than the sky, but she didn't find them. Mountains served as compasses in the desert, each range a distinct shape clearly visible under wide open skies. They must be in a depression, with just enough trees and land above them to block the view.

Shouting from the house made Jessica fear pursuit. "We have to go faster."

They picked up speed, and Jessica almost flung herself into a barbed-wire fence, seeing the faint shine of metal talons in the moonlight just before she crashed into it.

"Stop," she yelled, a little too loudly. She immediately worried they'd heard her. The only advantage she and Claudia had would disappear once the people searching for them could pinpoint their direction. She flung her arm out, but Claudia had already halted.

Jessica stepped on one of the three strands of rusted wire. It easily sagged under her foot and probably hadn't held back livestock in years. She lifted the top wire and encouraged Claudia to ease her way through. Jessica followed, one sharp tine scratching along her back.

Beyond the fence lay a badlands of desert crisscrossed with trails. Animal? Motorcycle? She couldn't tell. But at least each step took them farther from the house. She heard more yells and whistles, each one sending a pinprick of fear into her heart, but she wouldn't stop running, would never let someone jail her again.

"It's too hard," Claudia said. "You have to slow down."

Jessica hated being mean to someone so kind. Hated motivating with fear. But she did it anyway. "If you ever want to see your son again, you won't give up. We have to hurry, or they'll find us."

"No." The sound escaped Claudia like it came from a wounded animal, all heartbreak and terror. But the warning worked as she surged forward with renewed energy.

After ten minutes they came to a steep sand uprising. As they neared, Jessica watched it grow from a rise to a small hill to an almost clifflike steepness rising many feet above them. Water had eroded parts of the face into chasms. They could attempt to climb it, but anyone shining a light in their direction would easily see them.

Left or right? Jessica had no idea, couldn't have dropped a pin anywhere near their location. She chose left. The heady smell of the salt cedar pricked her nose, and the tang of dampness cut through her senses. They had to be near water. It might be a river or a pond. The Mexican state of Chihuahua, on El Paso's southern border, took pride in its reputation for cattle ranching. Cattle needed water, and ponds dotted the Mexican desert. Salt cedar always found its way to the water, surrounding banks and stealing all the moisture it could. But deep in her heart, Jessica hoped the smell meant the river. The border. Safety.

The cliff to their right lost some of its height as they ran along it. Jessica slowed to a walk as the terrain became too uneven to chance jogging in the dark. Eventually, she found a trail meandering up the bank that looked doable, and she started up. The sounds behind them had faded, not that she felt more secure. If she didn't hear them, she didn't know what they were up to.

Her lungs burned as she climbed, and her energy faltered, running, as it was, on adrenaline instead of food. Claudia's heavy panting reached her as well, although she hadn't lagged since Jessica's threat. It took forever to crest the rise, and Jessica cursed every step. When she finally stood on flat ground, she bent over, hands on knees, and sucked in air like she'd never breathe again.

"Look," Claudia said, pointing in the direction they'd come.

Pairs of lights traveled every which way. Headlights. They had vehicles, likely four-wheel drive since they seemed to have no trouble in the sand. One of them headed toward them. It had to be the people from the house. The coyotes.

"Let's go." Jessica took off across the sand, crossing tire tracks. The cliff they'd climbed was a levee and it was certainly the Rio Grande on the other side, but the trucks that hunted them would find the road that led directly to where they stood.

Jessica scuttled across the levee to where it dropped down on the other side. Unlike the river near home, with its manicured channel and flat acres of grass on either side, here the levee dropped to a jungle of salt cedar. She couldn't see the river through it, couldn't see the flat desert of the United States except far in the distance. Shit.

At least the salt cedar and other brush would hide them from the trucks, although it might be filled with snakes and who knows what other kind of vermin. And of course they had to make it down the extremely steep slope.

She walked to the edge, certain her depleted muscles wouldn't hold her up. They'd gotten so far. They'd escaped. She couldn't give up now, but she didn't know how to go on.

"We have to go down that?" Claudia said in a trembling voice.

Jessica could only nod.

"I'm going on my butt." Claudia squatted and then sat at the edge of the slope just as the roar of an engine approached. She didn't see lights and decided it must be on the other side of the levee, still too close for comfort.

Claudia pushed off and slid down the levee on her rear. Jessica dropped and followed. It hurt, probably as much as trying to climb down on her feet. Somehow it looked like Claudia slid, but to Jessica, the ride was neither slick nor smooth. Still, she jerked and pushed her way down.

Somehow, they made it to the bottom and Jessica dusted off her sore ass. Between the running and sliding, she'd used muscles she didn't know existed, and every part of her hurt. Her mood soured. Why did she always end up in these stupid situations either chasing or running away from people she should never be around?

"I ripped my pants." Claudia's hand covered nothing but underwear on one cheek.

Jessica needed to stop complaining. "You were really brave to do that. Now, we've got to make our way through this swamp to the river."

"It's the Rio Bravo, isn't it?" Claudia asked, using the Mexican name for the once mighty river.

"It has to be, but I don't have any idea where we are. Do you?"

"We could be anywhere," Claudia said. "But if there are coyotes involved, we're probably in the Valle de Juarez or further south."

"Well, that's a blessing and a curse," Jessica said. "The good news is we won't have to figure out how to get over the border wall. The bad news is we are a long way from civilization."

"Maybe we'll get picked up by the border patrol."

"We have to make it across this swampy forest and the river first." And both of those could be trouble. "Let's get started. Stay close."

"Don't worry. I'm not letting you out of my sight."

The women stepped forward. Dry sand ended roughly two feet from the base of the levee. The muck they stepped into pulled at their shoes. Jessica could barely keep her boots on, and Claudia lost her fashion sneakers with almost every step.

Soon, the salt cedars closed around them, blacking out the sky. The usually scrubby plants had grown into full on trees, and roots and branches reached out to trip and pull at them. The smell of muck and decay assaulted Jessica's nose, and the rough bark scratched at her. But greater than the discomfort was how slowly they traveled, especially when she heard a truck barreling along the top of the levee.

It drove past without stopping but then that truck or another came back from the other direction. Jessica plowed forward, wanting to put as much distance between it and them as possible. The truck couldn't drive down the levee, not that there was a road here anyway. And there's no way anything but the biggest of tanks would make it through the salt cedars.

Step after careful step, she moved forward, praying she wouldn't hear human voices descending the slope behind them. The truck hadn't moved on and her heart rose into her throat with fear. They'd no doubt be armed. She didn't want to die without seeing Angus. But she'd throw herself in front of a bullet before she became a hostage again.

What drove her just as much was her need to save the woman behind her. She didn't want another child growing up without its mother. Jessica had only spent part of her life without hers, but it had scarred her, keeping her from becoming the woman she should have become a long time ago. Just one foot in front of the other.

Finally, surrounded by darkness, with branches in her hair and scratches on her skin, with no idea how much further she had to go, the vehicle started up and drove away.

She let herself pause and breathe. Exhaustion took root in her feet and traveled up her body in waves, turning her legs into liquid unable to hold her up. She leaned into the nearest tree almost hugging it and letting it exfoliate her arms as she sank to the ground. Her butt hit roots and soft, smelly mud, but she didn't care. The cocktail of relief and fatigue practically knocked her out. A bottle of tequila wouldn't have put her on the floor faster.

Claudia dropped down beside her. "I'm so tired. Do you think it's much farther?"

"I honestly don't know. Every inch feels like a mile. And we've still got a river to ford and a desert to walk through. *I don't know if I can make it*, she wanted to admit. She'd have given almost anything for a meal and a bottle of water. Even the crappy old energy bar that had been floating around in her truck for years sounded delicious.

But she wouldn't give up. She just needed to sit for a minute, get a little energy back.

"Jessica. If they're coyotes, they're probably going to cross people tonight. They have to get across the same river. What if we run into them?"

The same fear had nagged at the back of Jessica's thoughts. Could they get that unlucky? "I don't think they'd bring someone through this jungle. It's too risky. There have to be easier ways to get to the river. We'll be careful when we cross. On the other side, depending on where we are, there might be a lot of flat open desert between the river and highway. It would be easy to spot us."

"Should we rest here until morning?" Claudia asked. "It would be a lot easier to navigate this forest in the light."

"I'm afraid to stay here." Jessica rarely told the truth in situations like this, but her weariness, or maybe her fear, ripped the words from her lips. But she wouldn't say more, wouldn't tell Claudia she feared not only that they'd be found, but that if she didn't get up and keep moving, she might languish here forever.

With that thought, she rolled to the side and pulled herself up to her hands and knees. She wanted so badly to pitch forward into the mud and rest. Instead, she pulled one foot beneath her and then the other, and using her hands for balance, she stood. She wiped her hands on her pants, then reached her still filthy palms to Claudia and helped pull her from the ground.

They struggled forward. At least Jessica thought it was forward. Who knew in such a dark place? They could be walking in circles, but Jessica wasn't about to acknowledge that fact. It felt straight, but they'd also been at it a long time.

They slowed, no longer as fearful of someone following them. The panicked blood rushing through Jessica ears slowed, and her ragged breathing eased. She heard cricket song, the hoot of an owl, and their footsteps. While the ground still gave way under their weight, a thick mat of plant matter covered the mud that no longer sucked the shoes from their feet. They stumbled on, one step at a time, arms raised to keep from running into low branches.

The plants thinned somewhat, and Jessica heard the unmistakable rush of water. She crept forward slowly until she could see the glint of silver on the river's surface. It had to be the Rio Grande, but it ran so much slower and deeper here than the river Jessica knew. How far were they from El Paso?

"It's the river." Relief permeated Claudia's voice.

"You're right. We must be in the Valle de Juarez or further south."

Was it better to be lost in a valley known for violence, or possibly hundreds of miles from civilization along an almost deserted river? One step at a time. First, they needed to cross, and then they'd find help. Of course, they had no water. She didn't want to end up like so many migrants who crossed the river only to die of thirst after reaching the so-called safety of the United States.

"I'm not a very good swimmer," Claudia said. "But we'll make it."

Jessica glanced at Claudia then looked back at the river. Her father had taught her to swim. Not that she'd done it lately, but determination was a great buoy. Still, her battered, hungry body clamored for rest.

"Let's stop a while," she said. Then she crawled under a cedar whose branches canopied over the riverbank.

Chapter 15

Jessica woke to Claudia shaking her. It took long seconds to get her bearings and realize her cheek rested on dirt, she wore filthy clothes, and she lay mere feet from the river she needed to swim across. Darkness still surrounded her.

"I hear people," Claudia whispered, terror in her voice.

"Shh." Jessica sat up and put a finger to her lips, not that Claudia could see her in the smothering darkness.

Then Jessica heard it too. Gruff male voices speaking Spanish. Fear shivered along her skin. They seemed to be giving orders, and they weren't yelling. They had to be close. Too close.

Jessica peered through the tree's draping branches. The river glowed with the light of the stars and scant moon, but light barely penetrated their hiding place. She looked Claudia in the eye and put a finger to her lips, quietly shushing her. Waiting it out was the only choice.

Jessica began to parse different voices, one gruff and low, another with a nasal tone. Then she heard a child's cry followed by a mother's shush. Other voices entered the fray, low and muttering as if trying to communicate without being noticed. She heard the movement of a group of people, footsteps and rustling clothing. She focused on slowing her breathing and calming her racing heart.

In this location, in the middle of the night, it could only be immigrants looking to cross to the United States, and it seemed like a relatively large group of them. A splash sounded, and then another, as a loud, harsh voice directed people into the river.

The child's cry grew louder, and at least one other person began to sob. Claudia stiffened beside her. Jessica turned to her again and shook her head. They couldn't help these people. The men ushering them into the water surely had guns. Opposing them would be a death sentence.

Jessica watched the river and saw the crossers a mere twenty yards downstream. Heads bobbing, darker than the silver water and arms flinging to pull people further in, interrupted the river's quiet flow.

A shriek split the night, followed by a woman's call. "Gloria! Gloria!"

"Cállate," the gruff man said, telling the woman to shut up.

The pitch of the murmuring voices shifted upward, and raucous splashing ensued, followed quickly by hacking coughs. Hopefully, Gloria.

A few people tried to turn back, but someone Jessica couldn't see told them to continue or die. Jessica imagined a gun pointed toward the water.

She'd always assumed migrants who crossed the river did so quickly and quietly, the opposite of this calamitous night. But she'd imagined the crossing on her familiar river with its wide berth, frequent sandbanks, and almost no place where someone would be forced to swim. Sometimes the river had no water at all. But in springtime, when the mountain snow melted, the New Mexico reservoirs fueled by the mighty Rio Grande released enough water for the river to flow again.

Eventually, the last person made it across, hauled up the far bank by waiting hands. The men leading the group called to each other across the water. Then they disappeared into the Texas desert.

The crossers might be gone, but the danger had not passed. At least one man, a nasal-voiced one, remained on this side of the border. Jessica didn't hear him walk away, and the fear he'd find them made it hard to breathe. This might have been the group Don Octavio had warned about, perhaps even the same men who'd hunted them in their trucks. They might be hunting for them still.

They could do nothing but wait. They had no phones or watches. Jessica tried counting the time, but her calorie-deprived brain kept forgetting her place, forcing her to start over again and again.

The night seemed endless, but finally, the sky brightened. During the escape, she dreamed she'd be home in bed by now. They'd delayed their plans, but at least they'd lived through the night. Now, Jessica's gratitude for the morning and the light of day filled her with hope.

"I'm going to see if anyone's around." Jessica pushed herself to her knees silently.

"Please don't leave me here," Claudia's voice sounded as rusty as Jessica felt. They hadn't said a word to each other after they'd watched the crossing. They hadn't slept. They'd barely breathed.

But they couldn't stay in hiding forever, and Jessica desperately needed food. She'd considered gnawing on a branch of salt cedar, but plants in the desert often contained poisons to guard their precious water. Cacti had spines to do the same, and Jessica had waking dreams of the sweet, wet fruit beneath the spines much of the night.

"I'll be back," she said, then crawled out of the hiding place, knowing the risk, but also guessing the coyotes wouldn't wait around until full morning. Hopefully, the coyotes had moved on, even if they believed Letty's story.

The memory of the house, her prison, caused a shudder. She wondered if Letty had survived the coyotes, if Tres remained breathing and hooked to his machine. She sure as hell wasn't going to be the one to check.

Slowly, quietly, Jessica crept along the riverbank. She came to the place where the people had crossed. A rutted dirt road ran to the bank, then a wide path cut through the steep side as it dropped to the water. The churned-up dirt provided evidence of the night's activities. She saw no sign of the nasal-voiced man, or anyone else.

Jessica turned to the water, searching the opposite side for a landing place. She found it, a cut in the bank several yards downstream. She surveyed the water, seeing its eddies and swirling currents as the sky lightened. They needed to cross now, before daybreak would make them easy to spot.

She trotted back to Claudia, who stood just outside the tree's draping branches, a worried look on her face. Claudia wore filthy athletic shoes, wide-legged, ankle-length jeans crusty with mud, and some kind of black wrap top that Jessica imagined she'd bought to camouflage the belly she hated. The jeans and shoes would drag her down.

Jessica also wore jeans, although hers hugged her figure. Normally, she'd have had on dress pants for work, but the wind-blown, sandy day she'd last seen home, she had chosen more casual attire. The dust storms would have given her black pants an orange hue. Somewhere along the way, she'd lost her jacket, but her form-fitting, once-white sleeveless tee remained. Her boots and jeans would also be a problem.

"Take off your shoes and jeans," Jessica said, stripping her own jeans from her body.

"Why?" Claudia asked.

"They're too heavy and might drag you down."

Claudia did as she was told and soon stood barefoot in black boy-shorts and her shirt. Jessica shoved a shoe in each pant leg and tied them around Claudia's waist.

"Nice choice in underwear," Jessica said, her own ass hanging out of the magenta lace thong she'd once thought so sexy. Ridiculous fucking undergarment. She tied her boot-stuffed jeans around her waist as well.

"Hopefully, the shoes will stay in the legs of the jeans," Jessica said. "Although, I've certainly never done anything like this before. If the pants get too heavy, it's a loose knot and you should be able to drop them. Plus, we'll be there to help each other."

"Good idea," Claudia said. "I am not walking into El Paso half naked, not to mention you can't walk through a desert without shoes."

She wasn't wrong. Even in spring, sand could get hot, not to mention cacti, scorpions, and other dangers.

"Okay, let's go." Jessica headed down to where the others had forded the river.

"Why don't we cross right here?" Claudia asked.

"I think it will be safer to cross where the others did. There's probably a reason they have people do it there. Plus, here the bank on both sides is a steep drop. There we can just walk in. We need to go now before it gets too light. I don't want anyone to see us."

Claudia nodded and followed her.

When they approached the water, Jessica walked straight in without stopping.

"Wait for me," Claudia called somewhat frantically.

"Food and family are on the other side." Jessica took one more step, but no river bottom met her foot. Instead, she plunged into a hole of rushing liquid. She sputtered up and Claudia was right there.

"It's deep," Jessica said, starting to float downstream. "Jump out and swim to the other side."

The current grabbed Jessica, and she tried to lie on top of it and swim. Claudia splashed beside her, arms pushing her forward and a determined look on her face.

Jessica spit the brown water from her mouth. She'd probably get some horrible gut disease, although a part of her wanted to drink deeply and sate the punishing thirst she'd lived with the past few days.

She battled the river every stroke as it tried to push her downstream. A part of her wanted to let go, rest her starving muscles and let the water carry her all the way to the Gulf of Mexico. But she could not let that happen. *Angus* she thought, flinging one arm forward. *Tela* her inner voice screamed to propel the other arm.

She kept her eyes on Claudia who fought toward the far bank, sweeping her arms and kicking her legs like her child's life depended on it. The far shore drew closer, and finally Jessica's foot hit bottom right before the river dragged them past the exit path. She grabbed on to Claudia and shoved the shorter woman toward the bank.

Chapter 16

Claudia climbed up the embankment on her hands and knees, and Jessica followed exactly the same way. She pulled herself up the last few inches and then hacked up river water and bile. Tears stung her eyes, but she wouldn't let herself cry yet. They still had many miles to go.

Both women lay in the sand, their breath heaving. The sky had turned from slate to the gray-blue of morning just before the sun rose above the horizon. As much as Jessica wanted to lie there until someone found her so she wouldn't have to expend another ounce of energy with nothing to feed it, they had to walk.

She rolled over, pushing herself up again. She'd never had to think about getting up from the ground before, but now, each hand and leg had to be in a certain position, stabilizing or pushing, to maneuver to standing. She dusted the sand and pebbles off her backside.

Her jeans and boots had made it across the river, but between damp skin and soaked clothing, she might not get them back on. Claudia sat on the ground beside her, shoving her legs through wet denim. Jessica tried balancing on one leg and almost tipped right back down to the ground when she tried to dress.

"Hang on," Claudia said. Once she'd pulled her jeans completely over her feet, she stood and wrenched them up to her waist. "This isn't ideal. I can feel every grain of sand trapped under my pants."

"Nothing about this is ideal, but at least we're alive and free."

"Lean on me," Claudia said.

Jessica did, and inch by inch pulled her tight wet jeans over her damp body. Her feet squished water out of her boots as she stepped into them. By the time Claudia had her shoes on, the sun had crested the horizon. Heat, then thirst, would soon follow, but for now, cool morning air accompanied them.

Jessica surveyed the area. They'd exited the river at a wash, a dry creek bed that would turn into a torrent with rain. While flash floods proved deadly, today the depression had a base of tumbled rocks and sides of loose sand. If they left the wash, anyone out there could see them. If they stayed in it, they wouldn't know their location.

They had likely outrun and outwaited their enemies, but Jessica couldn't be sure, so for now they'd stick to the wash. The further into the US they traveled, the safer she'd feel.

"The Rio Grande divides Texas from Mexico along its entire length," Jessica said. "So we have to be in Texas. I'm certain we're not south of Big Bend because the geography changes. This looks like the El Paso desert, but we're nowhere near the city." The two million people who lived in the El Paso/Juarez metroplex stretched miles along the border. The area where they stood looked like it had never been inhabited.

"I'm pretty sure we'll hit the interstate eventually," Jessica said. "As long as we keep walking away from the river."

"You're probably right," Claudia said. "Although it may take a while. Let's start. I miss my baby."

The sentiment clawed at Jessica's heart. She missed Angus and Tela and her mom and her friends. But if she'd had a child? Her heart almost broke thinking about it. She could hardly make it two months without ending up in some dangerous situation. No child should have a mother like that.

She tried to leave her thoughts behind as she focused on putting one foot in front of the other. Within a few yards, a gravel road crossed the creek bed.

"Should we take the road?" Claudia asked.

"No. It runs along the river. People on either side of the border might see us, and we don't want that. We have no idea whether the men who chased us are still out there searching."

"And bullets cross borders," Claudia added.

Yes, but Jessica wouldn't have said it. Bullets could travel a long way in the desert. Once, a gun fight in Juarez had resulted in a bullet piercing a window on the tenth floor of El Paso's City Hall. That time, no one had been hurt.

They continued up the wash, the creek bed changing from rocks to loose sand. The footsteps of those who'd come before remained visible in the churn. Jessica hated every step. Her stomach had hollowed, and her body ached like it was consuming itself. The wet jeans dragged her down, even though she knew they'd dry quickly in the moisture-free desert air. And her throat and lungs burned with every breath.

She concentrated on putting one foot in front of the other, taking tiny steps that barely moved her forward. She longed to climb up the side of the embankment and get her bearings. If she could see the mountains, the freeway, she'd know where they were and how far they had to trudge. Another road crossed the wash, this time an unmarked paved one. It seemed no more than one lane wide and must belong to whoever owned the land.

Her heart longed to give up, to travel down the smooth road instead of fighting the landscape. But she didn't know if the road ended in the lair of friend or foe, and she didn't know whether a right turn or a left would lead her home. She glanced at Claudia and saw her desperation mirrored in the other woman's eyes.

"Forward," she croaked.

So many steps. She counted each one until she reached one hundred, then started over. She saw a path rising up one side of the creek bed. Her need to know overcame her apprehension.

"Stay here. I've got to find out where we are."

Each step upward sent a new wave of fear through her. What would she find at the top? A person? A bullet? But when she reached it, no one was there. She spun around slowly as a breeze ruffled her hair. In the distance the sun lit El Paso's mountains like a beacon. They had to be less than a hundred miles away. Maybe fifty? She couldn't tell, but if they kept walking, they'd reach the highway. She couldn't see it, but it was there, following the border on its long journey across the state.

Jessica slipped back into the wash, her heart beating with hope for the first time in days.

"We're not too far from El Paso. I can see the mountains. We'll hit Interstate 10 if we keep walking." Each short, jerky sentence sprang from her, driven by excitement because of their proximity to home and by the dull fear that she wouldn't make it. She'd sleep for a week if she successfully finished this trek, waking only to eat and drink everything in sight.

"I'm so glad. I have such bad blisters, I think my feet are bleeding," Claudia said, the crack of tears in her voice.

Jessica understood. Since they'd left the river, her left knee had begun aching. She hadn't remembered twisting it, but every step sent fire racing from the back of her knee up to her left hip and down to her ankle. But it didn't matter, they had to keep going.

"Do you want me to look at them?" Jessica asked, praying Claudia said no because she did not want to slow down.

"No, If I take my shoes off, I may never get them back on. I'll deal with it later. When I'm with Cinco."

Good girl. Fight through it. Claudia had taken each challenge remarkably well. Steel underlaid her kind heart. Tomás did not deserve this woman. Jessica respected her enough to keep her mouth shut. If Claudia could deal with this, perhaps she had the fortitude to deal with Tomás as well.

The banks of the wash gradually shallowed. Jessica could now make out the mounds of sand topped with creosote and sage stretching beyond the banks. Spiney ocotillo and the oval paddles of prickly pear cactus dotted the landscape. Occasionally, a dirt road crossed their path, but they stuck to the creek bed. Nature was sure in the direction she carved. Water always headed to lower ground. A human road could lead anywhere.

A rooster tail of dirt sprang up on one side. Someone drove toward them, probably on one of the crisscrossing dirt roads. Panic sparked in Jessica. Friend or foe?

"Someone's coming," she said, hating the fear and urgency in her voice.

"There's no place to hide." Claudia's agitation matched her own.

The vehicle approached quickly, with the roar of its engine and the shaking of metal traveling over washboard ridges. A row of clearance lights crossed the roof of the big black truck. She imagined them lighting up a swath of desert or a dry pond bed at night. They made the vehicle look more like a creature native to the desert than something manmade.

Jessica pulled Claudia behind a scrub brush on the edge of the wash. Not that its sparse branches and their tiny leaves hid much. She prayed for the truck to fly past them, traveling on to some other destination. But, of course, it slowed.

Two men occupied the cab. The truck pulled half into the wash, its back tires still on the wide dirt road as if it had cornered them. The passenger window rolled down.

A thick-set Hispanic man in his thirties with slicked back hair leaned toward them. "Hey ladies. What are you doing out here in the desert?"

Jessica recognized the deep, gruff voice. He may or may not have been at the house last night, but he had definitely led the group of migrants who'd swum the river. He was a coyote. Fear plunged like a sword, eviscerating her. "We're just out for a walk." It took all her strength to keep her voice steady.

"It's dangerous out here, and you two don't look so good. Let us give you a ride."

No, no, no. She'd rather die than go back to that house. Would probably die if she went back there. Her eyes flicked about the truck to the bright yellow globe that lit a cloudless blue sky. The sunny day did not match the sheer dread that grabbed hold of her.

"We're fine. Thanks for the offer." She kept her voice chill, despite the flames of fear licking her insides. Claudia trembled beside her, and Jessica spied a new vehicle making its way through sand trail still clinging in the air from the first truck. There was more than one of them. They had no chance.

"It wasn't a suggestion," the man in the truck said, now brandishing a pistol.

Claudia let out a soft moan, then her body dropped to the ground. Jessica stared at her, the woman's arms splayed unnaturally, and her head lolled to one side. Had they shot her? Jessica glanced back at the man in the truck who now wore a scowl.

"I think she fainted." Jessica turned to Claudia, knelt down and put her fingers on her neck looking for a pulse. The truck door opened and the thud of feet hit packed sand.

Claudia's chest rose and fell with her breath.

"Vámanos. Alguien llegue." A different voice yelled the words.

At first, Jessica thought they were telling her to come. But *alguien llegue* meant someone was coming. Someone or something these two didn't want to encounter. Jessica stayed by Claudia's side as the truck door slammed again and the engine revved. The truck took off.

Jessica shook Claudia's shoulders. "Wake up. You have to get up."

Claudia moaned and half opened her eyes. "Where am I?" She looked around, looked at her clothes, and then turned to Jessica. Recognition, then fear lit her eyes.

Finally, desperation took over. "Are we still alive?"

"For now," Jessica said.

A green and white SUV stopped on the road. Border Patrol.

From the other direction, where the truck had gone, Jessica saw another trail of dirt coming their way. A black and white SUV approached. The sheriff's department. Jessica had never been so happy to see law enforcement. She'd take a jail cell in the US over that hellacious cinder block prison anytime.

The border patrol officer approached, a young woman with a severe face and a scar slashed across her face. Her hands rested on the heavy belt at her waist that likely held a gun, handcuffs and other tools of her trade.

"What's going on?" the officer, Renteria according to her badge, asked.

Jessica pulled Claudia into a seated position, then looked back at the woman. "We were kidnapped and held across the border. We escaped."

"You crossed the river?" the woman asked.

"Yes," Jessica said, no warmth in her voice. For some reason this woman irritated her. "We are tired and hungry and really want to see our families."

"Does she have any papers?" the woman said, nodding at Claudia.

For fuck's sake. They were both half dead and this woman was concerned about citizenship. Jessica bit back the stream of curse words that came to her lips.

The sheriff's office vehicle came to a stop near them. Jessica almost dropped Claudia back into the dirt as Deputy Guerra, Keith, stepped out. Was it possible for this day to get any worse?

The border patrol officer strode toward Keith with her hands on her hips. She didn't look happy to see him. Jessica would have normally felt the same, but literally anyone was better than the guys in the truck.

"I'm not sure what we've got," she said. The two officers faced each other within easy hearing distance. "I was following the truck that just barreled through here, when I came upon them." Her head tilted Jessica's direction. "We've got two women here, a Caucasian and a Hispanic. I've just arrived."

"Yeah, I heard you radio in the call. These two are missing persons cases from El Paso. I'm happy to take them in."

"They don't have any documentation on them, and they look like they've just crossed the river."

"We're right here," Jessica said. Their idiotic conversation infuriated her. She needed food and water, not two cops arguing over jurisdiction and paperwork.

"Ma'am, we'll be with you in a minute," Renteria said.

"The hell you will be." Jessica exploded. "I've been fucking held prisoner in a house in Mexico for the past I don't know how many days. The woman who kidnapped me poisoned the food, and I'm so hungry I might start gnawing on my arm. And I'm thirsty too because the last thing I drank was river water. Which might kill me. And speaking of killing, that asshole in the truck that was just here crossed a bunch of people last night and just threatened us with his gun. So, I don't know what you two are arguing about, but I need you to get us out of this goddamned desert. Right now."

"Trust me," Keith said to the other officer. "You do not want to deal with this woman. I'll take them in."

"Fine. But I'm going to report this." Renteria tramped back to her vehicle.

"Do you two need help?" Keith asked, tucking away his pissing-match demeanor and pulling out something more caring.

"I want to see my baby." A sob wracked Claudia, and then she collapsed in tears.

Tears rose in Jessica's eyes, but she shoved them back down where they belonged. She got it. Something about a rescue coming after such a harrowing experience shredded the determination that got you through the trauma. Ten minutes earlier, she had no doubt they'd make it to the freeway. Now, she might not make it to Keith's vehicle without assistance.

Her body started powering down, every ache blaring its presence and her hunger and thirst overpowering everything else. And that didn't compare to the mental shutdown. A heavy blanket cloaked her thoughts, relief pushing down and making her drowsy. She wasn't sure she could still form words.

Keith helped Claudia up and walked her to the car with an arm steadying her. Claudia leaned into him as if she could no longer bear her own weight. Her tears didn't stop. Jessica trudged after them.

Once he had Claudia settled in the back of the SUV, he turned to Jessica who'd stopped near the front tire. "Are you all right?" he asked, concern etched across his features.

Jessica felt like a ghost of her former self, as if her bones and flesh had turned to dust and blown away. Only a shrinking cord tethered her to reality, and she held on to it with everything she had. She definitely wasn't all right.

"I'm. . ." She didn't have the words to finish the sentence. She was worn out, worn down, worn away. A bout of dizziness came for her, and she locked her knees. She just had to make it a little longer. She inhaled and pulled her disparate parts back together. "I'm okay."

He put a hand on her back and directed her around the vehicle. To the back seat. Her rage came flaring back. Funny how that was the thing that kept her together.

"Are you arresting us?" she asked, allowing the flame to ignite her voice.

He sighed. "No, Jessica. I'm saving you."

She looked into his black eyes and strong face, and for a moment his words seemed true. They'd needed saving, caught in that frightening house with horrible people. She'd needed someone to save her when she thought they'd be shot dead running across a field in the night and hiding in a scrub forest. Hell, swimming across the river she'd have given her soul for a rescuer. But no one had shown up. No knight in shining armor, no guardian angel, no superhero. She and Claudia had saved themselves.

"If you want to take the credit, show up earlier next time." She grabbed the door handle and pulled herself into the back seat.

Claudia sobbed quietly beside her. Jessica took her hand to give what comfort she could. It was okay for her to break now. She'd been strong when Jessica needed that.

Jessica slumped against the seat, too exhausted to keep her eyes open. "Will you let Jaime Castro of the El Paso Police Department know we're coming in. He's been involved in this case, and he'll notify our families."

"On it. There's been an APB out for you, and Sergeant Castro came by the department and shared what he knew. After finding you out at the reservoir and then learning you'd disappeared while working on a case with Mexico ties, I just had a feeling if you were anywhere, it'd be out here."

Jessica tried to make the words make sense. "You thought I'd be here?"

"We're not far from the reservoir. It's north about five or six miles. But I didn't know you'd be exactly here. The border patrol has all kinds of tracking instruments out here: sensors, drones, cameras. I've been listening to their radio communications. This part of the border is a popular place for migrant crossings because there's no wall and it's relatively close to civilization."

"We're close to the reservoir?"

"Yeah." Keith nodded, then picked up his radio receiver. He also brought a computer in the car to life.

Alarm bells went off in Jessica's mind. Was it possible the coyotes she'd barely avoided last night had also crossed the Guatemalan girls from her earlier case? If so, did they realize she knew about their crimes? How many people in the sheriff's department had connected those dots? After all, Keith had arrested her once before, and the sheriff himself knew about Jessica's involvement in that case.

She listened as Keith reported to headquarters that he'd picked them up. He asked that Sergeant Castro be notified. Then, he took the rutted gravel road east, toward the El Paso mountains shining on the horizon. She wanted to stay vigilant, make sure he took them home, but she could no longer open her eyes or keep her head up. Instead, she let sleep come for her and trusted the universe to keep her safe.

Chapter 17

Claudia shook Jessica's shoulder and practically screamed at her to open her eyes. Her head hurt. No, her whole body hurt. She peeled her eyelids apart.

The sun still shone absurdly bright. Had they gone anywhere yet? Yes. They'd parked in a lot surrounded by similar vehicles. They must be at the sheriff's department headquarters, in the far east of the city. She lived on the west side of the mountains, and it would take a long time for Jaime or her family to get here. Keith opened her door and offered his hand.

She must have looked at him like he had three heads, because he slowly drew his hand back and shoved it in his pocket. Raising her leg to exit the car was as hard as climbing El Paso's highest peak. Her jeans had dried as stiff as cardboard, which didn't help. Fuck it. It didn't matter if she was slow. She just needed to keep moving.

She met Claudia at the back of the vehicle, and they clasped hands and leaned into each other as they walked toward the large sand-colored building. The trauma they'd survived together had forged a bond between them.

Keith led them into the building. The air conditioning sent a chill through her, but gray industrial carpet, buff-colored walls, and the sheer plainness of the building put her at ease. It could have been a call center, or the front offices of some super boring factory, and this normalcy soothed her emotions.

He left them in a conference room with a particleboard table and wire framed plastic chairs. Jessica and Claudia sat across from each other with nothing to say. Tears streamed down Claudia's face, but she didn't sob or make a sound. She'd grown unnaturally still. Jessica understood. They had to endure a little longer before the ordeal ended and they could fit themselves back into their old lives.

Keith returned with four bottles of water. Jessica drank her two immediately. She needed twice that, or more.

She looked at him. "More please. And food."

He returned first with a case of water, then came back with four packaged sandwiches, clearly from a vending machine, and half a box of donuts. The chocolate one had a bite taken out of it. Jessica didn't care. She shoved the whole thing in her mouth. After ingesting river water, there's no way a few germs left on a donut would make her sick.

"You might want to slow down there, Champ," Keith said. "Eating and drinking so much that quickly might make you sick."

She managed a thanks instead of lifting her middle finger. She might be grateful for his help, but her hunger preceded everything.

Claudia unwrapped a sandwich while Jessica destroyed another donut. She could hardly keep herself from snatching the donut box away so Claudia couldn't reach it. Food deprivation had turned her into a monster.

The door opened and a different deputy stepped into the room. Tall and thin, he easily had four inches on Keith, who had to be six-three. Probably in his forties, his thinning brown hair had begun its retreat, and arctic blue eyes stared through Jessica instead of looking at her.

He took a seat at the head of the table and gestured for Keith to sit as well. "Jessica Watts," he said, fixing those unnerving eyes on her. "I'm Sergeant Mayfield. Keith has briefed me on why he brought you in, and I've got some questions for you. Let's start with who your companion is."

Jessica still had half a donut in her mouth, and she stared back at him while slowly chewing. The sugar had given her quick energy, but the last thing she wanted to do was answer hours of questions. She took a long swig of water. "I'd like to thank Deputy Guerra for finding us in the desert. And for providing food and water. That's something I haven't had in a while. Is there any chance we can wait until Sergeant Castro arrives? He's familiar with this case, and it might save us some time."

"Ma'am, I need you to answer my questions." The words sounded polite, but the delivery was all bully.

"I am Claudia Garcia."

Mayfield's brows rose as he studied Claudia. "Oh, you speak English."

"For fuck's sake," Jessica muttered under her breath. But not quietly enough.

"Ms. Watts, do you have something to add to the conversation?" he asked.

"It's nothing." She rolled her eyes at Claudia.

"Good," he said, turning to Claudia. "Are you a US citizen?"

"No. My husband and I are permanent residents. We are both from Juarez."

"I see. And why are you in the US?"

Claudia tilted her head at the question, clearly confused. "We live here. We have a house here, and my husband's companies are here."

"But you don't have any documentation on you?"

Jessica seethed with fury. "This isn't Nazi Germany. She's not required to walk around with papers or a fucking star on her chest. Why don't you start asking questions that matter?"

The icy eyes swung her way. "Ms. Watts, you are currently here as our guest. Are you interested in changing that status?"

What a jerk. Jessica inhaled slowly to compose herself. "I was kidnapped in El Paso and taken to . . ." She stopped. She had no location to give him other than hell. "I was taken across the border to somewhere near where we crossed and where Keith found us. Later, Claudia was kidnapped and put in the same room with me. Then a guy was killed, I think, and then, somehow, we managed to escape and cross the border."

She almost added the part about the guys in the truck who'd threatened to kidnap them again, but the story already sounded completely unbelievable. Let blue-eyes process this first.

He looked bored. "Okay. Back up. So, you think you were kidnapped?"

Suddenly, loud voices echoed from outside the room. The door swung open, and Jaime barreled through. It thrilled her to see him. He'd believe her, and hopefully, he'd move things along so she could go home.

"Jessica. Claudia. I'm so glad to see you two." Jaime looked as grateful as Jessica felt.

"Excuse me," Mayfield broke in. "We are questioning these women. You can't just burst in here."

Jaime's eyes narrowed when he looked at Mayfield. "These two are subjects in missing persons cases in El Paso. Why are you interrogating them? Our department is the lead on this case.

"They were found outside of the city limits." Mayfield closed the folder on his desk as if he didn't want Jaime to see its contents.

Jaime stared at him, and the silence grew uncomfortably long. Jessica shoved another piece of donut in her mouth.

"Fine. Have a seat. We were just getting started," Mayfield said. "Ms. Watts said she was kidnapped in El Paso and taken across the border. I guess the same happened to Ms. Garcia, and they ended up together and escaped."

"No." Claudia spoke up. "That is not what happened and not what she said. I met with Letty in Juarez. She's the one who drugged me and took me to where Jessica was. My father-in-law is still trapped there."

Jaime blew out an angry sigh. "These women look like they have been through severe trauma. I've never seen Jessica so gaunt, and she's obviously filthy, as is Mrs. Garcia. Questioning them now is inhumane. I believe they both should be escorted to the hospital immediately to be examined and to have blood panels run. They said they were drugged. I'm happy to have the chief talk to the sheriff if you disagree."

Mayfield looked suddenly uncomfortable. Jessica glanced at Keith and saw anger in his eyes as he stared at his superior. It looked like Jessica wasn't the only one who thought this guy was an ass.

"I've got just a few more questions, then I'll turn them over to your custody." Mayfield opened his folder again. "Deputy Guerra picked you up at approximately 8:45 this morning in El Paso County. How and when did you cross the border?"

He'd looked at Jessica when he asked the question. What answer would get her out of this room the fastest and still be truthful?

"We managed to escape the house last night by overpowering the woman who'd drugged us. Right after that happened, we saw a bunch of trucks come up the driveway, so we ran."

"Why?" Mayfield asked. "You could have asked them for help."

Was this guy stupid? As if anyone showing up to a kidnapper's house would be the good guys. She stopped her eye roll. Barely.

"I'd overheard that a group of coyotes would be using the property last night. We weren't going to stick around to find out if they'd be happy to see us."

"Is that when you crossed the river? Illegally?" Mayfield's questions grew more annoying. Jessica's law training kicked in. His leading questions gave away how he wanted to shape the narrative.

"We didn't cross last night, because we were afraid of being caught by the coyotes. Instead, we hid in a grove of salt cedar. A group of people did cross during the night, but we waited until morning. Then we walked up the wash, heading for the freeway."

The next part of the story Jessica hoped the sheriffs could help with. "Before Deputy Guerra reached us, we encountered two guys in a truck. They had a gun and ordered us into their vehicle. Fortunately for us, they fled when the Border Patrol showed up."

"Someone found you and tried to kidnap you again?" Jaime asked.

"Likely story." Mayfield sounded skeptical.

"I recognized his voice. He helped cross the immigrants the night before."

Mayfield went white as a sheet. After a heartbeat, he closed his folder and stood. "Fine. We're done here. Guerra, get them processed and handed over to Sergeant Castro." He practically ran from the room. Something was off, and Jessica wanted to know more.

"What was that about?" she asked Keith.

"I honestly don't know." He shook his head and seemed to consider it for a moment before meeting her eyes again.

"Let's get you two out of here," Jaime said. "Your families can meet you at the hospital. I'll need you to make statements, and I'll contact the Juarez authorities about Mr. Garcia, but let's make sure you're healthy first."

"And clean," Claudia added.

"I'm really sorry about this," Jaime said, glancing around the room.

"Would you mind sharing what you learn with me?" Keith asked. Seems Mayfield leaving had loosened his tongue. "I'm really worried about guys with guns trying to kidnap people in the desert. It sounds like someone preying on border crossers. We need to know more."

Jessica sighed. "I want to know why we were able to freely enter the US so close to El Paso. Supposedly there's a crackdown on immigration, yet where we crossed, there were paths into and out of the river. That place is clearly used all the time." Threads of the question had rumbled around in her mind for hours, finally assembling. Surely, the Border Patrol, the sheriffs, someone, would watch that area closely. Yet at least a dozen people had crossed last night, and she and Claudia had followed this morning. No one had intercepted them.

"It's a good question," Keith said. "You were a good mile past the river when the Border Patrol found you."

"Agreed," Jaime said, focusing on Keith. "I'll put a call into the police department and get someone to check the history on that area. Can you look into your files? Let's go over the data later."

Keith waited a moment before nodding. Jessica smiled. It looked like Mayfield was on a need-to-know basis.

But she could worry about that later. Now, she just wanted family. And a lot more food.

"Hey, Jaime," she said. "Can we stop by Taco Cabana on the way to the hospital? I'm starving."

Jaime glanced at her and the sugary donut detritus on her napkin.

"You bet. Let's go."

Jessica followed him out the door, hoping to step easily back into her normal life.

Chapter 18

All hell broke loose in the hospital parking lot. Angus waited with Jessica's mom, his face somehow shining with both relief and concern. Her mom burst into tears the moment she saw Jessica.

Tomás stood beside a woman with Claudia's features on an older, more petite frame. That woman held Cinco, and the keening from Claudia as she saw the baby and leapt from the car sliced through Jessica's heart.

Claudia sobbed as she hugged the child, causing him to cry as well. Jessica glanced at Tomás's face and saw a whirlwind of emotions. Relief. Anger. Was that guilt? She couldn't tell as Angus opened her car door and swept her into his arms. Her body melted into pure exhaustion in the safety of his embrace. She could set down the fear, responsibility, and desperation she'd shouldered.

Her mom came up and rubbed her back as Jessica leaned into Angus. Her legs might not work without him there to hold her up. She'd never experienced fear the way she had in that horrible room. The time had dragged on so long it wore her bluster away, turning her from someone fierce into a pile of mushy dread. The emotions of the past days rushed into her, taking away the sweetness of the moment. She pressed her feet into the pavement and dug her claws into Angus, grasping on to what remained of her sanity before emotion overwhelmed her. She took a deep breath, telling herself she had survived.

Jessica pulled back and looked into Angus's eyes, which were filled with tears and desperate love. She mashed her mouth into his, not caring that she hadn't brushed her teeth or showered in days. He was here. She was alive.

"No." Claudia's sharp voice crackled across the hospital entrance.

Jessica turned to see Claudia step away from her husband. She held the baby with care but had fire in her eyes.

"You negotiated for me." The words dripped daggers. "You wanted a better deal, wanted to talk to your attorneys first. Letty threatened to kill us, and then these horrible men came after us. I'd be dead without Jessica. Your son would grow up without a mother. Is that what you wanted?"

"You're back, and you've been through a lot. Everything is okay now." Tomás's retort smacked of conceit. "Let me take you to a better hospital."

"I will not leave Jessica. She saved me." Claudia took another step back.

"Mr. Garcia," Jaime said. "I need to get a statement from your wife and would like her to stay here while she's examined." His tone held none of the kindness evident in the hand he'd gently laid on Claudia's back.

Jessica gave her mom a quick side hug and told her she was fine. Then, not letting go of Angus's hand she approached Claudia. "Let's go inside. One more journey together."

At Claudia's insistence, the women ended up in a room together. Jessica had her mother close the privacy screen so she didn't have to see Tomás. A nurse asked if she needed a rape kit. Jessica shuddered, grateful, and said no.

Jessica showered, then had blood drawn, and was hooked to an IV. She had to work to keep her eyes open. Soon, Jaime came into the room. He asked that only one person stay with each woman. Claudia chose her mother while Jessica sent hers away. She might never let Angus out of her sight again.

She grabbed her mom's hand. "Thanks for being here. I'll see you soon."

They opened the privacy screen, and Jessica saw that Jaime's partner Clint had joined him. The officers sat in chairs facing the two women. Jaime's eyes locked onto Jessica.

"Angus called me when you didn't come home three days ago. What happened? No glossing over it like you did at the sheriff's office."

Only three days. It had seemed like years, a lifetime. "The day of the big windstorm, I was bored and wanted to get out of the office. I drove to Letty's house, not intending to do anything." She paused. Too many of her stories started the same way. She hadn't meant to seek danger, but she always found it.

"I would have stayed in the car, but the wind blew over one of the trash cans, and I thought I'd just look and see . . ." Her story stopped again, this time because she didn't want to relive the next moments that bled into the worst days of her life. She kept her eyes locked on Jaime and took a breath.

"The can had all kinds of vials, needles, and bloody gauze. It was a real hazmat scene. I meant to return to the truck to get my phone so I could take pictures and call you, but when I stood up, I think someone hit me in the head. Maybe with a shovel. That part is a little fuzzy."

She touched the side of her head, where even now pressure brought pain. The memory of the headaches, of waking in that horrid room almost made her sick.

"According to the doctor, you've got a contusion and maybe a concussion, although they're not sure. What happened after that?"

Jessica shook her head, wanting to lock those memories in a lead box instead of taking them out to examine. Angus squeezed her hand.

"I woke in a room. All cinderblocks. One bare bulb overhead. A bed, a bucket, and me." The memory of those first moments turned her stomach. "I didn't know I was in Juarez. I thought I was in the house in El Paso. At first, I didn't think I'd be there long. I thought you'd find my truck and rescue me."

"Your truck wasn't there."

"What do you mean? I left it at Letty's house. On the street. Just one house down."

"It's gone. We've had an APB out on it for days. Hopefully we'll find it."

Losing the truck pushed Jessica over the edge. She needed the truck for work, and they couldn't afford a new one. The insurance company probably wouldn't give them much due to wear and tear, but no amount of money could replace the memories she'd created in that vehicle. She sniffled and wiped away a tear.

Angus pressed a hand on her cheek and turned her toward him. "It's just a truck. It doesn't matter. You're the only thing that matters, and you're here."

The tear that ran down his cheek, mirroring hers, broke her heart. She'd almost lost him. Almost lost herself.

She told Jaime and his partner the rest of the story. For Angus's sake, she left out how hungry she'd been, how desperate, how she feared she wouldn't survive.

After she finished, they asked Claudia for her version of events. When Claudia spoke about meeting Letty in Juarez, her hands worked the sheets and her voice stuttered. "I had to meet her to save Jessica."

"I see," Jaime said. "So, let me make sure I understand. Letty called you and told you she had taken Jessica prisoner, and you went to meet her in Juarez without telling anyone."

"Yes. That is what happened." Claudia ducked her head and crimson lit her cheeks.

"You met her in the lot and got into her car?"

"Yes."

Jessica ached for Claudia, for the story she would reveal. Would the officers see the fierceness in the woman through her desperation for the right body?

"And then you were drugged?" Jaime continued his questioning. "How exactly did she drug you?"

Claudia paused, then glanced at her mother before answering. "She gave me an injection."

"Where on your body did she inject you?" This time Clint asked the question.

"In my arm." Claudia grasped her upper arm.

Jessica looked at her forearm where a needle pricked her skin, delivering fluids and antibiotics. If Claudia sat in the front passenger seat, then perhaps the back of her left arm would have been an easy spot for Letty to sneak in a shot.

"Did you see the needle before she drugged you? Did you have any idea that was going to happen?" Jaime asked.

"No. I . . ." Claudia went silent. "I didn't know she was going to drug me."

"But you saw the needle." This time Clint spoke. The two policemen tag-teamed the questions, and it seem to knock Claudia off balance.

"I asked for the shot." Claudia turned her head toward Jessica. "I'm sorry. I didn't tell you that part. I really did meet her to try and save you. She told me everything would be fine. She'd take me to you and call Tomás and work everything out. But also, when I knew I was going to meet her, I stopped breastfeeding. It was past time. Cinco is over a year old. I told you she helped me lose weight before I met Tomás, and I have been so fat since I had the baby, and . . ." Her words faded.

"I don't understand how you can be afraid of her one minute and let her inject you with who knows what the next. She could have killed you," Jessica said. Something cold and dark snaked through her veins. She hoped Claudia understood that her accusation-filled voice included the words *she could have killed me too.*

Claudia began to sob. The child in his mother's arms stirred, stretching to look into his mother's face. But he didn't cry. Claudia touched his cheek and calmed.

She took a deep breath before speaking again. "I know it was wrong. I almost didn't do it. But she made it sound like everything would go back to normal. She'd let Tomás see his father. She'd let you go. In fact, she told me she'd never wanted to kidnap you in the first place. Don Octavio saw you snooping around the house. She said he wasn't a trusting man, and he's the one who hit you. I believed her. I really thought everything would be okay."

Jessica heard the truth spewing out of Claudia but didn't want to believe her. How could anyone be so naïve?

"I want to go." Jessica looked at Jaime. "Are we done here?" The hospital only added to her stress. She needed to go home and rest, pet her dog, and try to forget that the last few days had actually happened.

She'd dispose of her relationship with Claudia and Tomás, forever this time. The only question she wanted answered was whether Letty and Tres had survived. Well, that, and had the man with the deep voice also led Angela and Mari and their families across the river? Was the gun he'd flashed at her the same one he'd used to kill the girls' families?

Did he know who she was?

A new fear coursed through her blood, one born of living minute after minute knowing each could be your last. She wanted to drain that newfound fear from her body. Wished the IV hooked to her arm delivered the antidote to her increasing anxiety. She liked the old, bold version of herself. Maybe after a week of sleep and plentiful food, that Jessica would reappear.

Jaime said they only had a few more questions. She tried to listen to the rest of Claudia's words, but they rehashed a story she already knew. Claudia thought a phone call to Tomás would solve everyone's problem, her own, Jessica's, Letty's. She thought they'd be rescued within the hour.

But her white knight didn't arrive. Sure, he was on the other end of the phone hidden behind lawyers and excuses, but he had no intention of riding in to save someone until the negotiations ended in his favor.

"I need to leave." Jessica's voice rang out across the room. All eyes turned to her.

"They haven't released you yet," Jaime said. Captain Obvious.

Jessica fumed. Never again would anyone else decide when she got to leave a room. "I have been a prisoner for days. Do not try to tell me I can't leave when I want to. Now someone please get the nurse before I rip this needle out of my arm." Overly dramatic, certainly. But she should never have to worry about escaping again.

Angus and Clint jumped up at the same time. "I'll go," Clint said.

"We've got a few additional questions for you, Mrs. Garcia," Jaime said. "Plus, I'll need both of you to sign statements about what happened. It's important to keep a formal record since this is an ongoing case."

It might go on for the police and the Garcias, but Jessica was done. The nurse came in and asked if she'd wait for the doctor. Jessica said no. The last fumes of her energy had run low, and she needed to sleep. At home. Angus squeezed her hand in solidarity.

While the nurse removed her IV and prepared her to leave, Jaime asked Claudia where she'd go when the hospital released her. When she answered back to Juarez, Jaime asked if she could possibly stay in the US for a few days, for the case and for her safety.

For the first time, Claudia's mom spoke up, whispering to her daughter in Spanish. Maybe she didn't know that everyone in the room spoke Spanish, except, perhaps, Clint and the nurse.

Claudia's mother agreed with Jaime, but Claudia didn't want to stay in the house with Tomás. In a steely voice, the older woman said, "Me encargaré de ello."

Jessica bet she'd take care of it. She doubted Tomás had a chance of staying in that house. The men in Juarez might seem to run everything, but nothing compared to the network of mothers among the city's elite. If only they would use their power for good, like convincing young women that attractiveness did not equal skinny. Fucking weight loss drugs. Jessica couldn't believe Claudia had willingly let that horrible woman jab her with a needle.

Jessica left the room in sweats and a T-shirt Angus had brought. The conversation between the police and Claudia hadn't ended, but Jessica's appetite for it definitely had. They took the elevator to the first floor where they found Linda rushing through the automatic doors.

"Oh, my god. Jesssica. We've been so worried about you." She swept Jessica into a hug.

"I'm fine, or I'm going to be," Jessica said to her boss, hoping it wasn't a lie. "I just need to get some sleep, and I'm already hungry again."

"You take all the time you need. Whenever you're ready, I'm here to lend an ear or a hand. And your desk will be waiting for you once you've recovered."

"Thanks. I really appreciate it." Jessica tried to stay upright and put a little pep in her voice, but she wanted to sink to the floor and close her eyes. Adrenaline, donuts, and mainlining Diet Coke had kept her alert so far, but not even those tools could keep her going for long.

"I need to get her home," Angus said. "But thanks for stopping by."

"I'll see you soon," Jessica said as Angus wrapped an arm around her waist and pulled her into the sunny day.

She must have slept on the way home, because they seemed to go from the hospital to the driveway in seconds. With the last of her energy, Jessica pulled herself from the car and trotted to the front door. She had to wait for Angus to open it. She no longer had keys, phone, or a wallet.

"We've got to get the door rekeyed and the credit cards changed. Everything was in the truck."

"I'll take care of it. You just take care of yourself." He opened the door. "And Tela, who's missed you terribly."

The dog launched herself at Jessica, and she would have fallen back out the door had Angus not steadied her from behind. Then, seeming to understand that Jessica didn't feel well, the dog spun in circles then crouched on the floor. Jessica dropped to her knees and wrapped herself around Tela, finally letting go of all the emotion she'd kept trapped inside. It seeped out her eyes, fingertips, and pores, then dissipated into the air and sank through the floorboards.

When Jessica and the dog finally had their fill of each other, Angus led her to the kitchen. He sat her at the table and put a chocolate milkshake and container of fries in front of her. He must have bought them at the Charcoaler drive-thru on the way home. She hadn't even known they'd stopped.

When she couldn't eat any more, he led her to the bedroom. The old Jessica wanted to joke and tell him he had no chance of getting laid. But a quieter version of herself took hold. Or she perhaps let go of needing to control everything. Angus asked for nothing, only gave.

He opened her pajama drawer, but she requested his softest T-shirt instead. Then he led her to bed. He tucked her in, then settled Tela in front of her. He snuggled into her back and wrapped an arm around her, cocooning her in safety. Each time Angus stroked her shoulder, or she laid a hand on Tela's head, she uncoiled a fraction more, winding down until only sleep remained. Finally, she could close her eyes in safety.

Chapter 19

For three days, Jessica slept and ate and played with the dog. Every time she woke, Angus rested beside her. When she hungered, he had special treats delivered. He played gatekeeper. Her mother and friends stopped by, but they would ask how she was. She wasn't sure. Sometimes, her memories dulled as if a scab had formed. Other times a sound, a smell, or the recollection of cold concrete beneath her cheek sent panic crashing through her. Then, she only wanted Angus or Tela to see her weakness.

Someone must have covered for Angus at work, because he stayed by her side. Most importantly, he didn't ask her to talk about the abduction, although a new darkness in his eyes told her he wanted to know. He'd ask, eventually, when she wasn't so broken. And she'd tell him. Until then, she'd use the reprieve for recovery.

Her limited waking hours she spent in the backyard where the huge desert sky refused to box her in. Or eating. She wondered if she'd ever feel truly full again. She shoved food in her mouth, and too soon her stomach would distend and hurt. She'd have to stop, but she craved more, even when she couldn't eat another bite.

Thoughts of women starving to be thin plagued her. Did they feel this way, like they would never be allowed enough food to sate their hunger? Was that what Claudia went through? Her body set the limit on what she could eat, but what if she asked her mind to do the same? To force herself not to eat despite driving hunger. Perhaps the drug Claudia took kept the hunger from gnawing at her the way it did at Jessica.

Once sleep and food had restored her energy, another hunger claimed her. She had survived, and she wanted to feel it, to prove it.

She reached for Angus in bed, kissed him greedily. He patted her hair like she was Tela, which turned her passion to fury.

She grabbed his hand and bit the fleshy pad below his pinky. "I want you to fuck me, not pet me."

"Are you sure?" He looked scared, like he might damage her instead of restoring her to the living.

She wanted to scream that she wasn't a doll that would break. She needed him inside her, deliciously hard and slamming awake all her dulled senses. Instead of rough words, she ripped her shirt off and pressed her bare breasts into him, wrapped an arm and a leg around him, pressed her lips to his, and channeled her need directly into his soul.

She watched his face as she kissed him, felt his body respond even while the question remained in his eyes. Finally, he shut his eyes tight, kissed her back, then grabbed her ass and pulled her even closer. Joy exploded through her. She was alive, and it was brilliant.

He rolled her onto her back, finished undressing her, and kissed every part of her body. He ran his hands along her stomach and legs and skimmed his tongue along her inner thighs on the way back up. It wasn't enough.

"I need you in me, now." Her voice sounded strangled.

He looked into her eyes, still questioning.

"Right now. I have to feel you. All of you." The savageness of a wild mountain lion ran through her. She wanted to scratch him with her claws and tear through his skin with her teeth.

He entered her slowly and carefully. She wrapped her legs around him and pulled him hard into her.

"Harder. Faster." She groaned the words and dug her fingers into the soft skin of his back. He obliged, driving into her until the headboard rattled, then slammed against the wall.

God, to feel this alive, to crave more and more with every cell screaming for pleasure. "More," she cried, wrapping her arms around the sweet sweat of his body, pulling toward him until all of her body touched his. He rose to his knees and pulled her onto him like he was just as desperate as she, and it threw her over the edge of pleasure. She lived.

Chapter 20

Monday morning when Linda bustled through the door, she startled at Jessica sitting at her desk. Bored with home, unable to sleep any more despite the dark circles still decorating her eyes, Jessica had chosen a different path. She reopened the door to the Jessica of the past. She wanted courage, bravery, and a give no fucks attitude. She would become that woman again.

She had made progress, even if that room still haunted her dreams. But she'd had days to recover, along with lots of food, dog cuddles, and sex. So much sex. Who knew bedroom antics cured fear. Not that they'd confined things to the bedroom.

"What the hell are you doing back here already? I thought you'd be out for at least a few weeks." Linda's enormous satchel thudded to the floor, and she sank into the chair across from Jessica.

"I can't stay at home another minute. Before we go any further, I did something I should have asked you about." Jessica's eyes crept toward the large brown dog bed next to her desk. "I brought my dog, Tela, to work today. She's a really good dog, and she's in the backyard right now. She can stay on the dog bed when she's inside. I promise, she won't bother you." Jessica finally shut up, realizing how desperate she sounded.

"No problem. It will be nice to have a pet here. But we need to do something about the backyard. Why don't you call a couple of landscapers for a quote?" Linda's smile tightened like she wanted to appease Jessica. Like she thought Jessica needed the dog here.

Jessica blew out a sigh. She'd have to tread carefully. She didn't want to be seen as weak, but she did want Tela with her. The conversion from an old house to law office meant Tela could play in the fenced yard. Sure, Linda hadn't maintained it, but why would she? No one went back there, and Tela sure as hell wouldn't care.

"You don't need to worry about landscaping. She's a dog. She'd probably dig up any nice plants you put back there, and the dirt makes it easier for her to rut around." Jessica didn't want Linda spending money on something like that—on something meant to help her get over her trauma.

"Please. The yard is an embarrassment. I'm always worried clients will see it and think I put that little thought into their cases. You'd be doing me a favor."

Jessica could tell from Linda's arched eyebrow that she wouldn't win this one. "Fine. I'll call a few people. Now catch me up on where we are with clients."

"Catch you up? You've hardly been gone." Linda shook her head, then stared at Jessica in a way that made her uncomfortable. "Speaking of favors, Tomás and Claudia Garcia came to see me on Friday. They want to buy you a truck to replace your old one."

Jessica didn't know where to start with that statement. Angus had dropped her off this morning and would pick her up early so he could get to work on time. They'd talked about going used car shopping later in the week. While neither of them looked forward to the expense, they'd find a way to make it happen. If only next semester's tuition wasn't due. But she couldn't tolerate owing the Garcias anything.

And a bigger question astounded her. "They were together?"

"Yes," Linda said, looking confused.

"The last time I saw them, Claudia was furious at him for stalling our release."

"They must have worked it out," Linda said. "They didn't seem entirely comfortable with each other, but I figured the kidnapping had terrified them. Anyway, they said they wanted to either gift you the truck directly or give it to the firm if that worked better."

"I certainly don't want to take a gift from Tomás Garcia."

"Why? It seems like a solution to a problem."

"Tomás and I have a long history. Plus, he was willing to get his wife killed in lieu of giving up his inheritance. He is not a good guy."

"He wants to hire us to continue working on this case. I told him I'd have to talk to you first."

"And the plot thickens." Jessica took a deep breath, completely unprepared for this discussion. "Let's take a break for a minute so I can try and wrap my head around this one. Stay there, and I'll get Tela and introduce you two."

She left Linda sitting in front of her desk and strode through the office just trying to inhale and exhale without screaming. She had hoped to leave this case behind forever. Yet, she'd wondered for days what had happened to Letty and the old man. And every time she thought about the coyotes, it plunged her into a mystery from the past that still needed resolution.

In the kitchen, she poured a cup of coffee for Linda before opening the door and calling Tela. The dog ran to her from across the yard and bounded into the house in a leap that ignored three steps.

"Sit," she said, her voice stern. This dog needed to behave. Tela obeyed, but her skin twitched in excitement, probably from the thrill of exploring a new place. "Be calm and behave." She used her firmest voice.

Tela whined in complaint.

"Heel," Jessica ordered as she headed toward her desk. That particular command had never worked with Tela and didn't now. The dog darted for Jesssica's desk.

Fortunately, Jessica could see all the way to the front. Tela stopped in surprise as she passed through the conference room door. Then her whole body wiggled in happiness, and she disappeared from view, probably on her way to accost Linda and her perfectly tailored Armani suit. She definitely wouldn't win any guard dog awards.

"Hi, girl. Aren't you an interesting looking dog?" Linda said, patting Tela on the top of her head as Jessica walked into the room.

"Sorry, she's a little rambunctious because this is a new place. She'll calm down soon," Jessica said. The dog started bouncing, and her next move would be to put her paws in Linda's lap. "Tela. Bed."

Tela looked at Jessica as if she never let her have any fun, but she listened. She made her way to the pad and perched in a sitting position as if she'd be let loose to chase a fallen duck at any moment.

"She really is fine," Linda said. "I'm glad you brought her in. Now, let's talk about the truck and our relationship with the Garcias. I'm happy letting it all go if that's what you want."

Jessica handed Linda her coffee, then dropped into her seat. "What exactly do they want us to do on the case? Letty might not even be alive, not to mention Tomás's father."

"They think they might be. Someone meeting her description admitted an older man to Hospital Angeles in Juarez yesterday, and Tomás plans on visiting him this afternoon. Because Letty and Tres were married in the United States, Tomás would like us to research the history of similar manipulative marriage cases in Texas."

"Regarding his inheritance?" Jessica asked. In the end, she assumed everything led back to money.

"Yes. That and the legitimacy of the claim. I remember a case out of East Texas involving a big landowner. He'd only been married to his second wife a few months before he passed away. His kids tried to sue, but I don't recall whether they succeeded."

The East Texas case, and its similarities to Letty and Tres sounded interesting, but working for Tomás did not. "I'm not sure I can work with him. Again, he's not a good guy."

Linda ran her teeth along her bottom lip, seemingly lost in thought. "I hear you, and if you don't want the firm to take this case, that's fine. But, Jessica, you don't have to like your clients. I would never consider a case that I thought crossed an ethical line. After all, I spent the first half of my career as a police officer. But I don't think this one does. They have legitimate concerns given how quickly Tres married this woman and his rapid health decline after the wedding. It's actually kind of fascinating."

The questions spinning through her head overwhelmed Jessica. "What about the fact that his stepmother kidnapped his wife? Will that be prosecuted? Also, if the marriage/inheritance thing went to court in the US, would the fact that she kidnapped me be a conflict of interest? Is anyone even pursuing my kidnapping?"

"Those are all great questions. Jaime is preparing your case for the DA. I thought he had talked to you about it."

"He did. Last week." Jessica sighed. She'd pushed Jaime away, unwilling to handle the update. "I wasn't ready to discuss it then. I thought I'd catch up with him today or tomorrow."

"Regarding Claudia's kidnapping, that would be handled by the Mexican police. I think Tomás considers the threat of arrest a tool for getting Letty to concede on the inheritance. "I'm sure he's also concerned about how the publicity of the kidnapping would affect his father's businesses and his wife's family."

"It's really impressive that he's more concerned with reputations than his wife's life." Jessica's hatred of Tomás mixed with worry about why Claudia indulged the cockamamie plan.

"You're right. Let's take a step back. I'll call Tomás and tell him we won't work with him. I apologize if I've put you in a difficult position. I thought staying involved might help you work through what happened, but I misjudged the situation."

"It's okay." Conflict raged through Jessica. "I do want to know how this story ends. I also want to make sure Claudia comes out of this okay. She tried to save me, in the most naïve way possible. But still, I owe her something."

"I think she feels the same way. It was her idea to get you the truck. She'll probably reach out to you and try to convince you to take it. She's like a dog with a bone on that subject." Linda chuckled and glanced at Tela.

"I can handle that. Thanks for understanding."

"No worries," Linda said. "Now let's go through the rest of the cases."

Jessica tried to listen to her boss, but her mind kept wandering back to Claudia. How could she have returned to Tomás, when he hadn't cared about the danger she faced? Just days ago, Claudia had worried that her son would grow up motherless, and now that seemed to be forgotten. She longed to talk to her, perhaps to understand her thinking, perhaps to convince her of her mistake. But reaching out might mean engaging with Tomás, and she'd delay that as long as possible.

Calling Jaime topped her list, but she kept procrastinating. The thought of trying to prove who kidnapped her when she remained foggy turned her gut. Remembering the torturous hours in that room was a whole new circle of hell. She tried to shake the thought away. Even if she got through that, she'd have to endure a criminal proceeding for a chance at justice. The prospect loomed over her, waiting to suck away all her energy.

She preferred to focus on something other than herself. For days she'd fixated on survival. Then she spent even more days concentrating on recovery. She was fed up with herself and longed to turn her gaze outward to other issues.

Her mind needed to roam, otherwise it would return to the confines of the prison she'd endured. Each time she tried to force her thoughts away from the room and back into the open. But it was like the time she'd tried meditating, only opposite. Then, her mind had wandered the second she forced it to focus on her breathing. Now, instead of wandering, it constantly returned her to those four walls.

Jessica shook her head and pulled her thoughts back to the present, determined to get through this funk. Action would help. Knowledge also. She picked up the phone and dialed the sheriff's department, asked for Deputy Guerra. When she told the person on the other end of the line that she needed to speak with him because he'd saved her by rescuing her from the desert, a useful exaggeration, they patched her straight through.

"Jessica. How are you?"

"I'm doing much better. Thanks for your help last week. When you picked us up, you said the spot we were in was just a few miles from the reservoir. I'd like to know more about that."

"Sure. I can stop by and show you the exact location of both."

"That would be great. Are you going to be downtown in the next few days?"

"Yes, I'll be there this afternoon. Would you like me to stop by your office?"

"Sure." A thread of trepidation hummed through her as she thought about seeing the map. But overwhelmingly, she yearned to turn nightmares into nothing more than points on an aerial photo. Real images instead of the ones running through her head sounded like relief.

Chapter 21

When Keith arrived, Jessica took him to the backyard while she let Tela play. She had already pulled a couple of kitchen chairs into the dirt. Tela darted back and forth between them, seemingly happy to see the deputy again.

"I hope you're okay out here," she said. "I just needed to feel the sunshine."

"I can't imagine what it would be like to be locked in a room for days."

"It's not that. The day is beautiful, and it's nice to get some fresh air." She sounded defensive, but people didn't need to assume that the kidnapping had changed her. She would make sure it didn't.

"Fine," he said. "Let me show you what I've got." He pulled his chair beside hers and turned on the electronic tablet he carried.

"This is where I picked you up." He pointed to a spot on the aerial image.

The dirt road intersected with the wash with parallel tire tracks that stood out from the surrounding desert littered with clumps of sage and cactus. They'd made it more than halfway to the freeway. They would have had to hitch a ride from there, and given the way they looked, they might not have easily found a ride, but they'd have made it. Unless the guy with the gun had taken them first. Jessica shoved him from her mind.

She could not keep thinking about the terrible things that might have happened. Instead, she let the warmth from the sun seep into her skin and turn her black hair hot against her scalp. She pushed her feet into the packed dirt and rested her eyes on her multi-colored dog.

"Where were you coming from when you found us?"

"I had gone back out to the reservoir we walked. I checked out the smaller one too, the one farther from the freeway. I didn't find anything. Anyway, I was in the area, and when I heard the call come through on the radio, I thought I'd check it out."

"I'm glad you did." Funny how someone you once considered an enemy could quickly change into . . . She gazed at him, not exactly sure how to classify him. Colleague, perhaps. But one who seemed to have an uncanny ability to guess where she'd be.

If she didn't know better, she'd think he'd found a way to track her. But she'd had no device with her the three days in Juarez, so he couldn't have known. He must have just gotten lucky.

"It's uncanny how you always show up where I am."

"I drove the area every day after you went missing."

An awkward silence fell. He had followed her, in a way. It creeped her out a little, but given the result, it mostly filled her with gratitude.

"Would you like to see more?" He asked, holding out the iPad-sized device encased in thick plastic.

"Yes. May I?" she reached for it. She scrolled south, down the wash. The river had a sharp bend just before the mouth of the dry creek bed intersected it. She slid her fingers across the screen until she'd enlarged the area as much as possible. "This is where we came out." Jessica hovered her finger above the northern bank. She tried to match the pixelized image to her memory.

After they'd entered the river, they'd floated downstream a few yards. She found a bare spot on the Mexican shore. "I think we got in here."

"I see," he said. "And where did you hide?

She pointed to the large swath of green nestled into the river's bend. "This is a salt cedar forest. It took us forever to get through it in the dark, but we eventually found a place to hide right next to the river. That's how I saw the people crossing in the middle of the night."

"You were lucky they didn't see you."

"I know." The words threatened to take her back to that night, but she wouldn't follow them. She called to Tela, who sniffed something at the back fence. The dog bounded over. Jessica rubbed her fingers into soft fur and satin ears. Her strength returned bit by bit as she survived memories of the trauma without further damage.

"Any idea why that crossing isn't patrolled more? I think it's used pretty often." The question had nagged at her for days. A heavily patrolled border. A ford in the river whose banks were scarred with use. Some person or device should have noticed the large group that crossed before she and Claudia did. Should have noticed them.

Keith's black eyes stared into hers as he chewed his bottom lip. "I just don't know," he finally said. It wasn't right, and they both knew it.

"Looking at the map, do you have any idea where you were held?"

Jessica looked into her lap. She pinched the screen, and land on both sides of the border came into view. She easily found the levee, but a ditch full of water between it and the farmland surprised her. "I don't remember this at all," she said, sliding her finger along the ditch.

"It's possible it was dry," Keith said. "They only fill the irrigation ditches when they have crops."

"There weren't any crops." She followed her mind back to that night. "There was a barbed wire fence and a round corral."

Keith lifted the tablet from her fingers and manipulated the screen. "Like this?" he asked.

The screen had changed. Jessica now had a drone's view of a perfectly round orange corral. She hadn't seen its color in the black of night, but the solid corral walls notched themselves into her memory. She saw the long narrow yard with clumps of dirt and rocks. They'd been lucky to run straight back without falling. With one tentative finger she touched the screen, sliding away from the back fence. A rooftop came into view. The house.

"I'm certain that's it." Her voice sounded completely normal, which was opposite to her roiling gut and trembling nerves. "We ran out the back door and around the corral. Even the front of the house with the long drive makes sense. I saw headlights from the trucks coming down the driveway. Then we escaped out the back."

"You went north over a mile before hiding in the trees. That's a long way."

"We ran as fast as we could. Then we jogged. We had to get as far away as possible if we wanted to survive. They chased us. It took a while, I don't know how long. But eventually, we spotted headlights coming our way. That's when we ran up and over the levee and dropped down into the salt cedar. We heard the truck up on the levee, but we kept pushing forward until we got to the river." A chill spread down Jessica's spine despite the warm sun.

"Damn you were lucky. I'm so glad you escaped."

Jessica shifted her thoughts away from the trauma of the escape. Why did he care? They had one stint working together in the desert. Then he had shown up right on time after she and Claudia crossed the river. But before that, he had arrested her. And she'd come damn near to accosting him the time she'd seen him near the courthouse. She didn't trust the sheriff. Why should she think differently of any of his deputies? Yet here he sat, acting as if he cared.

"Why are you doing this?" she asked.

"I'm trying to find out what happened to you."

"Why?"

His eyes clouded, and a line creased his forehead. "You accused me of not listening to you when I arrested you at Pastor Wright's ranch. That kind of stuck with me. I didn't want those girls to get hurt. I should have done more back then, and I'm trying to make up for it now."

He'd opened himself up to her most important question. "Why didn't you listen to me then? It would have only taken a few minutes to check the buildings and see if I was telling the truth." She'd told him she'd heard voices from inside the padlocked buildings. How could she have faith in him now?

"I should have, but we were told to get you out of there ASAP. It wasn't Wright's first complaint about you, and my instructions were to bring you in as quickly as possible." He paused as if he wanted to say something else.

When he didn't, Jessica returned her gaze to the device in her lap. "Do you think the coyotes Claudia and I saw are the same ones who crossed Angela and Mari?"

"There's no way to tell. What I don't understand is how they're getting away with it so close to El Paso." Keith echoed her thoughts.

"My bet is it comes down to money. If they can cross people, they can probably cross other things," she said. Like drugs. El Paso's long history of involvement in the drug trade included stories from the seventies about colorful people blowing cash in Las Vegas and blowing coke up their noses. At least until someone was shot in the middle of the night. She'd thought things had calmed down in the ensuing decades until her own father became one of those criminals, not the partying coke fiend, just the local district attorney who'd blow up his life, and hers, after his conviction for destroying evidence in a drug case.

She hated her ties to this underbelly of corruption. Her entire adult life she'd stayed as far away from the trafficking as one humanly could in this border megalopolis. But even if she ignored it, the drug trade hummed like part of the circuitry of border towns.

Her mind wandered back to that house, that prison. How could a person prove what went on in a place? Drug deals, murders, people crossing the border illegally in the dead of the night. Someone should tear that house to the ground, and Jessica would volunteer first for that task. But in the renowned Valle de Juarez, the illicit activity would likely move next door.

Lost in thought, she'd almost forgotten Keith by her side. His voice surprised her.

"There may be all kinds of crime happening in the house where they held you. There was a time, back when my uncle was a deputy, that our department worked closely with our counterparts in Mexico. Unfortunately, today's political climate makes that extremely difficult."

"So then, why bother?" Why bother with her case? After all, he likely had other crimes to solve and other places to patrol.

Tela, tired of running around the yard, harrumphed and lay down at their feet. Keith raked a hand across his fade cut hair. The black hair spiked back up as soon as his hand passed by like someone running a nail across a toothbrush. Was he her age? Younger?

"I'm not sure," he said. "This case has me all tied up. I want to be one of the good guys, the way my uncle was. It has you all tied up as well. That's why I found you in the desert looking for clues. When you disappeared, I thought the Guatemalan girls had something to do with it. Like maybe the kidnappers had seen us out there searching the reservoir and had taken you."

The concern in his eyes startled her. But, of course, before he picked them up, he'd known nothing about her work with Claudia. "I don't think I was kidnapped because of that case, even though we may have stumbled upon where they crossed. My kidnapping happened in El Paso when I was doing a little reconnaissance on another case."

"I heard that. Jaime Castro told me. I just . . . I worried that there was some connection." Again, his concern took Jessica aback. Did he know something he wasn't sharing?

Jessica handed him the tablet. "Thanks for showing me this." She didn't know what she had gained. Maybe the house would be less of a threat in her dreams now that she knew where it existed, could see it on a map. She hoped so.

"I wish I could go there," he said.

"Go where?" Trepidation pricked her skin.

"The house you were in. I'd like to look for clues and set up surveillance."

"Do not ever wish to be there." Not even the warm sun could stop her shiver. She hated that house.

The door behind them opened and Tela jumped up at the noise. Jessica turned to see Linda in the doorway.

"Hey, you two. Is everything all right?" she asked.

"Yeah. This is Keith Guerra with the sheriff's department. He's the one who arrested me a couple of months ago. He's also the one who brought Claudia and me in from the desert last week."

A worried look crossed Linda's face. "That's quite a coincidence. If it's okay with you, I need my paralegal back."

"Of course." Keith stood immediately, his cheeks going red. "Thank you for your time, Jessica."

"Sure. Let me know if you find anything new." Although she had no idea what that would be. So far, Angela and Mari's case seemed to be a dead end.

"Stay there," Linda said to Jessica. "I just want to make sure he makes it out okay, then I'll be back."

Chapter 22

When Linda returned, Jessica assured her she was fine. She assured herself as well. Then, Angus stopped by so she could drive him to work. He asked if she was okay. She had to get everyone off her back.

She dropped Angus at work, then walked across the parking lot to Starbucks to study. But her books couldn't hold her concentration. She pulled up Google Maps on her laptop and located the house in the Valle de Juarez. The barbed wire fence showed as a faint black line, while the levee road delineated cropland and civilization from the banks of the river. She couldn't take her eyes off the path they'd traveled.

Her phone rang. Claudia. She considered not answering. Claudia hadn't exactly returned to her captor, but by forgiving Tomás, she'd subjected herself to something less than freedom. But Jessica's need for answers overwhelmed her desire to punish the woman.

"How's it going?" she asked.

"Your boss told Tomás you wouldn't accept the truck and don't want to work with us. Why? Do you not want to be my friend anymore?" Hurt rang through each syllable of the formal diction common to the Juarez elite.

"Being your friend and working with you are two completely different things." Jessica paused. She liked Claudia, but something beyond Claudia's reliance on Tomás dug at her. Guilt. Letty might never have called Claudia if Jessica had kept her mouth shut. Letty only reached out to Claudia after Jessica had told her everyone was onto her. And neither kidnapping would have happened if Jessica hadn't visited the house.

"So, you're back with Tomás." The unrelated question bought Jessica more time as she struggled with her emotions.

Claudia breathed heavily, then shushed the baby. Jessica could picture him lying on her chest.

"He explained to me how the attorneys were trying to get me out. Get us out. Plus, my son needs his father. And I want my family intact."

It must be hard not to know you can make it on your own. Jessica's uncharitable thought stayed behind her lips. After all, as much as she told everyone she was fine, Jessica hadn't exactly recovered. And Angus had helped tremendously.

"The deputy who picked us up in the desert came by my office today. He showed me an aerial photo of the house." No need to call it anything else. Claudia surely had the prison tattooed on her brain the same as Jessica.

Claudia gasped. "Why would you want to see that?"

"I see it in my dreams every night. It was nice to see it on the screen. It's just an ugly, disgusting house, not a monster." Jessica would have preferred to hide her revulsion, but the truth wrenched itself from her lips.

"Oh, Jessica. You should get therapy. I am. But I do have some news. Tomás engaged the police and private security to search for Letty. They went to the house where they held us."

"And?" Jessica asked.

"The house was empty, but Don Octavio is dead. They found his body in the horse corral. We probably went right by it."

Jessica had no pity for the man who'd likely hit her in the head with a shovel and then stolen her away to Mexico. She hoped he'd rot in hell. But he also hadn't masterminded the scheme.

"No news of Letty or Tres?"

"We think she took him to a hospital in Juarez, but she took him out just hours after they checked in. Tomás's men didn't know about it until they were gone. The police have searched her home in the city, and now every hospital and clinic in Juarez is checking new patients to make sure it's not Tres. We are so worried."

As they should be. Who knows what that horrible woman did with him? "Do you think they're alive?" Jessica asked.

"Yes. At least we hope so. Yesterday, Tres's Mexican checking account was emptied. Tomás is certain it was Letty. We're trying to get the surveillance video."

"How much did she get away with?"

"Only a couple of hundred thousand. He kept most of his money in investment accounts or the business."

Jessica couldn't fathom the wealth that would make two hundred thousand dollars seem like nothing to worry about. "Well, hopefully that's good news, and she's using the money to keep Tres alive."

"I hope so." The worry in Claudia's voice pulled at Jessica's heart.

"I wish you'd reconsider and accept the truck. And I really wish you'd keep working with us. I don't want to lose touch with you."

"It sounds like you have a whole army out searching for them. And you don't need to hire me to stay in touch. Just call me. We can be friends." She almost added *as long as I never have to see your husband again*, but didn't. Claudia sounded strained, a mirror of Jessica's own feelings.

A long silence played between them. With no response from Claudia, Jessica looked at her phone to make sure the call hadn't dropped. She needed to say goodbye, to get back to studying. Or staring at the house.

"I would like to be your friend." Claudia's quiet voice managed to howl with loneliness.

"You already are." Jessica thought she heard a sob after her words. She wanted to comfort Claudia, but not today. She had trouble seeing past her own frayed emotions and worried about Claudia's expectations of a friend. Jessica had a few deep and abiding friendships, thanks to her friends working hard to keep her in their circle.

"Hey, I've got to go," Jessica said. "Keep me updated on the case, and maybe we can get together soon." There. She'd taken it as far as she could today.

She hung up the phone and went back to staring at Google Maps. In the busy coffee shop she didn't hear Angus approach.

"Is that the place?" he asked, sitting beside her.

She startled and considered lying, although she didn't know why. "Yes. I'm kind of obsessed with it."

"That's understandable. Does it help or hurt to look at it?"

Jessica considered the question. Other than seeming like a time suck, it didn't hurt. It turned the experience into something physical she could deal with instead of a mental trap.

"It's good. It just looks like a regular house. I wish there was another way to explore it, other than going there. It's so much less frightening here than in my mind."

"I guess you could fly a drone over it."

The notion intrigued her. She could explore the path from where Keith had picked them up, backward to the river. She could study where they exited the water and turn back the journey to the place they'd entered, the place they'd hidden, the levee they'd walked. If she could rewind time, maybe she could erase it from her psyche. Except that she'd reach the house. The drone couldn't see through the roof. It couldn't photograph an empty room, not one imprisoning a terrified woman.

But still, the idea appealed to her. The visuals gave her control over a place where she'd had so little.

"Maybe. That's pretty interesting."

"I'll ask around and see if anyone I work with has one."

She nodded, curious about how far a drone could travel. How close would she have to get to the river, and what would she do if the guys in the truck came back?

"If you do this," Angus said, "I want to be there. Do not go back out there alone."

Chapter 23

The next day, Jessica arrived at work determined to put the incident behind her. She filled every moment with tasks, and when she ran out of things to do, she pulled out a textbook.

The landscaper from Linda's condo association stopped by. Jessica had already put in calls to several landscapers, but it seemed her boss had taken control of the project.

Linda introduced her to Oscar, then dragged them both to the back-yard. Tela had come to work with her again and loved the play break.

While the dog trotted around the perimeter, sniffing at everything she'd sniffed an hour earlier, Linda shared her vision for the transformation. Oscar listened and took notes.

The backyard probably hadn't changed since Linda bought the place over a decade ago. A stone wall surrounded the property, common for El Paso which had a surplus of rocks and few trees. Other than the wall, the yard consisted of compressed dirt with a scattering of weeds and stones.

Linda seemed to want to fashion a paradise out of the rubble. She spoke of pavers for a seating area, a pergola for shade, twinkle lights, and a garden of flowering sage and other drought-tolerant plants.

"And no cactus. Nothing with thorns. We wouldn't want Tela to get hurt," Linda said.

"What about trees?" Oscar asked. "If you wanted ones that flowered, you could have a Mexican Elder, a Palo Verde, and a Mountain Laurel. White, yellow, and purple. It would be very pretty."

Jessica stood, arms crossed. Linda didn't need to do this at all and certainly didn't need to do it for her. The scrubby yard didn't need to change. If nothing changed, maybe she could work her way back to the fearless woman she used to be.

"That sounds beautiful. Can you draw up plans for us to review?" Linda asked.

Oscar nodded and began taking measurements, while Linda smiled as if this would solve the world's problems. Why now? This would cost thousands, and Tela sure didn't care if anyone replaced the dirt with lush plants.

As soon as Oscar left for a different part of the yard, Jessica turned to Linda. "Why are you doing this? I promise you, Tela doesn't care where she takes a leak."

"We should have a nice place. We'll be able to bring clients back here and even host events. I think it will be beautiful."

"Have you ever hosted an event here?' Jessica asked.

"Well, no. But maybe I'm turning over a new leaf."

"It's going to cost a fortune." Jessica turned back to the yard. Linda's reasons sounded like excuses. If Linda thought changing the yard would somehow help Jessica overcome what had happened in Mexico . . . well, she might as well keep her money in the bank.

Why was Linda so concerned anyway? Jessica loved working for her, but honestly, any paralegal could do the job. Plus, she'd worked here less than a year. That was hardly enough time for someone as tough-skinned as Linda to get attached. Maybe these dreams of a swank yard would go away once she got the estimates.

Jessica had seen the best of working relationships go south, such as with her former boss Alma, not to mention Tomás Garcia. The thought of owing her boss might strain the relatively new relationship.

As if she'd summoned a ghost, her phone rang. Claudia. Jessica winced. They'd just talked yesterday. As much as she liked the woman, she hoped friendship didn't mean daily conversations.

Jessica answered the call. "Hey, Claudia. What's up?"

"She's alive for sure."

A chill went through Jessica causing goose bumps to rise on her legs, then traveled up her spine. As long as that woman lived, the chance existed that she would get her claws in Jessica again. And Jessica could never let that happen.

"Letty?" she asked, just to confirm.

"Yes, we're sure of it. We confirmed that she was the one who withdrew all of the money from Tres's checking account. For some reason, the surveillance cameras didn't work, but Tomás talked to the bank manager, and the woman he helped fits Letty's description."

Fuck. Jessica whistled for her dog and held her phone against her chest while she told Linda she wanted to take the call inside. Emotions pummeled her, and she needed to sit.

Back at her desk, Jessica raised the phone to her ear. "What's next? Will Tomás try to have her arrested?"

"Only if he can find her. And his father. He's completely beside himself about this, but at least it's something to go on." Claudia took a long, deep breath. "I wish she was dead."

"Yeah. Or behind bars." Although, honestly, dead was preferable. "Didn't you say she had a house in Juarez? I assume Tomás had the authorities look there again."

"Yes. And she has a small property in Chihuahua. She's not at either of them, and it didn't look like she'd been to either property in a while."

Jessica thought about the El Paso house. It would make a good hiding place, and she'd already taken care of Tres there. If he was still alive. "I should call Jaime and have him check the place in El Paso."

"Would you? I'd really appreciate that. I know you don't want to work with us, but my mind won't be at ease until I know where she is."

"We can both agree on that. That's one woman I pray I never see again." Not that Jessica prayed, but she'd come mighty close while stuck in that room thinking its cinderblock walls would be the last thing she'd ever see.

"Okay. I'll call him now and let you know what he finds out. Keep me updated if there are any changes."

After she spoke to Jaime, and he assured her they'd send someone to the house again, she called Keith. She'd wanted to call Angus but didn't want to interrupt him at work, not when he'd already missed so much time to help her.

Keith answered on the first ring.

"Hi, it's Jessica. Letty cleaned out Tomás's father's bank account. They haven't found her in Juarez yet, and I've asked Lt. Castro to check her El Paso house. I, uh, I thought you might want to know." Why had she called him?

"I'm glad you called, and I'm really sorry no one knows where she is. That has to worry you."

"Oh, I'm fine," she lied, but he probably didn't believe her anyway. Somehow, he seemed to know about her trauma, even though she didn't want to admit to it. That's why he'd shown her the aerial view of the house.

And it had helped. Somewhat. "I never thanked you for stopping by and showing me the house, but I appreciated it."

"You're welcome. I thought it might help. I can't imagine what you've been going through, but you were incredibly tough to have survived that experience. Not many people escape their kidnappers. I really admire that you did. If I can do anything to help, just let me know."

His praise embarrassed her. She'd just done what she'd had to do, it's not like anyone gave her options.

"Well, I guess you could start by not arresting me again." Always better to joke when faced with an awkward situation. "Oh, actually, there is one thing. Do you have a drone?"

"Why?"

"Seeing the aerial view of the house really helped. I thought maybe if I used a drone, I could get a closer look at what happened." He probably thought it weird that she wanted to keep reliving her worst experience. Heck, she thought it was weird. But it helped her grapple with the memories from that night. Turned them from nightmares to past experiences.

"It's illegal to fly a drone over the international border."

Well of course it was. Damn politicians and their imaginary lines. That whole area was one ecosystem split by a river. Animals didn't recognize the international border. Fish didn't keep to their side of the Rio Grande depending on nationality. And birds, those fuckers didn't give a damn where they flew. They'd shit on either side of the border with equal abandon. And wasn't a drone just an electronic bird?

"Fine. Thanks." She didn't mean to be short, but honestly, who the hell would care?

"I don't have a drone anyway," he said, sounding contrite.

"Really, it's fine. I just called to let you know about Letty. I'll talk to you later." She pressed end. It wasn't his job to save her. It wasn't anyone's job. In fact, she didn't need saving. She remained completely intact, sitting here at her desk. She'd work during the day, then go home and study. After that, she'd have dinner with her husband and probably fuck him silly. Nothing was wrong.

She woke her computer and stared at the screen, willing something to happen. A new meeting, a case decision, anything that would force her mind toward business and away from the house in the Valle de Juarez.

A few minutes later, her phone rang. She looked down and saw Keith's number. She needed to cut this short. She probably shouldn't have called him in the first place. It's just that he'd been there at the end, or at least at the transition from horrible to wherever she was now.

"Hey." She didn't have anything else to say.

"Jessica, I know someone with a drone."

She kept quiet. What could she say? He'd already told her it was illegal. There's no way he'd be responsible for someone breaking the law. He was a little too straitlaced for that.

"My uncle has a place in the lower valley, and he likes to fly drones."

"But you just told me it's illegal to fly them across the border." What did he want from her?

"I'm not suggesting you should do anything illegal, but my uncle is happy to meet with you. He's got several models, and he said he'd teach you how to use them. He might have some good advice for you."

"That sounds intriguing."

"Intriguing is actually a good word for him. His name is Salvador Guerra, and he's a long-retired deputy."

"So he's just like you, only older?" She couldn't help a smile.

"Trust me. He's different from anyone you've ever met. I've known him my whole life, and I can't even explain him. Anyway, I'll text you his info."

"Thanks." She ended the strange conversation. If Salvador was anything like his nephew, then the whole circus seemed like a waste of time. But Keith acted just cagey enough to make her suspicious.

She shook her head. She'd discuss it with Angus tonight. It was about time she started including him more, and the way he'd acted lately, she'd have to. He'd always worried about her, but he also let her make her own decisions, even when they were bad ones. But now her reliance on him had shifted something in their relationship.

She'd promised not to go back to the border without him, and she'd keep that promise. She probably wouldn't go back with him either. Not with guys with guns roaming around in pickup trucks. Jessica had a habit of surviving bad situations. Angus might not have that kind of luck, and she'd never forgive herself if she put him in danger. He was the best person she'd ever met.

Maybe Jaime would call back and let her know they'd checked out Letty's El Paso house. Best case scenario, they'd find her and arrest her. Perhaps they'd even find Tres. Having Letty locked away might mean Jessica didn't need to go back to the river and retrace her steps to rewind the experience. That would be best. But best-case scenarios rarely happened.

Chapter 24

Jessica and Angus drove his ancient, dented Toyota the thirty miles to Keith's uncle's place. Angus worked in the afternoons and evenings, and when Jessica had asked Linda if she could come in late, she practically begged her to take the whole day off.

Jessica didn't want the whole day off, and she needed to figure out how to get Linda beyond this coddling phase. It didn't suit either of them.

Listening to the fifteen-year-old vehicle's engine, she half wished she'd taken Tomás and Claudia up on their offer of a new truck. They'd have to figure something out soon. What she wouldn't give to have her truck reappear. She and that truck had a lot of shared miles together, and aside from needing a new fuel pump every few years, it had run perfectly. Unlike Angus's car, which sounded an engine stroke away from leaving them abandoned at the side of the road.

"This is so cool," Angus said for like the fifth time. "He really said he'd teach us how to fly drones?"

"I don't think it's that hard. You've played video games before. How different can it be?" Not that she'd played a lot of video games. She'd misspent her teens and twenties in bars, not in front of a TV or console.

Angus cocked an eyebrow at her. "Yeah, like that's your specialty. You know how much drones cost, right?"

"Yeah." She'd done her research and seen the painful results. Even a cheap drone, one that could fly as far as she needed it to while filming, cost several hundred dollars. Money that could go toward a replacement truck. She had far more important things to spend money on, yet she'd made this appointment anyway.

Her obsession with the house verged on maniacal. But she valued its offer of a cure, a path back to herself. She wouldn't have to walk through its doors again, just look at them until they became so normal she could forget them. But she wouldn't cross certain limits.

"Look, we're not going to buy a drone so I can fly the thing into the Valle de Juarez one time," Jessica said. "Keith offered, so I thought we could at least meet his uncle and see what this drone thing was all about."

They'd turned off the highway and now drove down Alameda Boulevard, an ancient passageway that paralleled the river. Today's version of the road included four crowded lanes lined with used car dealerships, shops selling piñatas and candy, and some of the best Mexican restaurants on the globe.

"We need to stop for tacos on the way home," Angus said, somehow inside her brain.

"Definitely, turn at the next corner."

They wound through backstreets and then a residential neighborhood, seeming to travel back in time as they did so. The production year of the vehicles parked on lawns showed the age of the neighborhood like tree rings. The houses changed from modern cookie-cutters on miniscule lots to tiny adobes on long, narrow swaths of land. Substantial trees replaced decorative boxwood shrubs, and lawns morphed into pastures.

They eventually came to the address on Jessica's phone. A gravel drive punctured a high rock wall. Jessica squeezed Angus's thigh, relieved he'd come with her. Would she always feel so weak?

Angus smiled at her. "Thanks for bringing me," he said, like she'd done him the favor.

They drove into a vast yard, if you could even call it that. She couldn't see the back wall. Unlike most of El Paso, verdant trees arched over a sea of grass and behind a fence. A few goats and two llamas nibbled the lawn.

Jessica had heard about hidden oases like this in the city. There was the private investigator from the 1970s who had hooks for hands and raised lions and tigers on his lower valley estate. It could be near this one, although most likely it had been converted into houses. Another local legend featured a man who raised hundreds of exotic parrots, always searching for one as beautiful as his wife who had passed away in her twenties. Thousands of years of habitation in this valley had spawned witches and heroes and the lore to accompany them.

They pulled up to a rambling adobe house with white painted walls and Spanish roof tiles. It looked like it had sprouted from the land or perhaps was sinking back into it. It wouldn't surprise Jessica to learn the house had stood for over a century.

The man who walked out the front door was as worn and rugged as the home. Angus pulled into a parking area, and they got out of the car.

"Hi. Are you Salvador?" she asked, meeting him in the drive with her hand extended.

"Please, call me Sal. You must be Jessica. Keith has told me a lot about you."

Jessica wondered at that. Keith had plenty of bad to share along with the good. When Angus neared, Jessica introduced him.

"It's so nice to meet you," Angus said. "You've got an incredible place here."

"It's so lush," Jessica added.

"We're right off the Franklin Canal, one of the main waterways in this area. I lucked into the property decades ago. It's my little piece of paradise."

Jessica studied the man while he spoke. She could see the resemblance between him and his nephew. Both brawny, Sal didn't have Keith's height, but he appeared tougher. His leathery skin looked like it could stop a bullet, and he had eyes that peered at people as if he hadn't decided whether to befriend them or kill them.

"I really appreciate your taking the time to meet with us this morning. I'm sure Keith told you I had an incident over in Juarez." Jessica struggled over what to call it: kidnapping, trauma, hell incarnate. The experience loomed in her mind, but she didn't necessarily want to convey its importance to others.

"He did. That's a lot to go through." Sal's voice was as course as tumbled gravel.

"I'm getting over it. It helped when Keith showed me aerial photos of the house. It made it just a house. Now I have it stuck in my head that being able to retrace my journey with a drone, where I can see it in real time, will help." Fuck. She hated being so vulnerable. But it was time to move past this thing. She'd always heard about closure, even though she knew from personal experience that she hung on to hurts far too long just so they could fester. Not this one. She wanted this one out of her system ASAP.

"We know it's illegal to fly them across the border," Angus said.

"If you could just teach me to fly one, I think we can figure it out from there."

Sal peered at Angus, then looked back to Jessica, clearly trying to decide whether to help them. She hoped they made a positive impression. They'd driven a long way for this. If it didn't work out, she'd find a way to get her hands on a drone and do it all herself. Seeing that house had become far too important, but she sure as shit wasn't going back to Juarez.

"Come with me." Sal turned and led them around the house.

Angus held her back a little then whispered in her ear. "He looks just like Charles Bronson."

"Who's that?"

"It's my dad's favorite actor. You know, the one who plays the tough guy in all those movies he watches on Saturdays."

"So that means he was famous four decades ago?" she asked. Angus's dad hadn't quite moved out of the seventies and eighties. He watched old movies, drove a restored El Camino, and named his son after his favorite rock guitarist. But he was a great guy. And she could picture Sal in movies from that era, always playing the lonesome cowboy or tough-guy detective.

When they rounded the back of the house, Jessica stopped in awe. A keyhole shaped, blue-bottomed swimming pool sat in the center of an enormous back patio. Lounge chairs faced the morning sun, and a deep portico along the back of the house provided additional seating areas.

"This is stunning," Jessica said, as a drawn out "whoa" came out of Angus's mouth.

"Thanks. It took me years to finish. I did the stonework myself." He gestured toward the slate pavers. Then he opened a side door to the house and beckoned them inside.

They entered what had to be the cleanest garage Jessica had ever seen. Tools on pegboard lined one wall, and several machines Jessica had last seen when walking by shop class in high school claimed an entire garage space. An ATV took up another space, and shelving lined the back wall from floor to ceiling. Three drones of graduated sizes sat menacingly on one shelf.

"I've had a bit of a drone obsession over the past few years. We'll get you up and flying in no time," Sal said.

"This is awesome," Angus said, like a kid entering his first toy store. He slowly spun in place, taking in all the gadgets.

Jessica pulled on his arm. "Hey. We're here to work."

"Let's start with this one," Sal said as he pulled the smallest drone off the shelf. "She's pretty easy to maneuver. There's no wind today, so it's a good day for flying."

Jessica walked up to the machine which looked more like an insect than anything else. Sal placed it in her hands, the cold metal and hard plastic chilling her fingertips.

"That's the drone, and this is the controller." He waved what looked like a complicated gaming joystick in front of Jessica.

"Let's do it," she said, faking confidence. It would have been better if she'd been one of those gamer girls, but instead she'd spent most of her time getting into real-world scrapes.

They returned to the yard, where Sal explained the controller. It had two joysticks that she could move with her fingers or thumbs. One directed the drone up or down or spun it left or right. The other moved the drone forward, backward, and from side to side. Jessica concentrated on his words and the movement of his fingers, feeling like she was back in math class when the numbers didn't make sense. As if that weren't complicated enough, the thing also had dials that would cause it to point at different angles and go faster or slower.

"You look confused," Sal said. "It's not that bad when you start using it. In fact, it's a lot more intuitive than it sounds."

"Sure," Jessica said, wondering if she should tell him she'd already forgotten all his instructions.

He set the drone on the dirt twenty feet from them, then turned it on. The four small propellers whirred to life. Sal slowly went through the instructions again, this time coordinating his words with the movement of the drone. Maybe this wouldn't be so bad.

Jessica looked over his shoulder as he maneuvered the machine so high she couldn't see it. On the screen she watched the three of them shrink in size until they almost disappeared. Then he brought it back down and zoomed it around his property, at one point causing a llama stampede. She loved watching the world through the video screen on the controller. It gave her power to see anything she wanted to see. She could direct the drone anywhere and make it hover, spin, or maneuver any way she wanted until she'd sated her curiosity.

Sal landed the drone exactly where it started. "Now, who wants a turn?" Sal asked.

"Let him go first." She glanced at Angus. If he could do it, then perhaps she could too.

Sal handed Angus the device and gave him a few final instructions. When Angus lifted the drone off the ground, it jerked up, then hovered about six feet above them. He looked at the drone then squared his shoulders as if challenging it to a fight. It rose more smoothly after that.

"Keith tells me he's run into you a few times over the past six months." Sal had moved close to Jessica and kept his voice low enough that it wouldn't distract Angus.

She glanced at him and didn't see any malice on his face. "Did he tell you everything? Like the first time we met when he handcuffed me and shoved me in the back of a cruiser?"

Sal grinned at her. Mostly his eyes just crinkled, but the corner of his lips curled up on one side. "He did. You seem to get yourself into some interesting situations."

Sal kept one eye on Angus but studied her at the same time. What did he want to hear? That she was rash? That she rushed into save people, danger be damned? He didn't know the half of it.

"I try to help people who need it." It was her best answer.

He nodded. They both watched Angus tour the drone around the back yard.

"You know," Sal said. "Keith was pretty busted up that he didn't listen to you about the voices you heard when he arrested you. Especially given what happened."

She hadn't known that. Well, actually, she had. Why else would he have shown up at the dried-up reservoir where they'd found the shell casings? "I think he's made up for it. He helped me investigate a site where coyotes might have killed some border crossers related to that case."

Sal raised one eyebrow. "So he's still working on it."

"I think so. Plus, he found me in the desert last week. He's starting to pile up checkmarks in the good column."

Sal chuckled. "He's a pretty good kid. I don't think he'd ever knowingly do something wrong."

Jessica reserved her judgement on that one. Her trust meter remained stuck in the off position. Keith managed to be in the right place at the right time too often for someone who didn't believe in coincidences.

"All right, bring her on back now," Sal said to Angus. "I don't like getting too close to the neighbors."

Jessica peeked over Angus's shoulder and saw the drone fly over the road in front of the house. She couldn't hear its whir.

"Were you in Mexico when they kidnapped you?" Sal asked.

"No. El Paso. I had parked outside a suspect's house. Their trash can blew over, and I went to look inside. When I stood up, someone hit me. I woke up in Juarez, although I didn't know it at the time."

The drone now hovered above them. Angus spun it in a slow circle, then lowered it to the ground. Jessica's hopes lowered with it. She had to make Sal understand how badly she needed this.

"I'm probably used to a little more danger than most folks. Maybe not a sheriff's deputy, but I've brought plenty of trouble on myself. I found myself in other scrapes while helping others. I always got out of those tough spots, but last week, I didn't know if I would make it."

Angus turned toward them, focusing on their conversation now that the drone had safely landed. His eyes asked if she needed help. She set her lips. She could do this on her own.

"You did make it out," Sal said.

"I got lucky. And they kidnapped someone else. She put herself in danger for me, and I had to get her out too.

Sal nodded. "You need to know one more thing. I knew your dad."

"Who didn't?" She'd never get away from his reputation.

"I always thought he was a good guy. What happened really surprised me."

She shrugged. "I was only sixteen when they convicted him. He admitted his guilt, to me and to the prosecutor." Jessica paused for a moment. Surely, he didn't think . . . "I am not my father's daughter in that way. I don't deal with any part of the drug industry. In fact, I can't tolerate it because of what my dad did."

"It's true," Angus said. "And I've known her since kindergarten."

Sal glanced briefly at Angus, then focused on Jessica again. "I wasn't accusing you of anything. I just wanted to let you know I knew your father in case that was a sensitive subject."

"It's no big deal," she said. Even though she hated that most people seemed to judge her for her father's deeds. Not that anyone thought she'd committed that particular crime. Instead, they watched her as if they expected her to do something wrong as well. At least it had felt that way growing up in this community and trying to work with people who knew her dad. Add Sal to that list.

Sal took the console from Angus and handed it to her. "Do you remember what the toggle sticks are for?" he asked.

"This one is up, down, and spin," she said. "And the other moves it in a direction."

Sal nodded and released his grip on the console. It hardly weighed anything. No wonder people wanted to use these in war. Why build a tank or a fighter jet when something this small could wreak destruction?

"Thank you," she said, looking directly into Sal's eyes. She wanted him to know how much she appreciated this. She liked his seriousness, and how he had given her an opportunity just because his nephew asked him to. There should be more men like this in the world and fewer Don Octavios or threatening ones with pickup trucks and guns. She gripped the console firmly, then turned toward the drone.

"You're going to do great," Angus said.

Time to do this. Jessica pushed the left-hand toggle forward and the drone shot toward the sky.

"Too much," Sal said. He tried to keep his voice calm, but Jessica could hear the tension underneath it.

She released her finger from the toggle switch and stared into the sky. She lost the drone in the sun's path.

"Try looking at the screen, not the drone," Angus said.

Jessica did that, dropping her head and managing to knock one of the joysticks with her index finger. The drone lurched to the right.

"Straighten it out, nice and steady now." Sal spoke in the tone he probably used with bank robbers, toddlers, and irate llamas.

Jessica clutched the console and moved both toggles to what she hoped was center. The whirring sound neared, and she looked up. The black device dove toward them. She jerked one toggle forward to make the drone rise and the other to the side to get it away from them. It hit the side of the house with a crunch, then tumbled to the ground.

"Oh, shit. I am so sorry." Jessica took off toward where the drone had landed. Crashed.

She heard footsteps behind her, but she reached it first. The machine made some kind of death whine. One of its arms lay a foot away from the rest of the device. Another hung to the side, twisted and certainly beyond use. It had a crack across its carapace that she hadn't noticed before.

"Oh, man," Sal said, kneeling down and cradling the machine like a hurt baby bird.

"Shit," Angus said, drawing the word out.

"I'm so sorry. I'm so very sorry I crashed it." Fuck. Now she'd have to pay him for the damn thing, and they certainly couldn't afford their own. Not that she could fly it if they had one.

Sal reached over and grabbed the stray piece, then turned to her. "No problem. My fault. I'm clearly not a good teacher."

"Mr. Guerra, I destroyed your drone. I am truly sorry. Please let me pay you for it," Jessica said.

Angus sucked in a breath, probably thinking about the money, but nodded at her like she'd done the right thing. Sal actually smiled big and wide for the first time.

"Don't worry," he said. "I can probably fix it. But I do think we've found something you're not so good at."

"I'll say," Angus mumbled.

Jessica wanted to kick Angus's shin like she had when they were little. He definitely wasn't helping the situation. He also wasn't wrong.

"How can I make it up to you?" she asked Sal.

"How bad do you want to see that house in Juarez?" Sal asked.

"Bad."

"Then let's do it."

"Now?" she asked.

"I've got time now if you do."

"But you know it's illegal." Jessica couldn't ask a retired sheriff's deputy to break the law.

"It's only a felony if you use it to facilitate an illegal activity. You just want to look at a house."

"You're sure it's okay?" She felt caged. She wanted this so badly, but she'd promised herself and Angus she'd slow down, make better decisions. She glanced at him.

Angus nodded.

Something in her broke loose, releasing a cocktail that mixed the fear of the house with the excitement of overcoming that emotion. "Let's go."

"One thing," Sal said. "I'm flying the drone. I'll make it go anywhere you tell me."

They returned to the garage, where Sal set the broken machine on a worktable. He grabbed a padded, sectioned duffle bag and loaded it with batteries and the two larger drones. Then, he led them to his jeep. "I don't know that your car can make it off road, so let's go in mine."

"Thanks," Angus said, surely realizing his car was lucky to have made it down the driveway.

They hopped in Sal's Jeep, and he steered it toward the highway while Jessica pulled up directions on her phone. She dropped a pin at the location where they'd crossed the river and said a quick prayer to the Google gods to get them there.

One nice thing about the Jeep was the terrible road noise, which meant Jessica didn't have to talk much. After thirty minutes of driving east on Interstate 10, GPS had them take the Tornillo exit. It took about sixty seconds to drive through the unincorporated community. Then, they turned on State Highway 20, an empty two-lane road that carried them farther from El Paso.

The highway ran through agricultural fields that took advantage of the fertile river valley. Rows of bright green contrasted with the dark loamy soil. Occasionally, they drove through young pecan plantations, their branches not yet draping over the road the way they did a hundred miles north.

As they traveled closer to where Keith had found her, Jessica's nerves tightened with each spin of the wheels. She didn't want to be back here, yet she returned every night in her dreams. That had to stop.

"Slow down. We're almost at the wash," she said.

Sal slowed, then Jessica saw the empty streambed drop below them. He pulled the car to the side of the road. She looked down into the dry wash, a thousand emotions spilling through her. Angus, in the back seat, laid a hand on her shoulder. She wanted to curl into him, return to safety. But safety wouldn't exist until she conquered her fears.

A dirt track ran parallel to the wash. Sal turned down it. The Jeep bumped slowly down the road, drawing ever closer to the river. Sweat beaded under Jessica's arms and at the back of her neck. She wondered if Sal had a gun, just in case the men in the truck returned.

They passed places Jessica recognized. The dirt road where she and Claudia had encountered the men with guns, the border patrol officer, and Keith. They trundled past the place where she'd climbed out of the wash to figure out where they were and had seen the comforting mountains of home on the horizon.

The dirt track veered away from the wash when they reached the river. It couldn't be so soon. The trek had seemed to take hours. Jessica remembered forcing herself to put one foot in front of the other for what felt like half her life. What had seemed like forever sped by in just a few minutes by car.

Sal stopped the Jeep twenty feet from the edge of the water. It wasn't where they exited, the road had taken them just north of there. The water ran a brownish green in the harsh sunlight. The river looked small. It had seemed such an achievement to cross it that morning. Now, it looked like it should take a few minutes tops. Not that she wanted to try.

Jessica stepped from the Jeep, steeling her spine. She would walk into this like the badass she'd always assumed herself to be. She headed downriver, toward where she and Claudia had climbed out of the water, while Sal and Angus messed around with the drones.

As she stepped down into the wide mouth of the wash, she heard the ghosts of the hundreds, probably thousands, of people who had crossed over the millennia. They tickled her skin in their rush to get by. Perhaps it was just the breeze rattling the sage on the riverbank.

"Don't move." Sal's voice cracked through the air.

Jessica stopped, suddenly terrified. What had he seen? Men with guns? The drowned body of an unlucky? The stirring air whipped with concern.

On high alert, she heard a clink to her left and turned her head. Four feet away, a snake writhed against a large rock, a knife protruding from its head. Jessica scurried backward, praying no snakes lay in wait behind her. She couldn't take her eyes off the twisting reptile. A golden beige, it had dark brown diamonds the length of its back. It was twice as thick as her wrist and probably four feet long from its viper head to the end of its black and white, rattle-tipped tail.

She bumped into something and staggered forward before Angus wrapped his arms around her, steadying her.

"I've got you," he said.

"What the fuck?" Coherent questions didn't come to mind. In all the times she'd traversed the desert, she'd seen few rattlers. Yet this one threatened from steps away.

The snake's movements slowed. "Is it still alive?" she asked.

"Nope. Death twitches." Sal said as he approached the serpent.

Jessica heaved out a sigh, pulling herself together. She stepped from Angus's embrace. "That's your knife?" she asked Sal.

"You should have seen him," Angus said. "He whipped that thing out so quick and killed the snake before I even knew what he was doing. Perfect shot."

"I'd prefer not to kill them," Sal said. "But he had his eyes on you, coiled and ready to strike."

Adrenaline still coursed through Jessica, but her perspective shifted. Danger lurked everywhere, even on a sunny spring day. She could roll with it or walk around terrified. Her choice.

Sal pulled the knife from the snake's head and cleaned it in the sand. Then he grabbed the monster by its head, walked to the edge of the river, and threw it into the middle of the flow. The dead snake floated downstream.

"You're a fucking badass," Jessica said.

"Where do you hide your knife?" Angus asked.

Sal turned back to them wiping his hands on his pants. "Waist."

"I told you he was just like Charles Bronson Angus whispered. "My dad would love this guy."

"I think you're half in love with him yourself." Jessica smirked at Angus.

"Definitely."

"What's next?" Jessica asked, heart still pumping double-time, but ready to move on from the snake distraction.

"Let's launch the drone from near the Jeep," Sal said. "The ground is highest there. That way, we can use it to show us the path instead of tramping across the snake-infested desert."

"Good plan." Jessica returned to the Jeep far less scared about what she'd encounter on the video and ready to get it over with and end this field trip.

It took almost no time to set up the drone. Jessica stood next to Sal with a clear view of the much larger screen on this controller. He launched the device upward and maneuvered it to where she'd come out of the river.

"Honestly, this is a little anti-climactic after the whole snake thing," Jessica said. Still, she stuck to Sal's shoulder, eyes on the screen, as the drone crossed the river.

He lowered the machine close to the surface and scanned the bank on the other side, but she couldn't be exactly sure which tree they'd hid under that night. At her direction, he lifted the drone over the salt cedars and flew it to the levee and then the path they'd traveled. It all seemed so innocuous in the daylight.

"Raise it up more. We'll know the house by the round corral." She searched for butterflies knocking around her stomach or a general feeling of ill will, but the reality of day had divorced her foreboding from her nightmares.

"This one?" Sal asked, hovering the drone some distance from the property.

Jessica saw the dirty-orange corral. The squat house showed the door she'd exited on that frightful night and no back windows. It looked so ordinary.

"That's it. Can you get closer?" Sal lowered the drone until it skimmed just a few yards above the dirt. It glided past the corral where the Mexican police had found Don Octavio's body. No dead bodies today.

The drone continued toward the house. It didn't look occupied, although the lack of windows made it difficult to tell. Jessica remembered how she'd suffered, but this dumpy house in the middle of nowhere hadn't caused that. Not that razing it to rubble wouldn't make her happy.

"Do you want me to circle the house?" Sal asked.

"Sure," she replied. "Wait! That's my truck." Someone had parked Jessica's white truck under a tree. For all she knew, it hadn't moved from the day she'd been kidnapped. They might have even crossed her into Mexico in the passenger seat or bed.

Jessica turned to Angus. "They have the truck. We can get it back."

She expected his eyes to mirror her relief. Now, they wouldn't be forced to buy a new vehicle they couldn't afford. Instead, he looked at her with shock, eyebrows raised and eyes bugged out.

"You can't go back over there." His soft voice filled with worry.

What was he talking about? Just like with the drone, returning was the cure, not the disease. But he couldn't understand. No one could. They'd tried to break her in that house, and they'd almost succeeded. She'd spend her life rebelling against that if she needed to. And right now, she needed to.

"Do you know how much they took from me?" Jessica hated that her voice trembled. "They are not taking my truck."

"Jessica. I'll buy you a new truck. Hell, take the one from Tomás. But you can't risk going back."

"Son," Sal said, still holding the controller, but focused on Angus. "It's like getting bucked off a horse. It's best to get right back on. But we can make sure it's safe. I know people who will make sure the property is vacant, and I'll go with her for protection."

"Yeah," Jessica said. Relieved that Sal had a plan. She didn't want to do this alone. "Besides, he has mad knife skills."

"I'd prefer he have an arsenal of automatic weapons if he's going to take you back to that hellhole." Tension writhed through Angus's voice.

He was always so good to her, and she always pushed him beyond his boundaries. Sure, he didn't want her to go, but he'd never held her back. Now, she needed to be strong, for both their sakes. He'd fallen in love with the fierce, slightly feral version of Jessica. That's who she was in her heart. It had taken her a lot of years and many mistakes for her to realize that woman deserved love. If Jessica couldn't get that woman back, she'd revert to the self-loathing behavior of her past. The day she'd asked him to marry her, he warned her that he wouldn't stick around for that. This time, she had to save the best version of herself.

Besides. They had her truck.

"I want to get it," she said, directing the statement to Sal. "What do we need to do next?"

Sal had already started the drone on its return journey. He put it away, and they piled into the Jeep without addressing Jessica's next steps question.

As soon as they started bumping down the dirt road, Jessica pounced. "When can we go get the truck?" she asked.

"Would Saturday work for you?" Sal asked.

"That would be great," Jessica said.

"I have to work on Saturday." Angus's voice reached Jessica from the back seat. Anger and resignation laced his words. She'd heard both of those before.

"It'll be okay. I'll take the extra keys, and we'll be in and out before anyone notices. Right?" She turned to Sal for confirmation.

"Well, we're not going to ride in there like the damn cavalry. Your truck was the only vehicle there, and the house looks empty, but we'll make sure. But I agree, we don't want to spend any time there we don't have to."

Angus remained silent in the back seat. Sal turned the rearview mirror so he could look at him. "I know you recommended taking weapons over there, but we can't take guns into Mexico. It's illegal. Getting hauled into a Mexican jail probably wouldn't be much better than the situation she already experienced."

Still nothing from Angus. They drove in silence for a while. He loved her enough to let her make her own decisions, but she could tell he didn't want this. She hoped he wouldn't resent her choice.

"If you give me your truck's registration, I could go get it by myself. If that's what you want," Sal said once they hit the smooth pavement of the freeway.

"I think I need to go." Jessica had spent long minutes in the car debating this. Yes, she wanted her truck, and financially, they needed it. But of course, she could have someone else get it. Going herself would prove she'd recovered. It was a test of courage, and she'd made her mind up.

She turned around in the front seat until she could look Angus in the eye. "I need to do this."

Chapter 25

By the time Saturday arrived, Jessica had revisited her decision relentlessly. Sal had asked her not to tell Claudia or Tomás. He thought the fewer people who knew the better. Jessica agreed. She still didn't trust Tomás.

She hadn't told Linda either. Her boss's recent strange behavior had Jessica on edge. The landscaping in back of the office was underway, and she'd bought Tela a permanent, monogrammed dog bed and gourmet dog treats. Every day, she asked Jessica how she was doing with a desperate sparkle in her eye, and she constantly encouraged her to take paid time off.

While most employees might have loved that behavior, Jessica respected Linda because of her toughness. For some reason, Jessica's brush with death had transformed her boss into a different person.

Just yesterday, Linda asked her for the fifth time that day how she was doing. "Sit," Jessica had said. "I'm fine. Why are you acting this way? What has changed?"

"I almost lost you," Linda replied.

"Listen, I know I'm good at my job, but there are probably fifty people in this town who would do as good a job or better."

"Well, I like you. And I feel responsible for you." Linda wrung her hands, an action Jessica had never seen from the woman.

Jessica had figured out a way to get herself past the trauma of the kidnapping, but she needed Linda and Angus to believe in her again. The last few days, Angus had turned sullen. He wouldn't even have sex with her. He didn't want her to go. She needed to, even if it scared him. Neither relented.

The very people who anchored her, who kept her tethered to life when she thought she might go insane, had changed into people she hardly knew. She remembered all the lectures on patience. This needed to be her time for patience—with those around her. She owed them that. And she owed herself the chance to fully recover and not just reclaim her truck but reclaim the part of herself Letty and Don Octavio and that cursed room had taken from her.

On Saturday, she dropped Angus at work. She'd thought he was going to leave the car without saying goodbye. Instead, he turned to her and told her he loved her and to please come back safely.

She nodded. "I've always gotten myself out of trouble in the past."

Jessica watched him leave, still pretending this trip was no big deal. Driving away from him felt like leaving the best part of herself behind.

She drove east on the freeway, the worst of El Paso visible to her left and her right. The tangle of billboards, business signs, and commercial buildings with fading paint seemed to stretch to infinity in every direction. Gems of beauty existed in El Paso, but you had to search for them. Hideous things also existed in the borderland, and one of them called her name, beckoning her to return.

Her hands tightened on the steering wheel. Despite the clear sky, her breath became forced, as if wind and sand invaded the air. Her determination grew alongside the fear. She changed lanes and stomped on the gas, wishing away the heavy traffic that slowed her progress.

Finally, she arrived at Sal's. By this time, a light sheen of sweat coated her forehead and underarms. She rolled her tight shoulders as she emerged from Angus's car. She stood tall, took a deep breath, and girded herself for battle. The war between captivity and freedom had already been won, but it had taken prisoners. Today she would rescue her mind from that trap, not to mention her truck. It would require all her courage.

She stepped forward, knocked on Sal's door. He opened it, the smile on his face dissolving as he looked at her.

"Are you sure you want to do this?" he asked.

"Absolutely."

"How about you come in and have a cup of coffee first?"

"Can we go now? I want my truck back."

Almost exactly the same height, they stared each other down. Jessica's impatience became a physical thing, pressing at her back and trying to shove her into action. She ignored it.

"Okay, let's go." Sal led her through the house.

Her curiosity about this man kept other feelings at bay. The living area had rich terra cotta floors and low furniture that provided a view to the pool and land beyond. They turned left, and she spied a fully stocked bar along one wall. It called to her to come over and down a shot or two of liquid courage. She might have followed that siren song once. Not today.

They entered a kitchen with colorful Mexican Talavera tiles that brightened the counters and backsplash with sunshine yellow, cobalt blue, and sage green. The stainless steel appliances looked expensive. Jessica smiled. Sal needed to meet Jaime Castro. Both bachelors had great kitchens, and she'd bet Sal's cooking skills rivaled Jaime's. Her muscles relaxed a notch. Good men surrounded her. Angus, Jaime, Sal, maybe even Keith. She could do this. She wasn't alone.

Jessica saw a laundry room off the short hallway that led to the garage, then the brief interlude of exploring Sal's home ended. She pulled herself into the Jeep, then they were back on the road.

They crossed the border at the Zaragoza entry point. As soon as they reached Mexican soil, Jessica jolted with the memory of the warning never to return to Juarez. Not from the government, who waved them through without question, but from an old client. She'd escaped death that night. The woman who had dropped her at the bridge to walk back to El Paso warned her she wouldn't survive if she returned. Too late to worry about that.

"What is it?" Sal asked. He must have seen her jump.

"Nothing. Just haven't done this in a while." Not in years. Before that, she'd crossed often, even occasionally at this bridge so many miles from her home. Several large industrial parks flanked the Zaragoza border crossing, and in her prior life as an industrial real estate specialist, she'd often brought manufacturing managers from the Midwest looking to expand their operation to Mexico. That seemed like a lifetime ago, as did the threats of death. She'd faced so much worse since then.

Sal drove through one of the parks, then turned on Highway 2 which paralleled the river out of town. The four-lane road cut through the retail expected on the outskirts of any city: fast food restaurants, a grocery store, tire shops. Then the pavement narrowed to two lanes with little development save for the recreation centers particular to the edges of Mexican cities. Basically private parks, they usually had picnic tables, a swimming pool, often a bar and restaurant. They passed one with a small water park. Quinceañeras, weddings, corporate parties, the list of groups looking for space seemed endless.

The normalcy of the drive tamped down the dread. But then the commercial areas faded away, although she could still see the backs of newer housing developments not far from the road. Then even those vanished, leaving nothing but cropland and Jessica's twisted memories.

"So, your contacts say there's no one at the house?" Jessica asked for the third time.

"They've driven by repeatedly, and there hasn't been any activity there. They've even knocked on the door. There are two trucks on the property, yours and a green Nissan. You don't know what Letty or Don Octavio drove?"

"I think I saw Letty in a gray sedan once." The night Claudia had called her, afraid of someone staring in the windows, Jessica had seen the car with Chihuahua plates driving down the road in the opposite direction of the house. Not a sure thing.

"If anything gets sketchy, we're going to leave," Sal said.

"Sure." Jessica stared at the road ahead. Highway 2 shot straight as an arrow in front of her. The road ended one hundred miles southeast of Juarez in the small town of Porvenir. Beyond that, she'd heard legends about the dirt road that continued along the border, at times rolling atop mountain ridges, other times sweeping far from the Rio Grande as it skirted entire mountain ranges. Traveling that road sounded like a grand adventure, exploring wild lands where few people lived. But with today's drug wars and immigration battles, danger lurked not only in geography, isolation, and wild animals. Human monsters fed off Americans' insatiable desire for drugs and immigrants' desperation for a better life.

Those monsters also lived here, in the Valle de Juarez, and had occupied the house they motored toward. Jessica sat with her fear. Made friends with it. It could be a part of her, would be, but she needed to learn to use it to make her stronger. It could make her more patient, as long as it didn't mask when she needed to act. And she would need to act again. Maybe not today, but something in her bones assured her the monsters and the fear would find her again. She'd fought them with boldness and badassery in the past. But last time, even though she'd escaped, she hadn't won. Going back today would be a victory. Learning to live with and use her own fear as a weapon seemed the only way forward.

She looked at the man beside her. "Are you ever scared?"

"Sometimes."

The silence stretched between them as the miles rolled on. It surprised Jessica when Sal spoke,

"I was in the military before becoming a sheriff's deputy. Ran some pretty ugly missions. Soldiers are not supposed to be afraid but always are. We're taught to ignore fear or overcome it. When you're eighteen, it takes a while to understand you can die, and even longer to start caring about that. But then you start to collect things in your life. Friends. Lovers. Dreams about the future. At some point, you realize the fear you refuse to deal with can eat you alive. That's when I left the military."

She waited to see if he'd go on. He didn't, but Jessica wanted to know more. "So you became a sheriff's deputy? Was that better?"

"No, worse. Not as scary. Not always. But this is El Paso. These are my people. They expected more of me, and I learned to expect more of myself. The fear that I wouldn't turn into a man people could be proud of, that I could be proud of, haunted me. There are so many choices when you're a deputy. You can take more than you should from the people you protect. You can not work quite so hard. No one will know. You're still doing more than most." He sighed. "Those were the easy choices. There are a million ways to make money on the border. A thousand thieves in the night."

"It sounds like you're talking about corruption." Had she made a bad choice? She'd come here willingly. It would be impossible to escape the car, or his knife. The fear she'd kept mostly at bay hummed through her.

"When I chose honor as my highest calling, then everything else I'd worried about became a tool for achieving it. The greed, corruption, and hate in others fueled me. From then on, I trained my body and learned about, and acquired, the best weapons. But mostly I honed my mind. Fear hasn't left me, but I channel it into something useful, along with everything else I can't tolerate about myself. It makes me powerful, and deadly."

"You sound like a Jedi." Jessica's fear remained, but her mistrust of him disappeared. He understood mental weapons. She'd used her fury with her parents to mold her into something more fearsome than actual skin and bones. Her sense of justice became a sword, her desire to protect, a shield. She'd forge her fear into a mace or maybe into a superpower. She didn't know yet, but she could already feel it transforming as her body sculpted it into something new.

Before she was ready, they turned left, toward the river, then left again, back toward civilization, but only for a mile. Finally, Sal turned the Jeep into a drive, and they passed through an open metal gate that leaned off its rusted hinges.

She caught sight of the house, and her heart moved to her throat as if trying to escape her body. She swallowed it back down and told herself to be brave. Her truck sat to the left of the house beneath a large palo verde tree, its yellow flowers decorated the hood and surrounding dirt.

It should have been pretty, but the flowers transformed to insect carcasses in her eyes, and the house festered like a wound. Why couldn't she find peace? Damn it. She was not going to go through life like this.

———

Sal pulled the Jeep sideways behind her, truck keeping Jessica on the far side of the house. "I'm going to run a quick recon mission and make sure no one is here. You've got your keys?"

"Yes." Jessica looked toward the house. "Do you mind if I walk the grounds? This isn't just about the truck. I need to get past what happened here."

"I figured." He didn't grimace but came close. "Let me check the grounds first. I want to make sure we're not surprised."

"Fine." Jessica swallowed, then hopped out of the Jeep, landing between it and her truck. When she looked back to find Sal, he was already slinking along the side of the house. She hadn't even heard the Jeep's door close. The guy really was a Jedi. She scanned the front of the house, not seeing any movement through the window but wondering if someone inside watched her. A creepy feeling shivered down her spine. She didn't like being exposed. She followed Sal to the side of the house, although he'd already slipped around back.

She tucked in close, where the short eave created a shadow that hid her from the midday sun. Only a row of cinder blocks separated her from her prison. She set her hand against the wall and felt nothing but the rough texture.

She continued in Sal's footsteps, wanted to get a look at the backyard in daylight. But then she stopped as a deep shudder ran through her. A faint beeping that she'd never forget came through the wall. Tres's machine. The happy thought that he still lived was quickly crushed under the tidal wave of fear that slammed through her body. Suddenly, she remembered the hunger, the glint of Don Octavio's gun, the bucket. She heard the lock slide shut, cutting her off from the world and keeping her in a room she thought she'd never escape. She sank to her knees and slumped against the wall, locked in a prison of panic.

"Put your arms up!" A voice penetrated Jessica's thoughts, but she couldn't move past the paralysis of fear. Especially when she recognized the voice. Letty. Jessica tried to sink into the wall, afraid to even turn her head. She'd prefer to be shot than to die in that cell of a room.

"Lady. Please put the shotgun down. I'm looking for Chuy Soto. Does he live here?" Sal's voice reached Jessica, and the dread coursing through her multiplied. She'd brought him out here and endangered him. Her body seemed to fall into itself as if it were imploding. Time slowed as she pressed herself into the dirt and the wall.

"Keep your hands up," Letty said. "Are you out here alone?"

"Yes ma'am. Listen. I didn't mean to bother you. If Chuy's not here, I can come back some other time."

"Step back ten paces, then don't move."

Jessica could barely siphon air. Letty approached the Jeep and glanced at it while still keeping her gun trained toward the house. Any second now, she'd see Jessica. Letty turned, and Jessica would have sworn she stared right at her, but she didn't jerk in recognition or acknowledge her in any way. Instead, she refocused her eyes and the gun on where Sal must be.

"Walk toward the house." Letty's steely voice cut through the air.

"Ma'am, I'm really sorry. There's been some misunderstanding."

"Shut up!" Letty's voice cracked like gunshot.

The next thing Jessica heard was the front door as it closed.

She waited one breath. Two. The fear that had paralyzed her drained into the dirt, replaced by hopelessness. She could probably make it to her truck and drive away. But Sal wasn't the only one who believed in honor.

The thought brought her no joy or pride. Instead, she rose, zombie like. Why not, she was already dead inside. People didn't live through close range shotgun attacks. Jessica didn't even have a way to fight back. She'd never learned to use a gun and didn't have a knife in her waistband, not that she knew how to use that either.

She had the truck. Running an old truck into a block building would probably total the vehicle and leave the building unscathed.

But in the glove box, she had her taser. It had saved her once before, when she'd needed the flashlight to see in the dead of night. She'd used the taser on a man. It had been enough to buy her a few seconds, but she'd also had surprise on her side. And Letty would have her choice of people to kill.

Jessica's options narrowed to one stupid solution. She headed toward the truck, skirting wide and hoping to avoid any eyes looking through the front window. She appreciated Sal's parking job that blocked any view from the house as she opened the truck's driver side door and reached across to where she had the taser buried beneath gas receipts and her latest proof of insurance.

She trekked back to the house, keeping out of the sightline. Should she go in the front or the back? Should she knock? She wished for x-ray vision, or perhaps a life that didn't constantly find danger. Armed with neither, she crawled across the front of the house until she knelt beside the lone window.

"No one sent me, I swear." Sal sounded desperate, but Jessica doubted he was. Someone like him would bide his time for the right opportunity, then pounce. She needed that kind of patience to wait until the best opportunity presented itself.

"Stop talking and keep walking. Go in that room right there."

Jessica could picture the layout. Letty would force him into the room. He'd go through what she did, even if he'd handle it better. But he might not survive. They didn't have time like she did the first time. Angus knew exactly where she was. Hell, she had her phone in her pocket with Find My Friends turned on. No longer a secret outpost, this would be the first place searched. Sal wasn't a prisoner. He was a hostage.

The options weren't good. It had taken them a long time to get out here, and any force, especially one coming from El Paso, would take over an hour to arrive. Not that US law enforcement could just swing over and do battle in Juarez. Mexico was a whole different country, and one whose relationship with the US had soured.

"I really don't want to go in there. Why don't we reach a deal. How much can I pay you to let me leave and never mention this again.?" Sal's voice traveled through the glass. Stalling was a smart tactic.

Jessica slid her phone from her back pocket, keeping her other hand wrapped around the dual flashlight-stunner. First, she silenced it, lest the phone give her away. Then she texted Angus.

"At Juarez house. Letty took Sal hostage. Doesn't know I'm here. Sending Claudia's #. Tell her to have Tomás send cops ASAP. Call Jaime – same. Going offline." She hit send and tried to ignore the pang of guilt about Angus receiving the message. She had to focus on other things.

She turned her attention back to the house, refusing to think about what the text would do to Angus, who'd begged her not to come.

". . . plenty of money," Letty said.

"Well, if you don't need money, what do you need? I promise I'll make it worth your while if you let me walk out of here. I really just wanted to see my friend. I got the directions wrong. Wound up at the wrong house."

"Back up," Letty yelled. "If you take another step toward me, I will shoot you."

"Please. You don't want to shoot me. That kind of thing stays with a person."

"Ha!" Letty's voice came out as sharp as a pistol crack. "You think you'd be the first person I've killed? Not even close."

"Really?" Sal sounded intrigued with a hint of disbelief, like he really was some doofus who'd stumbled upon this place.

Jessica slowly chanced a peek through the window. She saw Letty's back, her arm crooked around the shotgun. Sal faced her but made no sign he'd noticed her.

How was she going to get him out of there? He might still have his knife. If Jessica distracted Letty, it could give Sal the chance to use it. But if she had disarmed him, Letty would probably shoot Jessica first and then kill Sal.

Jessica could wait, but what if the coyotes or someone else came by and saw her. That would hasten their deaths. Letty would hear the engine start if she tried to leave in her truck, spelling a death sentence for Sal.

She glanced at her phone. Three dots pulsed, but no response came through.

"What's that beeping?" Sal asked.

Jessica glanced in the window again. Sal hadn't moved.

"None of your business. Now get in that room before I shoot you." Letty's voice had gone so cold that Jessica shivered.

She looked at her phone one more time. "Left messages. Please stay safe."

The dots still pulsed. Poor Angus. He deserved someone who wasn't constantly getting into trouble. He probably felt her scrapes more deeply than she did. At least until that last one. But then he'd been putting her back together for years, never asking for anything in return. Except for her to stay safe—the one thing she couldn't seem to do.

She chanced one more look in the window, depleting any remaining luck she might have. Sal and Letty had moved halfway to the prison cell. Just a few steps down a short hallway and Sal's chance of escape would disappear. And then Letty would be one-on-one with Jessica, if she found her. The taser was a neat weapon, but it wouldn't stop a bullet.

Jessica debated sneaking in the front door. It seemed the only option remaining if she wanted to save Sal. If she was quiet, she could slink through the room and surprise Letty while she locked Sal up. Huge holes made the scenario more of a sieve than a plan. The light spilling in from the outside would probably alert Letty, spinning her around to shoot Jessica. If Jessica made it to her and tased her, she'd probably pull the trigger, most likely killing Sal.

"Why did you stop?" Letty screeched.

"I can't go in there." Sal's voice sounded panicked.

"Dying seems a worse outcome, but the choice is yours."

A double click from straight out of the movies reached her. A gun, that terrible sound that comes before the shotgun blast. Damn it. If she got out of this scrape, she'd definitely go to gun school. She moved as she thought, the mental exercise a distraction from her ridiculous plan.

Chapter 26

S he stood at the door and quickly but silently turned the knob. It swung inward, and she peeked around it in time to see Letty's back disappear into the hallway. Fuck. She slipped through the door, drenched in fear, although whether she dreaded arriving too late to save Sal or of dying herself, she couldn't tell. She tiptoed toward the hallway, grateful she wore sneakers instead of boots for once.

She heard the door to the prison cell open while Sal pleaded with Letty not to lock him in. His voice quavered, Oscar-worthy.

Her thumb hovered over the button that turned the flashlight into a painful taser.

"Go sit on the bed, right now. That is, if you want to live."

Jessica took a breath. She needed to attack Letty when she closed the door, that was the only time the gun wouldn't be pointed directly at Sal. She exhaled silently and moved as close to the hallway opening as she could without being seen.

The door closed with a thud. Jessica simultaneously crammed her thumb down on the taser's button, bringing it to life and charged through the doorway.

Letty started and turned toward Jessica, but Jessica got there first. She shoved the taser into Letty's side and kept moving until she was behind the woman. She flung her free arm around Letty and pressed into her back. The flow of electricity through the instrument reverberated into her hand. Letty's scream overshadowed the crackling from the device as her body jerked wildly.

The gun went off with explosive power, throwing them both to the floor. Jessica's head screamed with pain as it crashed into the hard cement, but she kept the taser pressed into Letty's side. How would she get out of this without getting shot?

The door to the room swung open. Sal emerged. His face registered no surprise. Almost more quickly than she could see, he swung an elbow into Letty's temple, and the woman went still. When Jessica looked up at Sal, he had the shotgun.

Jessica pushed herself up, then placed a knee in Letty's back and pulled the woman's hands behind her. "Let's find something to tie her hands with."

"Here. You keep the gun trained on her, although I think she'll be out for a while. I've got something in the truck that will work." Sal turned the butt of the gun to Jessica.

"I'm fine like this. You keep the gun in case someone else comes. The cops are on their way."

Sal looked at her a long few seconds, then spun the gun back around and stepped over Letty as he headed toward the door. Jessica breathed for the first time in what seemed like forever.

She glanced into the room. Nothing had changed. It smelled stale, the way she had. The cold from the concrete floor chilled her through the denim at her knee. Such a plain room, yet it ignited so many emotions. She wanted to shudder in fear but held herself still. She wanted to light the building on fire, drop a bomb on it, anything to completely destroy it so it would never haunt her again. But mostly, she wanted to finish this job and get the fuck out of here.

Sal returned and tossed her a roll of duct tape. Jessica wrapped it around the unconscious woman's wrists. She ripped the tape with her teeth and secured the loose end before standing.

"Here," Sal said, shoving the shotgun at her. "The chamber's blown out. It won't function."

Jessica stared at the weapon. Part of the metal had an unusual bulge, and a square patch on the side was missing.

"It looks like they put the wrong shells in it," Sal said. "Take a look at it."

Jessica didn't reach for it.

"What?" Sal asked. "You never held a gun before?"

"Not when I could help it. Although I've been meaning to learn to shoot."

Both his eyebrows traveled north, as if the revelation shocked him. "I'll teach you. I've got a range at the house."

Of course he did. And he carried duct tape in the jeep, a knife in his waistband, and who knows what else.

Sal stepped into the main room and tossed a small white packet on the table. Then he returned and hauled Letty up by her arms and carried her to one of the chairs at the kitchen table. Once he had her in the chair, her head and shoulders slumped over the table, he opened the packet. It looked like some kind of wipe. Was he planning on cleaning up the place? Jessica shook her head trying to figure it out.

Sal looked up. "Ammonia wipes. They work better than smelling salts."

"Okay, MacGyver." Where did he get this shit? Next, he'd be using paperclips to put together a bomb, or perhaps he'd have the drone deliver a lie detector kit. She never knew with this guy. Definitely not your average county deputy.

"Hang on a second," Jessica said, a new thought coming to her. "Let me check and see if Tres Garcia is still alive."

Sal nodded, and Jessica took off into the hallway. She opened the door to Tres's room and surveyed the area before stepping inside. No one else was there. She went to the bedside. While she recognized Tres, he looked even older than the last time she'd seen him. The machine beeped rhythmically, and its light moved up and down on the display in equal rises and dips. She looked at his chest and saw a shallow rise and fall. Let him sleep, he'd have a lot to deal with fairly soon.

Jessica certainly couldn't do anything to improve his situation. He seemed at peace, so she returned to the main room. "He seems fine," she said to Sal.

He held the wipe under Letty's nose. She jerked, then struggled to get her hands free. Finally, her eyes opened. "What the hell happened? My chest hurts."

"You need to answer some questions for us," Sal said.

"Nooo," she wailed, rocking like a child. Lipstick stained her face in a sharp plum line from her mouth to one cheek. Her mascara had smudged, but she looked younger than when Jessica had last seen her, her wrinkles less defined. Her black hair remained somewhat styled, probably thanks to a half bottle of hairspray.

Jessica noticed her clothes for the first time. A lush silk blouse the color of her lips set off a linen pantsuit. Her hair glowed with fresh highlights. Long red nails adorned each hand. Every time Jessica saw this woman, she looked more sophisticated and far less like the witch Claudia had called her. She had started to look like the Juarez elite, albeit one who'd had the shit beaten out of them.

"The police are coming for you." Sal's flat tone made Letty stop rocking and look at him.

"You were here for your friend?" she asked.

"Not exactly. I brought my friend with me." He nodded toward Jessica.

Letty turned her head and focused on Jessica for the first time. "La maga," she whispered, leaning away from Jessica.

Jessica didn't know the word. She looked at Sal.

"Sorceress? I think that's what it means."

Mage. Jessica thought. "La bruja y la maga," she said to Letty. "Perfect."

"I thought you were dead. They told me they'd killed you." Fear laced Letty's voice.

"Maybe they did. Maybe I came back to haunt you." If only she had that kind of power. She examined the woman in the chair. Loss, not fear, lit Letty's eyes. "You used to be the bruja. You looked like a real desert witch. Lately, you've tried to clean yourself up like a rich lady from Juarez. Are you trying to break through the millionaire's ceiling?"

Disdain colored Letty's features. "I was born there. I have always belonged there."

Jessica had punched a nerve. "But no one saw you that way, did they?" She remembered the story Don Octavio had told about Letty's father and Claudia's, about her raising Tomás. "Do you even remember the times before your father disgraced the family?"

Anger flashed in Letty, and she surged toward Jessica. Sal grasped her around the shoulders and shoved her back into the chair. He nodded at Jessica to continue.

"When they let you back into the family, they saw you as the help. They put you to work in the business and let you change Tomás's diapers. Your cousin treated you like a servant, didn't she?" Jessica stared into Letty's eyes, and the hatred emanating from them was like an uppercut punch.

"You hated them," Jessica said. The revelation hit home. Revenge fueled Letty, not greed. "Did you hate all of them? Tomás? Tres? Sofia?"

Each name narrowed Letty's eyes as if focusing the contempt. It became palpable, a physical thing that charged the room with tension.

"Did you kill Sofia?" Jessica asked.

Letty's mouth twisted, and Jessica thought she'd speak. Instead, a wad of spit flew from her lips, hitting the ground beside Jessica's sneaker.

"Hey," Sal said, giving Letty's shoulder a tug. "Watch it."

Jessica twisted the knife deeper. "No wonder they thought you were low class. Did you think hair dye, some Botox, and new clothes would change you? You must have been so jealous of Sofia. She was beautiful, wasn't she? Polished. She fit right into the world of wealth and luxury."

"Ladrona." Letty spewed the word into the charged air.

"Thief," Jessica repeated in English. "What did she steal from you?"

"Mi familia. Mi amor. Mi vida." The words came out in a lament, pain lacing through every syllable. My family. My love. My life.

The words plunged through Jessica, releasing a familiar pain. She'd risked each of them, almost lost them all. Except for love. She needed to text Angus. He had to be worried sick. She slipped her phone from her pocket. "We're okay. Letty disarmed."

Jessica put her phone away and glanced back up. Letty's demeanor had completely changed. Instead of buoyed by hate, she had deflated, becoming a mere shell of the woman Jessica had once feared.

"My father was a good man," Letty said.

"Really?" Jessica asked. "Good men can do bad and stupid things. My father broke the law and destroyed our family. That didn't make me hate others or want to kill them." It had only made her hate herself. But she'd survived the years she spent punishing herself and had built a good life from the ashes of a burned family.

Jessica shook her head and refocused on Letty. "Did you kill Sofia?"

"She had cancer. I eased her suffering."

"With deadly drugs?" Jessica asked.

"She would have died anyway."

"She had breast cancer. That's usually curable."

"She would have died someday. She got to live my life for a long time. It was my turn."

What on Earth was this woman talking about? "How was it your life?" My family, my love, my life. Letty's words reverberated in Jessica's head.

"Did you love Tres?" Jessica asked.

"I knew him first. From the company. He pursued me." Memories clouded Letty's eyes. Memories, not love.

"Then he met Sofia?" Jessica prompted.

"She was the boss's daughter. I should have been. My father was a better man, but his brother never gave him a chance."

"Sofia took your father's wealth and your lover." Jessica almost chuckled. "And then made you raise her bratty son."

Letty gave Jessica a sharp look. "I loved Tomás as if he were my own."

"Is that why you kidnapped his wife?" Jessica had tired of this game. When would the police arrive? Let them pull a confession from this woman. Jessica wanted to get back to her family. The adrenaline drained from her body, taking any energy she had with it.

"I'm going to sit," she said to Sal, before dropping into a chair far out of Letty's reach.

Exhaustion and ugliness overwhelmed her. Why did she always end up encountering the world's worst humans? She tried to spark her anger, to become furious at this woman who'd imprisoned her, almost killed her. But nothing came. The anger had run out.

She looked at Letty, trying so hard to be accepted by people who would never take her in. And for what? What would she get for their acceptance? Entrée into a circle of vipers? Jessica couldn't imagine anything worse than having to hobnob with judgy people who didn't even like her.

Actually, she could imagine a lot worse. She could imagine a life without Angus, without a job she loved and a boss who appreciated her. This woman had almost taken all of that from Jessica. And Jessica had walked straight into it. It was time to go home.

Eventually, she heard the rumble of engines. She went to the window, a little afraid of seeing trucks and guns. Instead, a line of Mexican National Guard vehicles traveled down the road. And a black Mercedes.

Jessica opened the door and stepped outside. Several officers hopped out of their vehicles, one of them with his gun raised. Jessica raised her hands. "We've got the suspect inside."

Tomás got out of the Mercedes. Of course. Jessica almost rolled her eyes. But, whatever. She just wanted to go home.

"Your dad's inside. So is Letty. My friend Sal has a hold of her."

"Thank you, Jessica." Relief crossed Tomás's features, and a tear came to his eye.

She would not feel sorry for him. "Come on." She led him inside.

The officers handcuffed Letty, despite the tape wrapping her wrists. One uniformed man held a gun vaguely pointed at Letty and Sal.

"Tomás, this is Sal. He brought me here to get my truck. We had no idea Letty and your father were here. Could you have the officers stand down?"

Tomás spoke rapid fire Spanish to a stocky man with a full mustache. The officer wanted to bring Jessica and Sal in for questioning. Over her dead body.

"Hey," she said, breaking into the conversation. "Letty is a wanted criminal. They should take all the credit and pretend we weren't even here. We'll just get my truck and go."

Tomás and the man started up again, with Tomás clearly directing what would happen. Money and power spoke louder on this side of the border. Eventually, several of the men took Letty away.

Jessica led Tomás in to see his father, and Tomás actually broke down in sobs. Jessica didn't think he'd had it in him. But she was done judging other people and those treacherous family ties.

Soon an ambulance arrived and carted Tres from the room. Federal agents still blocked Jessica's truck and the Jeep. Sal remained quiet, almost fading into a corner as action swirled around the small house.

Once the EMTs loaded Tres into the ambulance, Tomás headed toward the Mercedes. Jessica stood directly behind it.

"Tell them to move their vehicles so we can leave." Jessica crossed her arms and glared at Tomás.

"Everything's fine. Just like you suggested, they're going to pretend you were never here. I need to go to the hospital with my father."

"We leave before you do, or this is going to get ugly." Jessica turned her head as a shadow appeared beside hers. Sal stood at her shoulder.

"Fine." Tomás yelled at two of the officers standing in the drive. They moved the SUVs blocking the Jeep and truck.

"You first," Sal said.

Jessica headed toward the truck, feeling multiple gazes on her back. What would have happened if Tomás had just left? She didn't trust the Mexican agents. Frankly, she didn't trust Tomás either.

Thankfully, the truck roared to life as soon as she started the engine. Sal backed the Jeep away, and Jessica reversed out of the space and into the drive. As she left the property, hopefully for the last time ever, she saw Sal's Jeep in her rearview mirror, with the Mercedes following closely behind.

Chapter 27

Jessica and Sal recrossed the border without incident. Jessica pulled into the parking lot of the duty-free shop on the US side and Sal followed.

How did you thank an accomplice who'd joined you on a task to regain yourself? Except that she didn't feel stronger or braver. Letty would go to jail, although she should really be punished for the way she treated women like Claudia, drugging them so they'd meet some cultural ideal. That revolved around a clear right and wrong, unlike family ties.

Heavy with exhaustion, Jessica pulled herself from her truck and trudged to Sal's window. She peered into his lined face. "Thanks. That word doesn't seem like nearly enough for what we went through today, but it's nice to have the truck back." Worst apology ever.

"Jessica, I take full responsibility for everything that happened today. My sources were wrong about the house being empty, and I need to find out what went wrong with that. However, what you did today was reckless. You should have driven away. You endangered both of us by coming into the house and attacking her. Why didn't you go for help?" The glint in his steely eyes pummeled home his disappointment.

Shock swept through her like nausea. "I couldn't leave you there. I know what it's like in that room."

"You could have gone for help. You knew where I was. Other people did too, like Keith. You risked our lives. Also, do you know what it looked like when the federales arrived? It looked like we'd taken a Mexican citizen hostage. Thankfully, Tomás's connections got us out of that fix, otherwise we'd both be in a Mexican prison right now."

"But I did ask for help. That's why they came. She could have killed you." The desert swirled around Jessica despite the lack of a breeze. She'd done what she had to do. He'd risked himself to help her, and she couldn't have left him in that godforsaken house with that vile woman.

He looked at her for a long time, the creases across his forehead and beside his mouth seeming to deepen as he passed judgement. She shrank under his gaze, although her childish beating heart wanted to scream *I did it because I had to.*

Sal turned the Jeep off, and the car settled into the pavement as the motor died. "You are courageous, but naïve. You don't understand how to work with a partner, which involves trusting others to do their job. You clearly don't understand guns, or you wouldn't have attacked the way you did. I don't know what kind of milagros you carry, but it's sheer luck we're both alive." He slowly shook his head, each pass buffeting Jessica with disapproval.

Her voice disappeared, and only sheer will and the hardness of her bones kept her from collapsing onto the pavement. This had been a success, no miracles needed. Letty was in custody. Tres had survived. Jessica got her truck back. Today was a victory. They should be clanging beers together in a frothy toast.

And yet. Her new mentor's hard gaze showed his disappointment. Jessica's body hollowed out. The fear of the house no longer permeated her thoughts. The desire for vengeance had packed its bags and left. But for once, nothing remained. No sense of justice. For whom, Tomás? It's not like Claudia had gained anything from this. Don Octavio's murdered body lay underground, not that many would miss him. Letty stagnating in a jail cell would benefit the Juarez community, but she'd steep in her own hatred and sense of injustice until she died. And that left Jessica, cold and alone on a hot desert day.

"Well. Thanks anyway," she said as she turned from the Jeep. She rolled up the tattered flag of gratitude and stuffed it back in her heart.

***

Jessica drove the border highway toward home. The ugliness and beauty of the desert passed by the windows unseen. Her actions might not have been what everyone wanted, at least not in hindsight, but there hadn't been a choice.

Except someone else could have retrieved the truck. She could have gotten herself to safety and called in the appropriate reinforcements to arrest Letty and save Sal. She had told herself not to take the case, that had been the first decision. But the wind had blown, she'd walked out the door, and set something into motion she couldn't, or wouldn't, stop.

At least this day would end at home, not in a prison cell or a cinderblock room with one glaring bulb. She'd wrap her arms around her man and sink into the unburdened love of her dog. Every mile the gravitational pull toward home strengthened. She forced herself to ease up on the gas pedal so the local police wouldn't pull her over and slow her return.

She pulled off the freeway and made one of the last turns, trusting that home would replace the emptiness that had left her weak after Sal's dressing down. Finally, she turned onto their road and Angus's dumpy car shone like a beacon drawing her to the adobe cottage. Home. A place filled with love. These walls and the beings in them had healed her from the trauma of imprisonment and escape. Going back to Mexico had added to her misery, not healed it.

She pulled up beside Angus's car and her truck shuddered to a stop. The front door seemed impossibly far away. She'd been on Odysseus's tour, a ridiculous trek that brought her back to where she was supposed to be all along.

She swung the door inward, and Tela jumped off the couch and bounded toward her as if she understood how much Jessica needed her love. Jessica sank to her knees and embraced the dog, letting her lick her face and wiggle in her arms. The goodness of home welled in Jessica's chest.

Angus stood in the kitchen. Jessica glanced up and saw relief and pain reflecting from his eyes in equal measure. She couldn't keep hurting him like this.

"I'm so glad I'm home," she said, meaning it as much as she'd ever meant anything.

"I'm glad you're alive." He didn't start toward her, didn't open his arms.

"You were right. I shouldn't have gone back." What could she say to appease him? She just needed to find the right lever to help him understand she meant it this time.

"And yet you did anyway. Just like always."

"Please don't be mad at me. It's been a really long day." Her strength flagged. Tela whined. Jessica moved to the couch and the dog jumped up beside her."

"I'm not mad at you. I'm . . . I'm blank." His face didn't look blank. It looked permanently scarred with regret. He stood so still, as if moving would break him.

Jessica pushed herself up from the couch and crossed the room. Her fingers ached to soothe the worry from his face, to rip her shirt open and show him her beating heart so he'd believe she was fine.

He held up both hands as she approached. Not in surrender, but to protect himself. She could see it in his eyes.

"Angus?" *Are you there? Do you love me? Are we okay?* So many questions passed through her, but she could only form the sound of his name.

"Last week." He shook his head as if the memory caused physical pain. "I've never seen you so broken. There were nights I feared you'd never come back to me, never be whole again. And then at the first opportunity, you went back for more. It's like an obsession. A drug addict would be easier to deal with."

"What do you think I'm obsessed with? And look at me. I'm here. I'm fine."

He shook his head. "Maybe you're fine, but I'm not."

Angus stilled, as immobile as a rock. Or a wall. Impenetrable. A second passed. Two.

"What can I do?" she finally asked. "How can I repair this?"

He sighed as if he'd been holding his breath. "I lost my mind when you texted me today. Well, first I called Claudia and Jaime like you requested and sent them your location information. But then . . ."

His eyes raked across her. If she could only unlock his thoughts so she'd know what to say or do.

"When you told me Letty had captured Sal, I knew you'd go after him. I figured best case scenario you'd be captured again, and she'd steal another piece of your soul. Or she'd kill you." Angus's eyes turned hard. "You shouldn't have been there. There was no reason. But you had to go. Anything to put yourself in danger."

"It's not like that. I didn't have a choice. I couldn't leave him there to die, not when he'd helped me."

"So you risked your life. You risked our future. When you shouldn't have gone at all. There were a hundred ways to get the truck back. Or you could have left it there. That truck isn't worth your life." The last sentence came out in a roar. Angus rarely raised his voice. Anger was her tool, not his.

"But I'm here. I came back."

"No, Jessica. Not really. You're here for now. But tomorrow, or the next day, or next week, you'll be back out there again looking for a new way to die." He ran his hand through his hair, exasperated, as if he spoke to a child.

It wasn't like that. It really wasn't. She didn't know how to explain it.

He took a deep breath and seemed to settle. "I think I liked it better when you were out fucking around. At least then I didn't have to worry as much about someone killing you."

His words broke her in two. She'd loved him for so long. Yes, she'd had years of drinking too much and sleeping with way too many guys. But even though they'd been friends since kindergarten and had an on-again, off-again, physical relationship, she'd always known he was too good for her. He should have ended up with a wife and two kids in the suburbs, not with someone so broken inside that she used tequila and anonymous sex to dull her sharp edges.

But she'd changed since then. Two years earlier, she'd stared death in the face for the first time. Almost losing it all had forged her into a new woman. She realized how much she loved him, how she didn't want to survive a life without Angus.

She made promises that night. She promised herself to fight for justice. And she promised him she'd leave her wayward self behind and be true to him—which meant finally being true to herself. And she had been. She hadn't meant to build a reputation brick by brick as someone who could solve crimes. Because the solutions came with their own dose of danger. And she knew he hated it.

"I can change," she pleaded. "I did it before." She didn't recognize the desperate woman who uttered the words.

"You can't. And I can't ask you to." He stepped toward her, wrapped her in his arms.

He would leave. She wouldn't let him. She grabbed him in a fierce embrace. "Stay."

"I can't. This isn't about you. I love how brave you are. You'll walk through fire to save someone, face any fear. But it's becoming your trademark, and I can't wait for you to come home each day knowing someday you won't."

"I will. I did. I'm here." She would not let him go.

"Jessica." His arms dropped from around her and he put distance between their shoulders even though she held his waist tight to hers. "You didn't need to go. You wanted to."

"But I didn't know it would be dangerous."

He grabbed her wrists, tugged them away from him. She wanted to hold on but wouldn't stoop low enough to fight him.

"That's how it's going to happen." Passion and pain fought in his voice. "You're not going to want to believe a situation is dangerous, and then you're not going to come home. I can't take that."

How could she turn back time? She didn't want to lose the best thing that had ever happened to her over one stupid mistake. But she had no words to combat his argument.

"What happens to your mom, your dog, when you don't make it back? Jessica, what if we had kids? You make it impossible to even have a conversation about family." A silent tear tracked down his face.

This time she shattered into a thousand tiny shards. The dream she'd had of a normal life with a man she both trusted and couldn't get enough of disintegrated along with her.

"I thought you weren't coming home." The whisper barely reached her ears.

Jessica searched his face, but he'd dropped his head and closed his eyes. He'd shut her out.

"I can't go through that again." His voice strengthened. "You thrive on fear. I want peace. Security. A love that won't end up bloody and battered in the desert. I don't want to have to identify you in a morgue, or worse, never know what happened to you or where your bones came to rest. I just can't."

He turned and walked into their bedroom without looking at her. The closet door squeaked open. The duffle thudded as it hit the bed. Drawers slid open. Each sound a separate torture. A part of her wanted to rush in there, scream and yell and pull his clothes from the bag. But it wouldn't work. And he'd see her as pathetic as well as someone he could leave.

She spied his keys on the kitchen table, grabbed them, and shoved them in her back pocket. Then she relocated them to her bra where they couldn't be seen. She wouldn't let him go easily, wouldn't let him go at all if she could help it. This was Angus, the one person who'd always been there for her through all the shit in her life. Surely, he wouldn't leave her now.

When he strode into the room with the duffle flung over his shoulder, he'd become a man she hadn't met before. Strong. Resolute. He'd bent to her so many times in the past, opened himself to share her pain. This man wouldn't do that. And fuck was it hot.

He glanced toward the kitchen table, then stopped and scanned the room. "Where are my keys?"

"I don't know." She stared at him in a challenge.

"Come on, Jess. I think we've both been through enough today."

She caressed her breast, moving her fingertips across the hardness of the keys. "Come and get them."

He grinned, but heartbreak shone from his eyes. "There's so much I love about you, but it's not enough."

Jessica's world stopped spinning. A tear cooled her cheek as it rolled down her face, then its pair dropped from the other side. She couldn't move, couldn't breathe. She wished she'd stayed in Juarez instead of coming home to this barren wasteland.

Angus stepped close and held out his hand, refusing to play her game. He was done. She gazed into his gorgeous brown eyes searching for some vestige of the love they'd shared and somehow fell in love with him all over again, just as he'd decided to leave.

She reached into her bra and pulled out the now warm keys. She might as well have tugged her heart out along with them. It didn't belong to her. It had always been his.

To keep from breaking apart in front of him, she bit her lip so hard she tasted the metallic tinge of blood. Slowly, she placed the keys in his palm, then curled his fingers around them.

She couldn't let go of his hand, so she looked into his eyes once more. "I love you."

"I know, and I love you too. But this is the only way I can stand to lose you. I'm sorry." He pulled his hand from hers, then left without even petting Tela on his way out.

Chapter 28

Jessica trembled, suddenly cold. She couldn't think about what just happened, couldn't let that kind of pain pass the blood-brain barrier keeping her alive. She stepped into the kitchen, carefully placing each foot so she didn't collapse to the floor in a puddle of remorse. She reached for a bottle of tequila on an open shelf and filled a third of a highball glass with the amber liquid.

Not even the burn in her throat as she swallowed made her feel alive. She put the bottle back. Some wounds not even her old standby would heal.

She trudged into the bedroom. She should shower. Instead, she saw the bed, still rumpled from the last time she and Angus had lain there. She stripped and crawled naked under the covers. Skootching over to Angus's side of the bed, she laid her head on his pillow and inhaled his scent. She wouldn't believe he was gone.

***

Jessica woke in the night. Tela had abandoned her dog bed and lay curled against Jessica's back. Loss overwhelmed her. She stood at the edge of a vast canyon in the dark of night. Alone. She closed her eyes, not caring if she fell off the canyon wall and tumbled to her death. At least that would bring empty relief.

She woke again in daylight, closed her eyes against the sun and crawled down under the covers. The click of nails on the wood floor approached the bed, and the heaviness of a dog's head dropped onto her hand. Tela whimpered.

Jessica rose and opened the back door for the patient dog. At least it got her out of bed. She kept the door to the backyard open so Tela could come and go as she pleased. Ever since an angry ex-mayor had burst into her house in a rage, Jessica had carefully locked every door. She no longer cared. Let someone come for her.

Jessica would not address the question in the dog's eyes. She couldn't explain that Angus had gone. Or why. Or if he'd ever come back. But Tela's stare emptied Jessica out even more. Her body became a dried corn husk, ready to waft away on the next breeze.

A part of her wanted to call her mom. They'd repaired their long-damaged relationship, and one phone call would bring her mom's love and understanding. But then Jessica would break, and she had to keep that at bay as long as possible. If she really considered what had happened, she might dwell there forever.

Instead, she and Tela walked to where the Rio Grande lay a few blocks away, splitting Texas and New Mexico this time instead of two countries. Unlike where she and Claudia had crossed, the river here had levees on either side and wide grassy shoulders stretching to the water. Here, the channelized, domesticated river created a safe space. People ran and biked along its banks under the happy spring sky.

But Jessica knew the wilder, darker river, and today's bright yellow sun couldn't match the storms raging inside her. She turned back to the house. Better to wallow in the torrents of her grief in private.

***

The next morning, Jessica jumped out of bed the minute her alarm went off. She took care of the dog, dressed for work. She didn't even make coffee, deciding to stop along the way instead. Palpable relief flooded her when she closed the front door, locking everything that had happened over the weekend inside.

She arrived at the office before Linda and turned on her computer, determined to get a head start on the day. A raft of emails awaited her. The first one brought her storms racing back. Keith asked for an update on the case. Hadn't he talked to his uncle? Surely Sal had told him about his disappointment in Jessica.

Jessica's phone pinged with a text from Claudia. "Have news. Stopping by at 9."

Jessica almost texted her back and told her not to come. This case had devastated her in so many ways. But too many people needed answers. Instead, she gave Claudia the thumbs up. She also texted Keith and invited him to the update. One and done. Everyone would learn what happened at the same meeting, and the case would be wrapped up before noon. Maybe then she could start thinking about how to get Angus back.

Linda rolled in soon after, with a chirpy, "You're here. How are you feeling?"

"Fine," Jessica replied before she could dig for an honest answer. "Claudia Garcia is stopping by at nine to update me on the case. I've invited Keith Guerra from the sheriff's office as well. I hope that's okay.""

"Of course. Do you mind if I sit in?"

"No." Jessica hid her trepidation in the short reply. She hadn't told Linda about returning to Mexico to get her truck. That decision had already cost her almost everything. If Linda found out, would she drop her as well? Maybe she could warn Keith to keep quiet. Although Claudia must know also since Tomás had shown up at the house. Fuck. What she wouldn't give to take back that decision.

A wrinkle crossed Linda's brow. "Are you sure you're okay?"

Jessica nodded with what she hoped was nonchalance. The emotions boiled inside her as if trapped in a pressure cooker, but she clamped that lid down hard.

Linda must have seen no way in and gave up. "Great. I'll be right back." Then she left through the front door she'd just come in. Jessica noted the oddity, but forced herself to breathe through the swell of emotions that made her want to vomit. Or curl up and cry. Not today. She'd make it through today. She'd make it through the morning. Or the next five minutes.

She reverted to a younger version of herself from when her parents had recently left, and she had to function on her own. She'd learned that time could be survived in ever smaller increments, but eventually they'd add up to an hour, a day, a week.

Of course, back then she'd had Alma, her attorney and guardian, at the house at night. So she hadn't been completely alone. And now she had Tela. She regretted leaving the dog at home today. Somehow in wanting to start fresh this morning she'd left a friend behind.

Her thoughts went to the next logical place, to Angus leaving her behind. A dagger stabbed through her chest that she couldn't breathe around. She sat in the pain holding as still as possible until it loosened its grip enough for her to inhale and then go on.

But go where? How? Somehow, she had to change. She'd skated by on luck so many times, promising to change, but never doing anything differently. No wonder Angus had given up on her.

Linda returned with a pastry box from a nearby bakery. Normally the aroma of warm bread and sugar would have enticed Jessica. Today, it repelled her, as if she shouldn't enjoy anything nice.

By the time Jessica had made a second cup of coffee, Claudia arrived. Tomás wasn't with her, a small win in the day. Neither was Cinco.

Keith arrived soon after, with Sal in tow. Fuck. Now Linda would certainly learn about Jessica's weekend activities. She might be the coolest boss ever, but she'd eventually draw the line. Just like Angus had.

Everyone settled around the table in the conference room. Jessica poured coffee, and Linda opened the pastry box full of Jessica's favorites: cinnamon rolls, apple fritters, and salad-plate-sized pan dulce with its multicolored crosshatched sugar coating. Angus loved that stuff.

She forced him from her mind by focusing on Claudia. Claudia looked at the sweets longingly but didn't take one.

A fit of rage pulsed through Jessica, making her want to take a pastry and shove it down Claudia's throat. How dare Letty and whichever women influenced Claudia teach her she couldn't have what she wanted because they thought she didn't look good enough.

Jessica grasped hard at the tornado of fury swirling through her, but it slipped through her grip. She closed her eyes. She was from the desert. She knew that. She was the desert. The storm receded. It wasn't Claudia, or Letty, or the women in Juarez who'd blown the winds around. It was her own ravaged heart. The wind died, along with the future she'd thought was secure.

"Split one?" Jessica asked Claudia. She pointed at the box. Claudia smiled, brightening her entire face. She nodded.

"Which is your favorite?"

"Apple."

Jessica removed the pastry from the box, then glanced around the table. "Dig in."

"Don't mind if I do," Sal said, reaching for a pan dulce. When he'd greeted her at the door, the anger and disappointment she'd seen Saturday wasn't visible, but she worried it lurked underneath.

Keith, on the other hand, seemed delighted to see her again and had embraced her in a half-hug. Awkward. Now he reached for the other apple fritter, while Linda took a cinnamon roll.

While Jessica sawed the fritter in half, Linda started the conversation. "Do I know you?" she asked Sal.

"You used to work for the police department?" Sal asked.

"Yes. I was a detective."

"I remember you. I was with the Sheriff's Department. I think I met you on the—" Sal glanced at Jessica then back at Linda. "On a case or two."

Linda's eyes grew big, and she glanced quickly at Jessica before locking her gaze back on Sal. "I'm not sure I remember you."

"Yeah, you were a real hotshot back then. I had only been in the department a couple of years, but you were unforgettable." Awe laced his voice.

Well, that was uncomfortable. The room seemed to stall, and bright red patches rose on Linda's cheeks. What was with these two? Linda was acting weird again, as if she overcompensated for something. And Sal's admiration seemed over the top.

Jessica needed to take control of the meeting. "Thanks for coming here today." She swept her gaze around the table. "I think we should get started. Claudia, do you want to update us on what you've learned?"

"Yes." She turned to Jessica. "Thank you for getting my father-in-law back. He's still in the hospital. Evidently, he had quite the cocktail of drugs in his system. We're still waiting for the toxicology reports."

"Where did you find him?" Linda asked.

Fuck. Claudia, Keith, and Sal immediately focused on Jessica. Then Linda turned to her.

"Sal and I went to Juarez on Saturday to retrieve my truck." Each word was a confession.

"You what?" Linda asked, her sky-high eyebrows creating a mask of incredulity.

"I didn't think . . ." The words trailed off. Didn't think what? That Letty would be there? That she'd risk her life? That she'd lose her love? That she'd have to sit in this confessional booth and bare her stupid decisions for all to see?

Linda fixed her stare on Sal, as if Jessica could no longer be trusted with the truth. "What happened?"

Sal recounted the story, wincing at the part where Jessica stormed the house to save him. "I never should have taken her there. I'm sorry."

"But if you hadn't gone, Letty would have probably killed Tres." Claudia turned from Sal to Jessica. "Thanks to you, Letty is in jail, and the doctors expect Tres to recover. We are so grateful."

Jessica grimaced, unable to shoulder the responsibility for the good or the bad twisting through the room. Yes, a few things had gone right. But at an unbearable cost.

A shaft of light broke through the room as the front door opened. Why was Alma here?

Linda rose from the table and went to greet her. Jessica strained to hear the conversation between the two attorneys, but Alma kept her voice low.

"What?" Linda gasped. "She didn't tell me."

Fuck. Fuck. Fuck. This couldn't happen. Somehow, this had something to do with Angus. She couldn't think of another reason for Alma's presence.

"Please come in," Linda said, leading Alma into the room.

"Hey, Jess. How's it going?" Alma asked, taking the seat beside Jessica.

Alma rested her hand on top of Jessica's and gave it a squeeze. Jessica jerked her arm away and nestled her hands together in her lap. If someone was nice to her right now, she would break.

"Everyone, this is Alma Rey. She's a friend of Jessica's, and a great attorney," Linda said. "Alma, I've just learned that Jessica and Sal here," she nodded to the man at the other end of the table, "went to Juarez last weekend to get Jessica's truck. They went to the exact same location where Jessica and Claudia were held hostage. It didn't go well. From what I understand, Sal was captured and Jessica went in to save him, pitting her stun gun against a shotgun." Linda sat back and crossed her arms.

Claudia gasped. "Is that true? Jessica, you are the bravest person I know. First you saved me, and then you rescued Tres."

"I agree with that assessment." Quiet until now, Keith looked at Jessica with appreciation.

Sal sighed heavily. "She was reckless, but brave. I should not have put her in that situation. She doesn't have the training, and I'm still trying to find out why my guy in Juarez thought the place was vacant."

An awkward silence fell over the room. Jessica looked around the table. Keith winked at her, of all weird things. Sal gave her a nod. Claudia gazed at her like she was some kind of hero. Linda looked at her with frankness. She now knew all of her secrets. Jessica couldn't look at Alma.

Alma spoke. "She's never had any type of training, and she always gets herself into these situations." And her husband left her because of it. Jessica heard Alma's unspoken words.

"Well, maybe we should get her training." Linda crossed her arms and looked to the other end of the table as if Jessica weren't in the room. "She's an asset to me, and frankly, to the community."

"Definitely," Keith said. "And her position allows her to investigate with more leeway than officials can." He addressed Linda's question, but his eyes strayed to his uncle.

"I'm not sure we should encourage this behavior. It's endangering her and affecting her relationships." Alma jumped in, her revelation making the room even more uncomfortable as eyebrows raised at the last comment.

Jessica belted herself against the stares, constricted her insides before they spilled all over the table. Emotion, pain, regret, desire. Especially desire, for the life she'd had, the man she loved. Breathing became hard.

"Jessica, what do you want?" Sal asked.

The room grew pregnant with expectation waiting for her response. What did she want, other than the ability to turn back time? Angus. Only Angus.

Should she get up and walk out? Would that bring him back to her? No. It wasn't the job he despised, it was her decision-making. What could she do differently next time? She refused to believe no chance existed for their relationship.

Jessica had waited too long to give her response. The concern in the room had ratcheted up to a boil.

Keith, sitting beside her, turned and rested a hand on her shoulder. "Hey. Are you okay? Do you need some time?"

"I need to keep my job." Jessica blurted the words.

"Well, of course you'll keep your job. You leaving is not an option." Linda's response came quiet and firm

"I bet." Sal shot the words across the table.

What was up between her boss and Sal? Linda's cheeks reddened again under the scrutiny.

"You haven't told her?" Alma addressed the question to Linda.

Jessica stared at her boss, currently sporting an expression so fraught it probably matched Jessica's own. What the fuck was going on?

Alma turned to her. "Linda worked on your dad's case."

Jessica's stomach dropped as if her cushy office chair had morphed into a rickety rollercoaster. Was her entire life a lie? She'd thought she'd earned this position, found a kindred spirit in her boss. Had she been a guilt hire? Did Linda want something from her? And most importantly, why did her past always come back to bite her in the ass?

She drew her eyes from Linda and slowly gazed around the room. Keith's grimace told her he knew. Sal stared at her defiantly. He must know, and that knowledge caused the back and forth between him and Linda. Claudia's face showed innocence and confusion. Finally, her gaze came to rest on Linda.

Her boss wore a frank, open gaze. "I'm sorry I didn't tell you. I was the arresting officer on your dad's case. I hated that case, how he became the fall guy for far more corrupt happenings. Not that he was innocent, he wasn't. To the prosecutors, he was a big fish in El Paso's almost waterless pond, but far more sinister people lurked under the surface. Only no one had the balls to go after them. That's why I became a lawyer, so I could right wrongs like that. What happened to your family, to you, was unfair."

"So I was a pity hire?" Jessica asked. Might as well know the truth since everything in her life sucked anyway.

"No. It wasn't like that. When you contacted me out of the blue, I thought maybe this was my chance to right a wrong. But you've been a really great hire. And your drive for justice reignited my desire to do more to right the wrongs in this community—like with the Guatemalan cousins."

"You saved those girls," Keith said.

Would he just shut the fuck up? Jessica liked it better when Keith hated her, arrested her. It's what she deserved. This ridiculous fawning had to stop.

"Thanks for getting everything out in the open," Linda said to Alma. She sounded far from thankful. Her eyes moved to Jessica. "I've been trying to find a way to tell you, but you get pretty uncomfortable when people talk about your dad."

"Yeah. With good reason." The pat response spewed out of her before she could stop it. "I appreciate everyone coming in today to talk about me like I'm not even here. Claudia, thank you for keeping us apprised of Letty's case. I'm glad she's in jail, and I hope Tres makes a full recovery. I take you've updated Sergeant Castro this?"

Claudia nodded.

"Unless any of you have something else, I need to get back to work." Jessica pushed her chair from the table.

"Jessica, don't." Alma placed her hand on Jessica's leg as if she could stop her from standing. "You can't keep running away from your problems."

"No." Jessica shook her head vigorously. "You don't have to walk into every room and wave the truth around. This isn't a courtroom, and some people like to keep their secrets."

She glanced at Linda, hoping to get a nod of agreement. Instead, Linda's gaze fixed on her like a laser. "It's personal," she said to her boss.

"It's also professional," Linda countered. "You got into this spot because you took on a case that had severe negative ramifications for your personal life."

"I didn't take the case on. In fact, I turned it down multiple times. Everything I did, I did on my own. And I'll deal with the consequences."

"What happened?" Keith asked.

"Is everything okay with Angus?" Claudia asked right after.

Fuck, fuck, fuck. She bottled her emotions, forced them to stay put with glass and steel and the power of the desert mountains. She would not break. She would not break.

But she couldn't respond either. To say a single word would let something escape its bind, and if a single word got free, the rest of the emotional disaster inside her would tumble out.

"I'm going to take Jessica out for a little bit," Alma stood and grabbed her wrist.

Jessica didn't even look back as she followed the woman out of the room, across the office, and out the front door. Alma continued to pull her down the street toward the courthouse. Two blocks later they reached a coffee shop and Alma turned toward the door.

Jessica kept walking, dragging Alma, who refused to let go, along with her. Finally, they reached The Tap, one of Jessica's favorite dive bars. *Coffee shop my ass.* This day deserves a gateway straight to hell.

She opened the door to cavernous darkness. Relief flowed through her as she disappeared into the cool bar. She could hide here. Hide from the bright desert sun, all her mistakes, and the people who wanted to help her. Except of course, for Alma.

Jessica grabbed a bar stool and even smiled as her favorite bartender emerged from the back. "Hey, Irina. It's like you live here."

"I could say the same about you. What'll you have?" Irina stopped in front of her. A tight white tank top hugged her generous figure and showed off armfuls of tats.

"A tequila. Whatever the house brand is." The worse the better. She needed to burn all the bad out of herself, and firewater seemed like a good place to start.

"Jessica. It's still morning." Alma stated the obvious.

"And a cup of coffee," Jessica said to Irina. "Since it's still morning."

Irina set two shot glasses in front of Jessica. One she filled with tequila. For the other, she grabbed a glass pitcher full of a thick red liquid from a nearby refrigerator. After pouring some into the second glass, she decorated it with a lime slice.

"Sangrita. On the house. Because it's morning," Irina said. "Pretend it's tomato juice."

Alma ordered her own coffee while Jessica downed the tequila and then chased it with the spicy, citrusy, tomato mix. Breakfast of champions.

"Talk to me," Alma said. "Tell me about Angus. What are you feeling inside? What are you going to do?"

"I'm pretty sure you learned a long time ago that you can't save me." She wanted another shot. Twelve of them, until she'd built a liquid moat of drunkenness around her that would keep Alma and anyone else from getting in.

"He called me and asked me to check up on you. He's worried about you. So am I. And from what I saw in that room, so is just about everyone you know."

The words hurt. It's not like she'd set out to scare the people she loved. She followed up on cases because she wanted to help people. And she did. "Claudia didn't seem too worried. In fact, she seemed pretty grateful that I found her father-in-law and helped put a criminal behind bars."

"It sounded like you got lucky."

"Fuck you."

"Stop pushing away the people who care about you."

"I didn't push Angus away. He left me." The pain of the words cleaved her in two. Everything she'd held inside spewed out her chest in a great wracking sob, while traitorous tears leaked down her face.

Jessica closed her eyes and mentally clawed the emotions back one by one. She forced her breathing to slow and straightened her spine. She'd made this mess, and she'd find a way out of it. She took one more breath, then opened her eyes, ready to face the world.

"Here." Irina placed another shot on the bar. "This one's on me."

Jessica circled a finger around the rim, then looked at Alma. "I'm going to get him back. I have no idea how, but I will."

"I believe you, and I'll advocate for you. I am your lawyer, after all. But I don't think it's going to be easy. You really scared him this time."

"Wait." A horrible thought rushed through Jessica. "Did he contact you because you're an attorney? Does he want a divorce?"

"No. He didn't mention it. Honestly, he just sounded concerned."

A shaft of light cut through the dark space as the front door opened. Linda and Sal walked in.

"I thought I'd find you here," Linda said, taking a seat next to Jessica.

"Figures. You're here as much as she is." Irina sniped from behind the bar. "What can I get you two?"

"I'll have an Irish coffee," Linda said.

Sal quickly held up two fingers, doubling the order. Jessica hadn't started her second tequila and took a long sip of coffee instead.

She wished she were anywhere else. These nice people would try to fix her. But their tools wouldn't repair the way she'd broken, only Angus could do that. And the rest of her didn't need fixing, at least that's what she'd always told herself.

"I understand that you might want your space right now," Linda said. "But I want you to know we're on your side. And, Sal and I have come up with a plan. You've got great investigative instincts, but you're short on skills. I know you don't have a lot of free time between school and work, but when you do, Sal's willing to teach you how to protect yourself and introduce you to some of the tools of the trade. You're taking too many risks right now. But we need you here and working."

When Linda finished, Jessica looked at Sal, and he nodded. His anger from the other day seemed to have dissipated. She turned to Alma, not sure how to respond to this new development.

"It's your call," Alma said. "Why don't you stop by the house after work, and we can talk about the other issue?"

Maybe it was the tequila, or maybe the support of the people around her made the world seem a little lighter. She'd survive this, just like she'd survived her parents leaving and a burning building and being held captive. These people would help, and somehow, some way, she'd repair things with Angus.

"I've got to get going," Alma said. "And it won't be great if I show up at the office smelling like a bar." She pointedly stared at Linda's drink.

"I cancelled my meetings for the day," Linda said.

"I'm retired," Sal took a sip of the coffee and smiled at Linda.

"Have fun, and I'll see you tonight." Alma slipped off the stool and headed out the door.

Jessica turned to her boss. "Thanks for giving me a chance. I . . ."

Linda held her hand up, stopping Jessica's words. "I should have told you about the role I played in your dad's arrest. I feel really shitty about that. But you're a good paralegal, and you've solved three mysteries since I met you. We need people like you in this city. When I hired you, I may have felt a little guilty about the role I played in your dad's arrest. But I also really needed a paralegal. Hiring you was a great decision. You're good at your job, are going to be a fantastic attorney, and your connections in El Paso and Juarez are good for business. Please stay."

Jessica rarely saw herself through others' eyes. Growing up, most people had seen her as a criminal's daughter, not a pleasant view. She needed the job, but she wanted to work with Linda, to learn from her. She glanced over at Sal. She had a lot to learn from him also. And there was still so much she wanted to do, like bring closure to the Guatemalan cousins.

She had so much to learn. Not just patience, but how to be safer and make smarter decisions. No more skating by without actually doing the work or making promises to learn new skills and then never following through. It was time for a change.

When she went to Juarez with Sal, she'd convinced herself she needed to recover her old badass self. Instead, she needed to improve the person she already was. If spending days locked in a room made her a little more cautious—well, that might not be a bad thing. And if she could layer new skills on top of her passion and drive, she could be herself, only better.

She couldn't think of finer people to work with. "I'd like that. And I'd like to work with you too," she said to Sal.

"Good," he said. "We can set something up on the weekends when you're free. Keith comes out a lot on the weekends too, so you may run into him."

Whatever. She had a different man on her mind. The first few tendrils of a plan started forming. It wouldn't be easy to draw him back into her life, but she would. He was the one thing she couldn't leave behind.

"Hey, I'm going to head back to the office. There's a lot I want to work on today, plus, I can get some studying done to make up for the time I've missed."

"Are you sure?" Linda asked.

"Yeah. And thanks for everything." She stood.

"I think Sal and I are going to stay here for a while." Linda smiled brightly at the man beside her.

Uh oh. Jessica glanced over at Irina who met her eyes and shrugged. *Not my problem*, Jessica thought, heading for the door.

***

Later that night, Jessica sat in her truck, which she'd pulled nose-to-nose with Angus's car outside the music school. The sun had dropped behind the western mesa some time ago, turning the sky tangerine and then blood red as it set.

A shimmer of gray light still lit the horizon, signaling someone else's day. Kids streamed out of the school carrying electric guitars and drumsticks. She waited until the instructors left, the dark shielding her from recognition. Finally, Angus emerged. He turned and locked the door, then stepped into the parking lot.

He stopped when he saw the truck. Jessica rolled her window down and gave him a small wave. She, of course, wanted to leap from the truck and throw herself into his arms. But that wouldn't work. Not that she knew what would.

He seemed to gird himself, then walked to her window, stopping a couple of feet away.

"Hey," he said.

"Hi." Then, suddenly she knew. "You waited for me for a long time. For all the years it took me to get my shit together. I'm going to wait for you too. As long as it takes."

"You think I don't have my shit together?"

She smiled. "You need to know that I'm not going anywhere. I'm always going to come home, someday, to you."

Anger flitted across his face.

"I know. I made a really stupid decision, and I've got to quit doing that. I will. I don't ever want to hurt anyone again the way I've hurt you."

His defiance buffeted her in waves. Of course it did. This was just the first day.

"And Sal's going to teach me how to protect myself. I know it's not enough, yet. But it's a start."

Angus raised an eyebrow. Interest instead of anger. She'd take it. "And he's got some pretty cool toys I get to learn about."

Angus crossed his arms as if trying to put something solid between them. She'd used the same tactic so many times to cover her own hurt and fear.

"I love you. And whenever you're ready, I'm here for you. For good this time."

THE END

Read the next book in the Jessica Watts Southest Suspense Series: *El Macho.* **When a friend calls after being abducted and left to die in the desert, Jessica is pulled into a mystery that ties together several past cases. But with bigger crimes come more malicious enemies, and she might not have the skills to survive the fight.**

I appreciate your help in spreading the word about this book. Tell a friend or submit a reader review. To join Kathryn Dodson for updates, events, book info, and more, visit www.KathrynDodson.com.

Other novels by Kathryn Dodson
The Jessica Watts Southwest Suspense Series
She's not a cop. She's not a PI. She's the woman who won't walk away.
Jessica Watts is haunted, reckless, and relentless when it comes to uncovering the truth. From missing women to buried bodies, every case drags her deeper into secrets that could destroy her. And some secrets are deadlier than the truth.

Unfinished Business: Stories of Bold Women
Midlife isn't the end of your story—it's the plot twist.
Meet a series of extraordinary women who prove that life's most powerful chapters are written after 50. In this compelling collection, discover what happens when women stop asking permission and start taking action. Three novels about what comes next.

Portrait of Deception
A photographer on the brink of fame. A dictator with a fatal agenda. A terrifying trap she may not escape.

Acknowledgements

Thank you to everyone reads this this book and the Jessica Watts series. You make my words come to life.

To say that I'm inspired by El Paso would be an understatement. Back in sixth grade when my parents told me we were moving to El Paso from Dallas, I thought my world was ending. It didn't, although I grew in ways I never expected. On the back of a horse, I galloped through the legendary river in this book, under a wide-open blue sky that let my creativity unfurl.

Later in life, I crossed the river daily for a job in Juaerz, Mexico, where I learned how people from two countries came togehter to make products for the world. I'm especially grateful to my boss Sharon Valdes who was a big part of that earlier time and who now supports me in this new career.

I worked for the chamber of commerce and the City of El Paso, each after stints away from the desert landscape that kept pulling me home. Kristi Borden from the chamber and the many incredible people I worked with at the city, including everyone from the economic development department, are a big part of my El Paso story. I also love following the career of Veronica Escobar, El Paso's amazing congressional representative, who I had the good fortune to work with when she served as a county commissioner.

El Paso is in my bones and comes out in my stories. I met my husband there and we took our son to live there when he was young. I return often, to see old friends, scout the locations I use in my books, and to see my parents. I am grateful that they introduced me to this city so many years ago.

About the Author

Kathryn Dodson

Author Kathryn Dodson

Kathryn has published seven books about women who become their own heroes - whether they're solving a crime or starting over. She grew up writing and riding horses in far West Texas, and had a full career running cities and chambers of commerce before returning to her college major, creative writing.

Kathryn loves to travel and has visited 30 countries and 44 states. This inspires her novels about interesting women in fascinating places.

Originally from Texas, she had the good fortune to live in Spain, Mexico, Tanzania, and several U.S. states, and the good sense to end up in Carlsbad, California. She loves travel, fiery food, hanging out with the neighbors in the front yard on Friday evenings, and reading. Join Kathryn for updates and extras at https://www.kathryndodson.com/.

www.ingramcontent.com/pod-product-compliance
Lightning Source LLC
Chambersburg PA
CBHW030137010826
48973CB00002B/603